The Caverns of Stillwater

M.R. King

Branching Realities
Independent Publishing, LLC

The Caverns of Stillwater
M.R. King

First Printing
April 2020

Branching Realities Independent Publishing aims to find the best in fiction of all genres from independent authors all over the world. To find more about us visit our website or send us an email. Please support the independents of publishing and writing.

Website: branchingrealitiespublishing.com
Email: branchingrealities@yahoo.com
Store: irbstore.co

This book is dedicated to my patient wife, Kristine, who had to put up with all the various drafts and edits, and who keeps me sane, and my daughter, Katheryn, who inspires me to write with her perpetual excitement about creepy monsters and eerie stories. Thank you both for all that you have done.

Chapter One
A Death in the Family

O my prophetic soul! My uncle!
Hamlet. Act I. Sc. 5

Thursday morning my phone rang, like it always does, never hinting that the call that would change my life. When I answered, a deep male voice responded. Each word was steeped in southern courtesy and tradition and boomed loudly over my speaker phone. Cletus T. Montgomery III, attorney at law, introduced himself. I scrambled to process his words as they were mixed with a variety of 'y'alls,' 'sons,' and 'fellahs.' By the time I had caught up, I realized he had told me his search for me had begun "Mundee last." Apparently, I was a relation of his client, John Lincoln, who had recently passed. My parents never told me about any uncles I had. I knew my family had been in Florida for the past several generations. Cletus, however, insisted I was his sole living relation. No matter how I argued, he replied I 'just about the only Bernard' that could be related to John. I figured that this was solely a notification call. So, I made obligatory noises showing just how sorrowful I was that Uncle John, half a country away, had died. I hoped it would get Cletus off the phone. Cletus would not let me off the line.

"I don't think you fully understand me, son," he said, pausing, "Mister Lincoln has done gone an' left you his entire estate."

That stopped me in mid-thought. "I'm sorry, his estate?" I took a sip of my still-searing cup of coffee. Suddenly I had much more interest in Cletus. As he continued, I frantically tried to dig up anything on John Lincoln from Stillwater, Missouri.

"Yes, sir, Mister Lincoln left you his house, his personal effects, his 200-acre homestead, and the residue of his estate."

The credit report I ran found some real estate in Missouri and a few bank accounts.

"OK." I said, still trying to figure out what this inheritance could mean. "What do I need to do? Can you email me the paperwork?"

"I still don't think you understand, son. So I'll go on and spell it out for you." Cletus paused, taking a deep breath. I got the feeling he was going to say something unpleasant. "Mister Lincoln had a little over $27 million in cash and various liquid assets, $12 million in stocks and bonds and $1.7 million in miscellaneous valuable loose gemstones."

I was stunned and the silence filled the line. Cletus gave me time think. After a few long seconds, I asked the only question that I could think of. "What's the catch?" I knew no one leaves anyone this kind of money without their being a catch.

"No catch at all, son. None at all."

"Really? I find that hard to believe." I began to wonder if this was some elaborate prank being pulled on me.

"Well, you do need to come to Stillwater to sign some paperwork, survey the property, and make arrangements, things like that."

"I would like to look around the property. After all," I paused, unsure of the right word, "he did put me in his will. I'd like take the time to get to know him."

"Up to you, son," he said, "I'm just Mister Lincoln's lawyer. But I suppose it would be the right thing to do."

He gave me his address, told me that the funeral would be on Saturday, and that he looked forward to meeting me in person.

After he hung up, I sat there, staring at my monitor. If what Cletus had told me was true, I would never have to work again. As I pondered my mysterious long-lost relation, the phone rang again. Maybe someone else left me their fortune.

"Bernard Devlin, how can I help you?"

"Mister Devlin, this is Chris with ArchUSA. We have an assignment for you."

ArchUSA was one of my best clients. I hoped, however, that it would not involve anything I needed to stick around Miami for. They needed a background check on a personal injury Plaintiff who was claiming $250,000 in pain and suffering from a slip and fall in her local supermarket. The report was ordered before I hung up.

I turned my attention back to my newly found fortune. Of course, it was not my fortune, at least not yet. Stillwater was a mystery. It did not seem to exist on anything but the most obscure maps. Back in the day it served as a railway depot.

It was worth a trip there, though. Forty million and change was certainly worth a few days off. I booked a ticket to Kansas City for the next morning. Despite the money, I chose a coach seat.

I called Susan, my office manager, into my office. She used to be my secretary before I promoted her to office manager. I decided to play this close to the vest until I knew more about the whole thing. I told her that my uncle had passed away, and that I would take tomorrow off and some of the next week, since I was named executor of the estate.

"You close?" she asked in a concerned voice.

"Not really, but most of my family will be there, you know how family is." I knew this would pluck the right strings in her heart—she was always taking days off due to 'family issues.' Her family issues, however, always seemed to arise on a Monday, though. I also knew she had no idea that I had no family.

"I'm sure I can hold down the fort while you're gone—you go take care of what you need to." I knew that her 'holding down the fort' meant coming in at ten, playing solitaire until lunch, and leaving at three. She was good at answering my calls and handling clients—which was all I expected from her since I was only paying her minimum wage.

"You'll be getting a report in about two hours. Can you fax it to Chris over at Arch? Thanks."

"I'll take care of it."

As I left, I could already tell she was planning on closing early. I walked to the parking garage in the mid-day Miami heat, and tried to process this development. Worry wormed its way into my thoughts. What if the estate is worthless—the bank accounts wrong, the property decrepit? There had to be a catch—no one would bequest that much money to a complete stranger. I just hoped it was a catch I could live with. Looking back, I now realize just how much of a catch it was.

As I passed a bus stop a vagrant walked up and asked for money. I usually ignore the bums since most of them are druggies washed out by meth or cocaine. Something in the guy's eyes, though, told me he was might be different. There was a clarity that you do not normally see in the addicted. I handed him a $10 and told him to go get a real meal. I figured it was like karma—if I helped out someone after my huge inheritance, maybe more good things would come my way. I could not have been more wrong.

His face lit up and he thanked me profusely and hobbled away. I watched him for a while, but lost him in the crowd of people on the sidewalk.

Two blocks later, I saw the guy emerge from a corner store with a large bottle in a paper sack. He made eye contact with me, raised the bottle in a mock salute, then took a deep swig. Trying not to let this disappointment bring me down, I turned by attention back to my uncle John. My parent had died years ago, and they had never been much about family. My mom drank herself to an early grave after my dad died in a fishing accident off Key West. My sleuthing skills had turned up little on John Lincoln of Stillwater, Missouri. Which was odd, since anyone with that much money, generally, leads a life that leaves a paper trail.

As is pushed my way into traffic, my mind switched to the fact that the last vacation I had taken was five years ago, which was also a lifetime ago. I had no idea just how many different lives I could lead. Occasionally I took a "sick of work" day, but I was never out for more than one day. Being a private investigator, every day I did not work was a day I did not earn money. With the kind of money I was supposed to inherit, I wondered if working was in my future.

Sitting still would kill me, though. I spend my spare time reading, working on my business, or watching soccer. A full day of idleness would kill me. After packing my "Go to Go" bag with jeans, t-shirts, button ups, and my "wrinkle-free" suit, I was ready to go. It was only five pm. Sitting at my home office desk, I realized just how empty my life was. I had few friends. Most had abandoned me years ago. My last girlfriend left me over a year ago—she said I was too distant. My life seemed to be a hollow shell of work and self-amusement. To beat my growing depression, I decided to treat myself to a steak dinner.

A master of self-deception and distraction, I turned my mind to the money and what I could do with that much money. Of course, I would not be unemployed—that seemed to be all I had that identified who I was. Finally, could take only those cases I wanted to; no more late-night stakeouts to catch some personal injury plaintiff walking down the block to buy beer when he claimed he could barely walk at all. I changed out of my slacks and into a pair of jeans and t-shirt, then headed beck to my car.

On my drive back across town, I called Bethany to see if she wanted to have dinner with me. My relationship with Bethany was complicated. We dated for a while. Then she broke it off, saying that she wanted to "really live." Whatever that meant. She kept in touch and, despite my reluctance, became just friends. It seemed we shared more as friends than we had as a couple. I knew she would not turn down a free steak dinner.

I thought over what, if anything, I was going to tell her about John Lincoln and my inheritance. I decided that I would not mention any actual dollar amounts–especially since I was not sure I was the rightful heir. I did want her opinion on the whole matter.

As usual, Bethany was late. However, she sure knew how to make her entrance. I could barely contain myself, she was wearing that slinky brown skirt that accentuated her legs and a low cut blouse that drew your attention away from her legs, and focused the attention towards her more voluptuous assets.

After we were seated, she asked what was up. She knew I was not the kind of guy to go out to dinner for no reason.

"Well, I guess you might say my fortune has changed," I said.

"What do you mean? What happened? Are you back—" She almost sounded excited for me, which made me suspicious.

"No, nothing like that," I replied cutting her off. "I got a call about an uncle who recently died, and left me his estate."

"Wow. How much?" She leaned forward, her eyes lightly widening. Assessing the news, she intuitively wondered whether I was going to be rich. That was the Bethany I knew.

"I don't know. The guy lived in Missouri in the middle of nowhere. I guess he had a farm, or something. We'll see."

She sat back, her eyes closing to hide her disappointment. "I guess congrats, is probably not the right thing to say, but... I don't see you as a farmer, though." She laughed at her own joke, which was a habit I found annoyingly attractive.

I did not know how to take her comment, so chose to ignore it. "Anyways, I have no idea who the guy was—my folks never talked about him."

"Hm." She was scanning the menu, and I knew she was merely humoring me. Bethany would much rather be telling me all about her life. "I'm betting the hick lawyer from Missouri screwed up. So you're going to Missouri? When?"

"Tomorrow."

"How long are you going to be gone?" she asked.

"Depends. The funeral is Saturday, and I guess the will and stuff will be handled, too. Then I thought I'd make whatever arrangements necessary to take care of the property and stuff. Then I'll come back. Maybe Tuesday."

"Take care of? Aren't you gonna sell it?"

"Probably." I paused as our dinner was brought by the waiter. "But I feel some sort of obligation to this uncle to at least look through his stuff."

She laughed, which always sent shivers down my spine, but in a good way. "Oh, Berns, you were always the sentimental type."

I smiled, doing my best to charm her. I still found her attractive. Part of it was her, but part of it was that, at least at one point, she liked me enough to consider me as a possible husband. Or at least I hoped that was how she felt. I never could get a straight answer out of her about us.

"What if it's a lot of money?" she asked quietly, returning to her second favorite topic of conversation, and trying to gauge if I thought it was a lot of money.

When I didn't answer her immediately, she pressed

again, "I said, what if it's a lot of money?" she repeated, "you know, like a million dollars or something."

"I guess, I'll buy a house and invest the rest. Maybe take a vacation." I hoped this dodge would put her off the scent of money.

"You're so boring," she laughed again, her smile cutting into me. I wished she smiled like that at me more often. "But seriously, you'd tell me if you were rich, right?"

"Absolutely," I lied. I decided to turn the conversation to her life. I knew she could not wait to tell me about her most recent boyfriend. "So, enough about me. What about you? How are you doing?"

"Well, you remember Bret?"

I nodded. She proceeded to go through her love life, dissecting and analysing each and every detail, from whether the guy kept a clean house, to his love-making routines. I immediately went into the passive listening mode. The occasional "yeah" and "huh" was enough to keep her talking. I focused on my meal to distract myself from the sordid details of her life. Besides, I had other things to think about—like just what was I going to do with the money?

I really did not mind being her listening board. For some strange reason, just being around her thrilled me. At the end of the meal, we walked out together. I even asked her over for a nightcap.

"Now, Berns," she said, her pitying look enough to send blood rushing to my face, "you know we had our fun, but it just didn't work. I appreciate your interest, though." She gently kissed me on my cheek and escaped into the evening. "Call me when you learn about the inheritance, OK?"

I went home, lay in my bed, and stared at the ceiling. My mind kept going back to my embarrassing pass at Bethany. I was stupid. I wondered how the money would impact my relationship with her. How it would impact my friends would also be hard to tell. I picked up a used mystery novel I had already read twice . Despite the fact I was in the private investigator business, I still liked mystery novels—even if they were far-fetched. About half-way through I finally succumbed to sleep, breathing to the never-ending hum of traffic in the city. Unfortunately, half an hour later, my phone rang, shocking me awake.

"Hello?"

"Hey, it's me,"

"How you doing Simon?" Simon was a private investigator associate of mine—I gave him the work I was too proud, or too busy, to handle. In exchange, he returned the favor.

"Not bad. What's up with you?"

"I'm heading out tomorrow to go to Missouri."

"Missouri? Big job?"

"Nah. Some relative of mine died; I got to go and administer the estate—maybe get a few bucks in return."

"Sounds lame. Guess you're not interested in a divorce job? I need some pics of the fifty-three-year-old wife cavorting with her 17-year-old boyfriend."

"Sorry, I'm gone tomorrow morning, not sure when I'll be back."

"That's cool. Keep me in mind if you need anything while I'm gone."

"You know you're my number one guy; it'll all go to you while I'm away."

"Later."

Thankfully, I fell asleep almost instantly after hanging up. Three hours later, the alarm clock woke me to the beginning of the next phase of my life. I ate a large breakfast, and took a taxi to the airport. I was not about to take my SUV to the terminal. I arrived at the airport the required two hours early. Of course, it took virtually no time to get through security; I had an hour and forty-five minutes to wait for my flight. Sitting at the gate was too boring for me, so I slowly ambled through the airport.

As I walked along the "B" concourse, I could feel the tension in the air; road weary travelers and newbies exude nervous energy into the recycled air. It seemed like everyone at the airport, including the Port Authority employees seemed nervous, but not about the same thing. The flaming aircraft crashing flickers at the edge of most travelers' thoughts as they sit at the gate, looking at this monstrous tube that apparently can fly. The Port employees seemed more worried that a traveler would get unruly; this was evident to me since they looked at all passengers with an eye towards trouble.

The thought of all that money was constantly gnawing at me while the airport atmosphere was keying me up. Coffee and a bookshop lured me in with the siren promise of caffeine and distraction. A large cup of drip and an apple fritter cost me more than they should have. I ate them while watching the piped-in airport television. It was a newscast about some IPO for some tech company that had shot up in astronomical proportions; six hours later it dropped like a rock, until it was worthless. The whispers in the back of my mind hinted that I might need to learn about stocks and bonds soon.

As I finished my second breakfast the news switched to a "feel good" story about kittens and a fire. I left and went into the bookshop. I browsed through most of the books quickly—they were all best sellers. I charged another used mystery novel by some unknown author and a biography about Jesse James.

As I walked back to the gate, my mind kept circling the issue of money. All money comes with strings attached. Some of those strings held as tight as chains, others are long enough to hang yourself with. The money pulled at me with a strange attraction. It was so much that I could ignore the chains that waited for me. But, sitting in the airport, I barely considered it. I had seen money do strange things to people. I had dropped everything and was off to the back roads of Missouri in pursuit of money. I justified it as not being based in greed, because I had never placed a lot of emphasis on money. It was more like a perverse lust of money. I knew what the money could do for me. I knew it would buy me access to new experiences. It would give me the freedom I yearned for.

I had so many questions and no one to answer them. Cletus had not said whether I was mentioned by name in the will. If it was, how did John Lincoln know about me? Also, what was John Lincoln doing in Missouri? How did he get that much money? What did he do for a living? Did he purposely leave out his other relatives? Would they be angry?

The biggest question I had was how did someone living in the middle of nowhere (or so I assumed), have so much money? Crazy theories flashed through my imagination. It could be a pot farm, or maybe he was a retired oil magnate. I hated to admit it, but the mere idea of all that money had started to change me. I was strongly tempted to upgrade to first class. I had no idea what lay ahead that would change me much more than any money ever could. I could get used to wealth and the comforts that it would bring. In the back of my mind, No longer would I be forced to cajole and persuade the people I wanted things from. I could simply make demands. Or so I thought.

I watched the flight attendant's pre-flight safety lecture. The water-landing instructions were laughable. We would be flying over Georgia, Tennessee, and other inland states—the chances of us falling out of the sky and hitting a lake had to be incredibly small.

I sat white-knuckled as the steel cylinder shuddered to life and ran down the runway towards take off. I hated flying. The next thing I knew we were cruising slightly above the layer of clouds and heading west. It was ironic, me heading west in my own personal gold rush. After the post take off jitters left me, I began to read—I needed to escape the questions gnawing at me about the money. Two and a half hours later, I had finished the mystery. The flight attendant passed by me several times, obviously intent on serving the first class cabin. She ignored me.

I tried to sleep, but the person in front of me had reclined his seat so it felt like he was laying in my lap. I chose not to recline—it seemed inhumane to pin someone in. I knew a long drive awaited me once I got to Kansas City. I drifted in the nether land between wake and sleep where reality and dreams meet. I kept thinking of all the things that I would do once I had the money. First, I would pay off my condo and my car. Next I would figure out investing so it would not run out. Maybe I would get a yacht. I always thought it would be fun to live at sea, free from the encumbrances of city life. Of course, I would have to learn to Captain a yacht—or maybe I'd have my own personal Captain.

A few hours later, I was violently shock awake by person behind me putting his tray table up in preparation for landing. I looked out the window, and watched the plane falling out of the sky to bump along the runway. The landing was worse than the takeoff, the pilot landed on one wheel, causing my seatbelt to strain against my stomach. Then he careened onto the next set of wheels, throwing me the opposite direction. He finally slammed on the brakes, sending me lurching forward. I wondered how anyone would consider traveling fun.

Once on the ground and out of the plane I had to figure out where my suitcase would end up. Two conversations with airport workers and one wrong turn, I ended up at the baggage carousel and waited for my suitcase to slide down on the conveyor belt. I could hardly believe the air conditioning pumping into the airport; it was a meat locker. My bag plopped onto the conveyer and I saw the blue tape that notified me that it had been searched by the TSA. From the looks of it, they must have hired gorillas to do the work.

Leaving the baggage area, I had to find a rental car. The major brands were full of travelers, but in a dark alcove, Dan's Rentals looked deserted. I wondered why. I decided to give it a try. The woman behind the counter gave me a free upgrade to a sedan because I was there on an off-peak time. I wondered if Dan's Rentals ever had an on-peak time. She did give me excellent directions to Stillwater. In a nutshell she said to take the 71 to the 7 then catch the 13, all headed south and watch for a sign to Stillwater. If I came across a sign that said, 'Welcome to Arkansas, Bill Clinton's State,' I would have gone too far.

"How do you know where Stillwater is?" I asked. After all, it seemed like the black hole of the state.

"Oh, I worked near there when I was in college at Mizzou. What brings you there? You're not a local-"

"My uncle passed, so-"

"I'm so sorry," she said, "Your Uncle was John Lincoln, right?"

I must have looked dumfounded.

"It's a very small town and John was, well, notorious." She eyed me closely.

"Notorious?"

"Everybody knew John, that's for sure. But you knew that, right?" She was prying for information.

"Actually, I never met him. I just got a call."

Her eyes widened slightly, "Oh, I see. Well, good luck, and I'm sorry for your loss." She handed me the keys, trying to close the conversation abruptly.

"Thanks, I uh," I stammered. "Can you tell me anything about John?"

"I'm sure you'll be told a lot about him when you get there. John was a good man, though. Notorious, but good."

The phone rang, preventing her from answering

any more of my questions. I left the counter to go find my upgraded sedan. The second I stepped outside I was assaulted by the oppressive August heat. If hell had an entry way, this must be what it felt like. It was not just hot—hot does not begin to describe it. It was muggy and violent; like you were being slowly roasted. It felt like the sun settled down on your back and slowly singed your skin. I found a late model Ford sedan that sat baking in the sun. I was immediately glad she gave me the upgrade. I was also glad the car had fabric seats.

Once in the sedan, I sat and let the air conditioning do its job, until the inside of the car was less like a blast furnace and more like an oven. I drove south towards my destiny. After about half an hour all signs of civilization were behind me. Gone were the steel and glass buildings pulsing with commerce. Gone too, were the suburban homes, with their neatly mani-cured and watered lawns. I was in "farm country." All around me were fields of wheat, soy, corn, alfalfa, and cotton. The fields were a patchwork of green, brown, and gold swaying gently in the summer heat. I could begin to understand why people would stay around this furnace.

I was surrounded by thousands of acres of crop-land. Occasionally, I would see a worn-out home off in the distance, its paint slowly mellowing under the sun's harsh rays. Sometimes I would pass cattle lazily grazing on the dry grass, looking hot, but content.

The highway, probably only traveled by supply trucks and locals, shimmered off in the distance, creating the illusion I was driving on black glass. Everything looked hot, dry, and burnt. Even the asphalt seemed liquid, as if the heat somehow managed to melt it back into tar. The black ribbon ran off to the north and south desperately seeking relief from the heat of the sun. It never ended.

Occasionally, I would see a sign for some town, but

I never actually saw any towns. It was like the road and I were the only two things living out there. It had been over an hour since I had seen another car. I realized that, despite the air conditioning, I was sweating. I hated to admit it, but I something was wrong. It felt wrong. An ominous gloom seemed to pierce my soul as each mile progressed. Despite the sun, it felt dark. The shadows moved and shifted, playing with my imagination. Back then I never listened to my intuition. I had to laugh at myself; it was just a road, like any other road. It eventually ended in Stillwater and my fortune. The siren's call of the inheritance was too strong, it pushed the fear to the recess of my mind. I had struggled for everything in my life. I had to beg, borrow, and steal to make it to where I was today. I constantly worried about how to pay the bills on my unpredictable salary. To me, this windfall was a Godsend. They say money is the root of all evil—but it is really the desire for money that leads to evil. I wondered what sort of evil this money might bring.

To take my mind off the feeling of impending doom I was fighting off, I turned the air conditioning up, and switched on the radio. All I got was static on the FM dial. When I switched over to AM, I got two stations. One played country music and the other was the farm report. So I listened to a man with a southern drawl discuss pork belly futures, cotton options, and grain forecasts for a while. The cadence was comforting, even if I had no idea what he was really talking about. These people grew something tangible. They actually produced something out of nothing. They planted seeds in the spring, cared for the plants in the summer, and harvested them in the fall. They actually saw what they made come to life.

It made my life feel irrelevant. I never produced anything, really. My work consisted of sifting through other people's lives and finding out the dirty little secrets we all hide. I produced nothing. I never realized how unhappy I was doing the dirty work for some other lawyer. I switched over to the country music station to take my mind of my total disgust with my life. I had to admit, I liked country music. Hank Williams was singing about a dark highway when I saw a sign that said Jefferson City, 25 miles. Then, I saw the billboard that all road trip drivers welcome with overwhelming joy: McDonalds, first exit in Jeff City. That meant a lukewarm burger, greasy fires, a watered-down soda, and bathrooms. It was a welcome oasis in the hostile traveler's world. I turned off my personal lost highway and into Jefferson City.

I found the McDonalds, ordered a supersized meal, two cherry pies, and a large coffee. I decided I deserved a break today, and chose a corner booth and read the local newspaper. Below the fold, but in large enough print to catch my eye, there was an article:

BONES OF MISSING TOURIST FOUND NEAR STILLWATER

Wednesday, Stillwater farmer, Ed Nile, found a pile of human remains along the southern border of his farm. He said he reported the find to the County Sheriff, and the remains looked like they had been stacked in a neat pile. He figured that the remains had been there, at the most, two months, since he had not been to that particular location since late May.

"It was the strangest, thing, though, them bones looked like they was stacked on purpose. But I figured that there was no way that could be, since it had to be some coyote got to them, and hoarded them there," Nile said.

County Sheriff, Tom Jones, issued a short press release stating that they had not conclusively identified the remains as those of missing tourist Steven Holcomb. He also indicated that the remains had been sent to the Missouri State Crime Lab for processing. The results are expected by next Wednesday.

Sheriff Jones would not say that Holcomb's disappearance, or the human remains found, were related to the other six missing or murdered people. He cautioned against jumping to any conclusions that a serial killer was responsible for the missing.

In the past ten months, seven people, including Holcomb, have disappeared in Southern Missouri. Three sets of unidentified remains have been found.

Locals speculate that a drifter must have passed through, hiding in the numerous abandoned farmhouses and caverns, and caused the disappearances.

The first disappearance was Leonard Wokowski, an Illinois truck driver whose truck broke down along Rural Route 22. Mister Wokowski's remains were identified approximately two months after his disappearance. His disappearance was followed by the disappearance of two University of Missouri Agriculture students, performing research for their senior thesis. Their remains have not been found.

Three other missing include Richard Stokes, a Stillwater resident, his common law wife, Nicole Ferigan, and Damian Stone, a traveling salesman, whose route ran from Little Rock to Kansas City.

The Sheriff's Office has missing person's files on these people. Anyone with information on these mysterious disappearances and deaths, are urged to contact Sheriff Tom Jones.

Stillwater sounded a lot more interesting than I thought it would be. Missing people, chewed up remains, a veritable hotbed of crime and death. It occurred to me that Cletus did not tell me how Uncle John had died. I hoped it was not murder.

I finished the second cherry pie, grabbed the coffee, which was finally cool enough to drink, and decided I should get to town before dark. If some lunatic was on the loose in these parts, killing the unaware traveler, I wanted to be locked behind my hotel door.

17

The food had calmed my nerves and I pushed it to make it there. Another hour and I was pulling off the highway and onto 13 towards Stillwater. It was about three in the afternoon and I was totally exhausted. The longer I drove, the more I liked the area. In Miami, people are surrounded by the ocean. Here, I could see forever; the horizon was a flat line. Even though it was really hot, it was Eden; lush fields full of grains, trees, gently whispering in the afternoon breeze. In the background there was a low hum of summertime insects. I could see why John Lincoln stayed here.

I almost missed the turn off to town because I was caught up in it all. A new place; a fortune. It was hard to take it all in. Once off Rural Route 13, I was "in town." Town consisted of approximately four square blocks of two story buildings, all on wide, two lane streets. Each street had its own name, "Elm", "Grove", and, of course, "Main." On the east side of town, just outside the "core" of town was a Wal-Mart. I could see the impact of the Wal-Mart on the town. There were several vacant storefronts with the faint outline of store names, like "Beverly's Dresses" and "Mort's Market." It was a sad town, its back broken by years of self-sufficiency undermined by modern commerce.

Behind the dilapidated store fronts and faded paint you could tell the town had been through hell, but was slowly emerging out the other side. It was not a sad place, just an age-worn, but hopeful survivor. You could tell that the town was not giving up—it was simply going to adapt to the modern age. In the same way, the town's people endured, despite the changing times.

Chapter Two
Skeletons in the Closet

History is little else than a picture of human crimes and misfortunes.
François Marie Arouet de Voltaire, L'Ingénu

Now that I was "in town" I had to find Cletus T. Montgomery III's office. As luck would have it I drove right past his corner office on Main and Grove. He even had parking out front. I pulled in next to a dirty Cadillac, which I assumed was his, and got out. I sensed the heavy presence of the town resting on me. The dread I had experienced on my driver here still itched at my mind. Adding to that was the simple fact that I was a stranger to everyone here. I guessed that there was not a single person who did not know I was here in the entire town. I shut the car door and glanced around. It was mid-afternoon and there were few people walking about in the heat. The town seemed unnaturally quiet, like something dark meandered through the streets dampening any happiness the town's inhabitants could have. The money's draw forced this foreboding, and I went inside, where I was immediately greeted by a woman dressed directly out of the 1982 Sears catalog with a 1950's hairdo.

"Hello. May I help you?" she asked pleasantly.

"I hope so. I'm Bernard Devlin, John Lincoln's great nephew."

"Oh, of course, I'm sorry about your loss. It was a shock that Mister Lincoln had passed.

"Mister Montgomery will be with you in a moment, please, take a seat."

As I walked to the old, worn leather chair, I heard her buzz Cletus and say, "It's *him*. He's here!"

Again, I wondered about John Lincoln. Through her tone I gathered they were expecting someone very different from me.

Cletus walked out of his office, lumbering like a wild animal in its lair, and began pumping my hand vigorously. "Well, boy, welcome. Welcome!" he smiled, "It's good to meet you. On the phone, you sounded, well, so much different."

Cletus, on the other hand, looked exactly like I imagined. He was old, with scraggly white hair and incredibly bushy eyebrows. He was at least three hundred pounds and wore bright red suspenders, a starched white shirt, and an antique tie.

"It's good to meet you, Mister Montgomery."

"Please, call me Cletus, everyone else does. Come on in, can I get you anything? Coffee? Tea?"

"No, I'm alright."

"Good, good. Have a seat, son."

"Thanks," I sat in a leather chair in front of his desk. I surveyed his office. Papers were scattered about in various piles that perched on file cabinets, credenzas, and his desk. Once corner of his office looked like a tornado had come through.

"Well, son, where are you staying," he asked, as if it were an inside joke. He dropped heavily into his chair, and I held my breath, hoping it would not collapse under his weight.

"I don't know, I just got into town. To tell you the truth, I hadn't even thought of it."

Cletus let out a huge guffaw, causing his belly to shake and said, "Well, son, I'll make it easy for you. You're staying at 'The Landing.' I took the liberty of making you a reservation." He snickered. "By the way, The Landing is Stillwater's finest and only hotel, motel, and inn."

I had to laugh too.

"Anyways, I suppose we should get down to business." He searched through several piles of documents on his desk. "Here is it." He put a pair of smudged reading classes on and reviewed the file. "First, Mister Lincoln's funeral will be tomorrow at 9:15 am sharp. It'll be held at the Lutheran Church on Harvest. You can't miss it—big red brick buildin'. I imagine there'll be a large turnout, everybody in town knew Mister Lincoln." He paused, as if he wanted to say more, and then continued, "After that, we'll come back here and I'll open and read the will."

"I'm sorry," I interrupted, "Read the will? I thought you'd already had..." I was crushed. I came here seeking my fortune only to find it snatched away by this lawyer who had misled me. It seemed strange that I would become so angry so quickly and I chided myself for overreacting.

Cletus said, "Oh, I see. No, I've not opened the will. Mister Lincoln left an envelope in my care that was to be opened upon his death. It contained instructions to call you, unfortunately the number he gave me was a little outdated. The letter said he'd left his estate to you and that I needed to contact you. It even had the amounts of his accounts. The letter was, oh, I'd guess six, seven years old. I imagine the estate's grown since then."

"So there's no guarantee that I'll inherit anything?" I asked, again much more sharply than I had intended. I figured the heat must be getting to me.

"Oh, I wouldn't worry about that. When Mister Lincoln said he'd do something, he would. He was a man of his word." Cletus eyed me over the frames of his glasses. He did not seem surprised at my anger.

"I'm sorry," I said. "It's been a long day of travel, and I'm not used to this type of heat—Miami is a lot different," I replied.

"Anyway, after that, I'll have Dean take you to Mister Lincoln's home so you can look around and such. Once evening comes on, I suggest you head back to town right quick."

"Why's that?"

"Well, you're not from around here, and, well, things are different out there. You see, Mister Lincoln's home is fairly remote." He paused, as if he had to speak of something unpleasant. "There's wild animals out there. They ain't afraid of people. They say that's how Mister Lincoln passed. I don't go out there after the sun goes down, that's for sure."

"How'd he die?"

"Well apparently, he was coming in from his yard, when something attacked him. Tore out his throat."

"Huh." It was more of a statement than a question. The wildest animals I encountered were drunk frat boys in town for spring break. Anything that could tear out a throat was something foreign and dangerous to me.

"Well, Sheriff Jones says it was likely a bobcat, but Zeke, the who found Mister Lincoln's body said he didn't think so. Said he'd never seen anything like that. And I'd take ol' Zeke's word over Sheriff Jones' any day."

"Why?"

"Zeke, was Mister Lincoln's good friend. He makes his living trapping and selling animal hides. Sheriff Jones probably never killed anything but a potted plant, and even then, he'd have to work hard at it."

A chill ran down my spine. "I see." It seemed like Cletus was telling me, in a backhand way, that John Lincoln might have been murdered.

"Enough about that." Cletus said, in a hurry to change the subject. "It'll take a few days for the estate to settle, then, it's all yours. I'd be happy to help you wind up the estate, you know, if you need to know who the best auction house is, how much the land is worth, anything, just give me a call." As he spoke he stood, his business card in one hand, his hand extended in the other.

I stood up, shook his right hand and took the business card with my left. "Thank you. I appreciate everything you have done. Really." I meant it. It was not every day you got to shake hands with the conduit for an untold fortune. Assuming, of course, I inherited the fortune. It struck me how solid his handshake was, especially for someone of his advanced years.

Cletus kept my hand and pulled me closer to him. His aged eyes were hard and sharp. "Remember what I said, about being out there at night. It's dangerous."

"I will," I replied, I had no intention of staying out there at night. After all, I was just a city boy; I had no idea how to deal with wild animals other than rats and roaches.

Ruby was standing in the lobby waiting for me. She told me she was more than happy to walk me over to The Landing. I figured she wanted to know all about the new stranger in town and I was not disappointed. Not five seconds after the door closed, she began the interrogation.

"So, you're from Miami, huh?"

"Yeah." I did not want to give her anything more than answers to her questions. If half of what was rumored about small towns was true, anything I said would result in rumors ten times magnified from the truth. I was irritated much more than I needed to be with her.

"What's it like?"

"Tropical. Not hot like this." I wiped the sweat away from my forehead.

She giggled like a schoolgirl, "What do you do there?"

"I'm a consultant." I was trying to be nice, but the pestering questions annoyed me.

"Really, how fascinating."

"It can be, that's for sure." I was doing my best to kill this conversation, without seeming too rude. The last thing I needed was a small town turned against me because I was from the "big city" and just here to get my inheritance, even if that was true.

Thankfully, we walked in silence for a little while, and then she blurted out, "You know Mister Lincoln was a good man."

My anger receded to be replaced with curiosity. "Well, up until yesterday, I didn't even know I had a great uncle. What was he like?"

"Well, no matter what some in this town think, I thought he was a nice man."

"What do you mean?"

"Well, he was, I guess you could say, unique," she stopped, trying to determine whether or not to continue.

"Don't worry. You won't hurt my feelings. I never met the man."

"No, no, it's nothing like that," she said, "Well, sometimes he was different."

"How so?" Now I was intrigued.

"I really shouldn't be telling you this. After all, the man is dead. It's inappropriate."

Great. Now she was going to clam up. "It's OK, really. You're just helping me get a picture of my long-lost relation." I hoped she would continue.

"Well, I suppose." She paused, trying to form her words just right. "Sometimes he'd, well, make unusual requests at the store."

"Unusual, how?"

"Well, once, I remember he special ordered an entire case of hot sauce. The hottest there is."

"That is kind of strange." I said. I figured John Lincoln must have liked spicy foods.

"And then there was a time when he came into the post office, covered in dirty overalls."

"Maybe he was gardening," I suggested.

"It looked like blood." She said quietly.

"Blood?" Great, not only was he insane, he walked

around with blood on himself. I wondered whether that would impact my ability to inherit the estate.

"Yeah. It was almost like he'd just skinned a deer or something."

"Maybe he had," I suggested, trying more to convince myself than her.

"Well, here we are," she said brightly, obviously glad that we were at our destination. That way she would not have to talk about the strange old man anymore. I got the impression she was testing me to see if 'crazy' ran in the family.

"Thank you. Do I need to move my car?"

She giggled again. "Nope. No one's going to care about it parked over there."

Over there was about 75 feet from the front of The Landing. I figured I could move it later.

"Now don't pay no mind to me, about your great uncle, I mean. I'm just a foolish old woman. I don't even know why I told you that."

"Don't worry about it, really. It's OK."

As she turned and walked back down the sidewalk, I wondered what she had thought of me. I knew the phone lines would be buzzing all evening long as details of our brief conversation were placed under the community's microscope.

I walked into The Landing and was immediately greeted by a man who looked like a line-backer, dressed in jeans and a button up shirt.

"Hi," he said.

"Hello, I'm-"

"I know, John's nephew, Bernard, right?" He smiled. "Little happens in these parts without the whole town knowing. Half the town hopes you're the marrying type for their single daughters. The other half hopes you're not as strange as your great uncle appeared to be." His smile disarmed the barb about John; obviously he knew John and was just joking with me.

"You can call me Berns, that's what everyone else calls me." Instantly, I liked him. He seemed honest and forthright.

"I'm Dean, my cousin Jessica, runs this place as well as Cowan's, the restaurant next door."

"Nice to meet you. I have to admit, I'm not used to small towns..."

"Not a problem. Jessica and I will do our best to take care of you."

"You don't have to do that..."

"It's OK. We were both John's closest friends and we feel it's the least that we can do. Besides, we figured you'd want to know about John, his life, his eccentricities, you know, about the man, not the town myth."

It was strange that a young man would be one of John's best friends. If he was, he might be able to give me some insight. "Actually, that would be great."

"You look like heck. You'd better freshen up, and I'll take you out to dinner at Cowan's."

"Sound's good."

He handed me a key to the room at the top of the stairs. It was a nice room, decorated more like a guest bedroom than a hotel room. The windows overlooked the quiet intersection. I wondered how long it had been since someone had stayed here. I quickly splashed cold water on my face to try to erase the worn out look on my face, and went back downstairs. Dean was sitting behind the desk reading *Missouri Farmer*.

He looked up and said, "It's $45 per night. $50 on weekends."

"I'm sorry, it was a really long day." I began to search for my credit card.

Dean smiled. "It's OK. I figure you're good for it. Just thought you should know."

I wondered how much he knew about John Lincoln. I figured he might know too much; maybe he had somehow figured out that I had been left a fortune. I hoped he was not upset by it. Hopefully, he was not expecting he was going to inherit John's fortune. If he did, he might resent me. The edge of anger bled into my mind once again. I could not shake the dark mood that had descended on me.

"Come on, let's get some grub."

Dean flipped the sign to "No Vacancy" and locked the door. We walked around the corner and there was Cowan's.

"Jessie wanted to be here to meet you, but she got called up to Jeff City on account of her parents."

"Her parents? What happened?"

"Oh, nothing, really. Every now and then they raise a ruckus and she has to drive up and visit them in the retirement home. She'll be back tonight. She wouldn't miss John's funeral."

He guided me into a back booth, "We'll likely want some privacy. The last thing you need is to have people stare at you while you try to eat. Not to mention try to hear every word we say."

Cowan's was a cozy café. There were several tables strewn throughout the restaurant, and booths along the interior walls. Six couples and one family were already eating. They all glanced at us as we walked by in the same way that one glances at a homeless man in a good part of town. Again, the ire flared in my head. Maybe I was being paranoid; maybe not.

As I started to look at the menu, Dean grabbed it out of my hands and said, "Trust me. You want the fried chicken dinner."

"Sounds good," I replied. It was hard to gauge Dean. On the one hand, he might be friendly because he was a close friend of John. Or maybe he was trying to size me up to see if I was worthy of John's fortunes. Then again, he might just be trying to see how easy it would be to take the money from me outright. He had a dangerous edge to him.

We made small talk until dinner showed up. As I

gnawed on a fried chicken leg, I brought the conversation back around to John Lincoln.

"John was a good man. Do not ever forget that. No matter what anybody in this town says."

"You're the second person to tell me that today." I left my question unasked.

"John's been around there parts since shortly after World War I. People 'round here are too young to remember him back then. They just saw him as a familiar fixture in town. You know, he was just a kid when he came to Stillwater."

"How do you know all this? It's not like you're much older than I am."

"My great grandpa and John were close friends. My family's grown up with John. I've pieced together the various stories both he and my dad told.

"Anyway, John started working at the produce stands in town when he first got here. He also gambled with it. Apparently he was a pretty good gambler. Soon, he'd saved up enough money to buy the land where his house now stands. Then he began to explore the caves."

"Caves? What caves?" I decided to act dumb. The article that I had read had mentioned them, but I might as well see what he knew about them.

"The property sits about a series of caves under the Ozark Mountains. Nobody's quite sure where they all lead.

"John went into those caves all by himself, and sometimes he was gone for two, three days at a stretch. He was always polite and gentle until you mentioned the caves. It was like a dark cloud passed behind his eyes and he'd grow real quiet. John's only rule was never go into the caves without him."

"Why was that? Was there something special about the caves?" My heart skipped a beat. This was the most interesting fact about John I had heard.

"Well, I can remember a time when my third

cousin, Elmer, came to visit over the summer. Elmer thought it would be fun to explore the caves. I don't know what happened to him down there, but he came out pale and had to be sent home. He never came back here. Last I heard, they had to put him in an institution because they thought he was crazy. Some of the locals say John scared the kid out of his mind. Me, I'm not so sure." He sipped his ice tea, letting the story sink in.

He continued, "These past few years were not so easy for John, that's for sure. It was, oh, five, maybe six years ago, and he changed. Both Jessie and I noticed it. His eyes became less and less kind and more and more dark. Sometimes you'd see him walking around town in his overalls, talking to himself. One time, I followed close enough behind him to hear him, but he was speaking gibberish. It was sad, really. But, he was in Church every Sunday morning, in his gray suit, front pew, center. Sometimes he'd just sit there, staring at the stained-glass windows behind the pulpit. Whenever someone would try to comfort him, he'd mutter, 'I'm OK. You just don't understand'."

"Understand what?"

"To tell you the truth, I'm not sure. It seemed like no one understood John. I mean, no one could understand the change in him. Combined with the fact that he was from a different age entirely. It was hard to say. At first I thought it was a sickness, but Doctor Stipek told me not to worry, John was in excellent health for a man his age."

"Doctor Stipek told you?"

"You've got to remember. Around here not too much is secret. If someone asks the Doctor if their close friend is OK, the Doctor is going to tell them the truth. We take care of our own.

"That's what happened to Jessie's folks. Her dad was diagnosed with Alzheimer's about a year or so ago. We all chipped in and helped them buy into an assisted living community up in Jeff City."

"What if they didn't want to go?"

"Her dad didn't want to. Like all of us, he was a proud man. Didn't want to admit that he was not the man he used to be. Her mom, however, knew that the only way they were going to be happy was to move so that he could have the medical attention he needed. So they did.

"Naturally Jessie felt guilty about the whole thing, which is why, whenever they call, she hightails it up to Jeff City."

I had just finished my second piece of cornbread when the waitress appeared.

"Will there be anything else?"

"No, we're fine, Cindy. Thanks." Dean replied

As she started to walk away, I asked for the bill.

"No friend of Dean's ever pays. That's the rule."

I protested as much as I could. I did not want any special treatment. It did not work. So I did the next most reasonable thing. I secretly placed a twenty-dollar bill under my plate as we were leaving. As we walked slowly back to the hotel, enjoying being full, Dean gave me a little background on the town of Stillwater.

Stillwater was founded in the 1840s by some outcasts from the State capitol. They objected to the Missouri government regulating moonshine stills. After that, farmers moved in. In the 1920s and 1930's the town had been a major rail depot for the southwest corner of the state. As usual, the rail caused the town to grow. Once the railroad was abandoned, the only thing left were farmers, one grocery store, one attorney, and a whole lot of real estate. Recently, even the farms were under increasing attack from large farming conglomerates. Every fall they came around preying on the farms whose harvests had not panned out. Dean thought the conglomerates sent saboteurs to break equipment and poison wells. Apparently, Dean did not believe in bad luck.

As we said our goodbyes, I thanked him for dinner and the information about John. The sun was sinking low in the western sky, and the earth seemed to sigh with relief as cool breezes floated through town. The crickets began to chirp and the night insects began to awaken. Their low hum set my teeth on edge and started sharp pains in my forehead.

We made arrangements to meet at Cletus' office after the funeral the next day and Dean left, headed off toward a beat-up truck parked across the street. I went upstairs to my room and flopped onto the bed. It had been a really long day. Despite my exhaustion, I could not drop off to sleep.

Then the phone range, startling me.

"Hello."

"Are you Bernard Devlin?"

"Yes. Who's this?"

"I'm Sheriff Jones."

I was instantly on guard. I had little respect for cops. "What can I do for you this evening?"

"You available for a brief chat?" I could tell that Sheriff Jones was not originally from around here. His accent did not fit with the local manner of speaking. "I would like to talk with you about John."

"OK, I replied." I could not put my finger on why I did not like Sheriff Jones, but I figured I could at least listen to what he had to say. He was another person who could shed some light on John.

"Would you like to get a drink?"

"Sure."

"How about I come by The Landing and we can talk?"

"I guess that would be alright." In my gut, something was wrong, but it was hard to tell just what gave me that feeling. I knew the last thing I needed was to have the local Sheriff mad at me for snubbing him. Any my headache was starting to get more severe, making even my eyesight get darker.

Not more than five minutes later, I heard a knocking on the hotel's front door. On the other side of the glass stood a uniformed cop that looked like he had just fallen out of a Hollywood blockbuster. Not a single hair was out of place, and his muscles pushed the fabric of his shirt taught against his chest and arms. I could see why Cletus and Dean did not like him. He was phony—I figured he must have seen too many cop movies and was trying to emulate the main characters.

"Thanks for meeting with me; I'm sure you're tired from your long flight and drive." He had a politician's shit-faced smile plastered across his face. "I figured the best time to talk with you would be tonight, since I'm sure you'll be busy all day tomorrow. I also wanted to let you know where I stand"

"On what?" His cologne snaked around me until it struck directly at my nose, causing my eyes to water and my nose to run. The anger began to surge through me and I struggled to keep it under control.

"On John. See, well," An artificial grimace briefly strained his face. "I think he is connected with the murders. Hey, you OK?" he asked, noticing my tearing eyes.

"Yeah. I think it's my allergies," I lied. Bile rose in my throat, but I swallowed hard. "You mentioned murders?" Sheriff Jones was being given enough rope to hang himself.

"You haven't heard about the killings, huh? Well, you see, there's been several killings around here these past few months. I'm pretty sure your great uncle was the killer."

My headache pounded mercilessly, while my anger continued to surge below the surface. "Why is that?" I desperately needed fresh air; the man's cologne was toxic.

Again, Sheriff Jones put on the politician smile. "John was a strange man. He kept to himself mostly.

32

I figured he was insane; he was as old as dirt. A while ago, I saw him in town in blood-covered overalls. At the time I figured he must have been hunting with Zeke. Then the first disappearance was reported."

I said nothing, gritting my teeth.

"It never occurred to me that John was the killer, until the remains were found about a month after the first disappearance. Then I was able to connect the murder with old John."

"How?" Despite my anger, I desperately wanted to hear the Sheriff's theory. The more I knew, the better off I would be tomorrow.

"The State crime lab did. I haven't told a soul about this, and I trust you will keep it confidential, but there was dust, consistent with the caves, on the bones of the victim. I figured that since old John was the only caver around, the murder must have occurred in his caves. "So the next day I went out to see if he would let me poke around in the caves. I figured he wouldn't object since he would want to clear his name. But he had none of it. Darn near chased me off his property. That's when I recalled the blood-stained overalls. I tried to get a warrant, but the local judges all said no. I needed something more."

He paused, trying to gauge the impact of his theory on me. "Now that old John is dead, I figure you'll want to seek justice and find out whether old John was the killer. I was hoping that you'll let me take a look in the caves and in his house. They say that serial killers usually keep trophies of their victims."

Rage coursed through my body, and my headache made it hard to think straight. I did not know what to say. I figured John Lincoln had a good reason to keep people out of the caves. "Gosh, Sheriff," I said, choking down my anger. I assumed my 'I want to help, but my hands are tied' tone, and said. "I would, but, well, I'm not executor of the estate. I can't give you permission, since it's not my house, yet. Maybe after the will is read, I'll be able to help you." I figured I could stall until I'd had an opportunity to talk with Cletus and Dean about this. They might have some insights into the whole matter.

"I understand, Bernard," he replied, barely concealing his disgust for my indecision. "I tell you what, I'll talk with you tomorrow afternoon. By then, you'll likely be the executor of the estate, right? Then you can give me permission." Again, the fake smile assumed its position on his face. "It's been real nice meeting with you. I can see that you're a bright man. I know you'll make the right decisions about old John's estate."

As he left, my headache improved slightly and my anger ebbed. I could not help but feel like I had just been tested by the Sheriff. Sheriff Jones had not given up hope that I would help him. He was unsure about me. At least the overpowering cologne was fading, though not quickly. My clothes needed to be aired in order to get that awful cologne out of them.

As I got ready for bed, so many different thoughts were reverberating through my mind. Sheriff Jones made a compelling case against John Lincoln. It was circumstantial. The Sheriff desperately wanted access to the caves and the house. However, he was not willing to risk an illegal search.

I could not figure out why John did not want to help the police. If he was innocent, why not cooperate with the Sheriff? It did not seem to be an unreasonable request to take a look in the caves. On the other hand, another perfectly reasonable explanation for John's ban might exist. Maybe he was just afraid of liability should someone get lost in the caves. That made some sense. Elmer's story came to mind. I wondered what was in the caves that would scare a man so much that he would go insane. Maybe he had gotten lost and became unbalanced because fear of dying overcame him.

If John was a killer, would Dean have known about it? Assuming that John was the killer, I wondered how many people disappeared over the past ninety-some odd years. As macabre thoughts trickled through my mind, I succumbed to exhaustion and fell asleep on the comfortable bed.

Chapter Three
Funeral Rites

Death is not the worst that can happen to men.
Protagoras

The next morning, I woke up at five. The sun streaming through the windows hinted at another hellishly hot day. Waking early was more of a blessing; a welcome respite from the dreams that had filtered through my headache. I carefully moved my head, hoping my headache was gone. A few slow shakes confirmed it was gone, but not yet forgotten. The slow nag of ache sat at the tope of my spine. I needed coffee. Even without my morning jolt, my mind turned back to all that I knew. None of my conversations yesterday gave me much confidence about John. It seemed two different John's haunted this town. The first was the town eccentric who was given leeway on account of his age. The other was much, much darker; the serial killer that flaunted his kills by walking through town in his blood-stained overalls.

Bloody overalls were never a good sign. I hoped hunting gear would be in abundance at the house. Maybe I could talk with Zeke to see if he knew about the overalls. Barring that, I was hard pressed to argue against Sheriff Jones' theories. Which lead me to I still did not know what I was going to do about Sheriff Jones' request. I hoped that Dean and Cletus would be able to offer some sage advice on the matter. I turned the television on, hoping to distract me from everything. The morning national news rattled on about the latest diet craze.

After I showered and got dressed in the only suit I had brought, I decided I would head over to Cowan's for breakfast. I was not really hungry, but I knew it was going to be a long day. I left the TV on, and as I left, I tripped over the local paper, which was put in front of my door. I gratefully picked it up. Now I would be able to hide from prying eyes behind the thin newsprint while I ate my breakfast.

Once at Cowan's, the morning waitress, Geena, seated me in a corner booth, expressing her condolences to me on the way. I thanked her and was glad she seated me in a corner booth. It seemed so strange that everyone in town would know John. I doubted half as many people would admit to knowing me, and I lived in a large city. As she took my order and walked away, I looked around the restaurant and saw quite a few people there already. They all were purposefully ignoring me.

I decided I did not care, picked up the paper and began to read. The headline article was about the County's decision to require a new permit before the planting of new crops to ensure "adequate and accurate" taxing on farms. It was obvious from the tone of the article that Stillwater did not care for the new permit idea. It transitioned into a discussion of the right to farm laws the agriculture industry wanted to enact.

After reading too much about farming, an article grabbed my full attention.

SHERIFF JONES PREDICTS MURDERS WILL STOP

Yesterday afternoon, Stillwater Sheriff Tom Jones held a press conference where he announced that he believed that the disappearances and murders will likely stop. When questioned, Sheriff Jones indicated that the person, or persons, responsible for the disappearances and murders are no longer in the area.

Sheriff Jones hinted that the murder was likely deceased, although, no names have yet been released.

The Stillwater Tribune obtained several reports from the Missouri State Crime Lab indicating that the remains found contained rock chips, dirt, and other trace evidence associated with the Lincoln caves. As many are aware, John Henry Lincoln was killed under unusual circumstances last week. One can only suspect that Sheriff Jones believes that John Lincoln was responsible for the murders, although no direct evidence has been obtained connecting John Lincoln to the disappearances and murders.

Bernard Devlin, John Lincoln's great nephew flew in from Miami, Florida yesterday. Mister Devlin is a private investigator in Miami. At press time he was unavailable for comment.

Now I was angry. How dare they suggest that John was a killer. Even though I considered it a possibility, I had no proof. For that matter, neither did the Sheriff. I wondered whether Cletus and Dean had seen the article—and whether they were as angry as I was. Gene brought the breakfast and I hardly tasted the food; instead I savored the anger. I leafed through the rest of the front-page section, searching for more information about the murders. There was none.

When I opened the crossword section of the paper, I found a handwritten note stapled to the top of the second page.

Bernard,

I'm sorry I was not around to greet you yesterday— I was forced to go up to Jeff City to see my folks. By now, I'm sure you have read the article about your great uncle. I can personally vouch for him that he is not a murderer. I'm sure you have lots of questions, and Dean and I will be more than happy to answer them truthfully. We hope, and pray, that you will believe us when we say that your great uncle is innocent. More than that, John was a great man.

I am also sorry I had to run this morning. Usually, I have hot coffee and some doughnuts for guests. But after I read this article, I had to go out to the house to make sure that it was still locked and OK.

Finally, I wanted to let you know not to believe Sheriff Jones. DO NOT TRUST HIM. Your uncle and he were bitter enemies and Sheriff Jones never got over it. Sheriff Jones has a personal vendetta against John. It has clouded his judgment.

I'm guessing that, by now, Sheriff Jones has asked to access to the house and the caves. Please, please, do not give him access until you have had a change to sit down with Dean and me and talk about John.

Sincerely, Jessica

Despite the fact that the handwriting was incredibly feminine, the note struck a chord in me. After what Sheriff Jones had said to the press, I saw little reason to help him. The note was confirmation that the Sheriff must be wrong, no matter what the evidence said. I could see where a personal vendetta might have caused the Sheriff to go after John Lincoln as if he were already a convicted killer. Even though I had not met Jessica, her note was sincere. Or at least is seemed sincere to me.

One thing still puzzled me. Why did everyone want to keep the Sheriff out of the house and the caves? Even if John was not a killer, he must be doing something illegal or else they would just let him in to take a quick look around. Visions of John's meth lab and pot farm kept running through my mind. That must have been how he got all the money. I hoped that whatever John and his cohorts were up to would not impact the inheritance.

After breakfast I walked over to Cletus's office to see if he had any insight into John and his many secrets. The sun had started heating up the air, but it was still a pleasant temperature. The town was unnaturally quiet. I was used to noise, the roar of traffic and tourists pushing their way to see the next trinket shop just off the beach. Here, I could hear the wind shuffling the leaves on the trees. I took a deep breath of the Midwest air, which seemed cleaner to me.

My peace did not last long. My rental, which had stayed parked outside Cletus's office, had four very flat tires. Scratches gouged deep into the blue paint all over the car. Both the passenger side windows were smashed in. Deep dents pockmarked every surface of the car. It had to be totaled. The anger that I had resisted yesterday forced its way throughout my brain, causing my headache to come back with a vengeance. How I ended up on someone's wrong side was a mystery. Not that it really mattered. I was leaving as soon as I go the money. When I got even closer, I saw a message scratched into the hood of the car. 'Go Away.'

It was a very compelling reason to leave as soon as possible; I was obviously not welcome in their town. I made a mental note to call and schedule my return flight.

"I'm sure sorry about that," said Cletus, causing me to nearly jump out of my skin. "I didn't mean to scare you, son. I saw that this morning and had gone over to The Landing to tell you."

I whirled at him, the rage pushing at my patience. Immediately, though, I saw sincerity and regret writ large on his elderly face; I knew then, that he did not do it, and he had no idea who would have.

I struggled to regain my composure. "Why?" I asked quietly. "What'd I do?" My anger was unusual. There was no reason to be upset, after all, insurance would pay for the damage. It bothered me deeply. It was a personal attack on me. I did not like it.

"I wish I could tell you, son," he shook his head.

"Who?"

"If I had to guess, I wouldn't. When I called the Sheriff, he was not too surprised about the vandalism.

But I got the police report process going."

"Thanks. About Sheriff Jones-"

Cletus gently took me by my arm and pulled me towards his office. "You don't want to mention the Sheriff too loudly outside. A good rule for a small town like this is to remember that there is always someone listening. Even if there isn't."

"OK." This town kept getting stranger and more hostile. "Did you see this morning's paper?" The anger switched targets, when I remembered how today had started. It seemed the town was conspiring against John.

"Yup."

His minimal response bothered me. "And..." I could not believe how calmly Cletus was taking this abuse of process. I wondered whether Cletus was in on John Lincoln's illegal activities.

"And what? It's horsefeathers. And everybody in town knows its horsefeathers. You see Mister Lincoln and the Sheriff went head to head for about a year over whether the city would shut down his caves on account of them being a public nuisance. At the time, the Sheriff wanted to buy land adjacent to Mister Lincoln's. He figured that there must be something in those caves of value since Mister Lincoln hadn't had a job in over twenty years.

"When the dust settled, the city allowed Mister Lincoln to keep the caves open and he bought the adjacent property outright for more than the Sheriff could scrape together. Since then the Sheriff has had a personal issue with Mister Lincoln. I was Mister Lincoln's attorney and was quite busy for awhile.

"Every time Mister Lincoln came into town with his car, the Sheriff would give him tickets for everything. Once it was that his rear fender was too low. Another time, his exhaust was too noisy. That's why Mister Lincoln took to walking through town. It was easier than constantly getting baseless tickets from the

Sheriff. Unfortunately, even then, he'd get jaywalking tickets. The judge even stopped making us come to court; he just dismissed the damn things outright."

"But what about the dust on the remains?"

"Oh, that. Here's what I think, for what it's worth. No question these people were killed. I guess their bodies were dumped somewhere in the wild. Scavengers got a hold of the bodies and took them back to their dens in the caves. Once the creatures were done, they took the remains back out of the mine and left them. That is how the dust got on the remains."

His rational explanation made my conjectures look foolish. I had to admit. It made sense. "Why didn't John voluntarily allow the Sheriff to search the caves, then?"

"I don't know, son. I always figured it had something to do with his past with the Sheriff." He glanced at his watch. "Come on, we'll walk over to the church, Mister Lincoln's funeral will be starting soon."

As we walked silently towards the church, I turned my thoughts away from my troubles and pondered Cletus's theories about John. It made more sense than the Sheriff's theory. It reinforced my sense that the Sheriff's evidence was circumstantial at best. The church was much like the rest of the town, a relic from a different time. It was small, painted white and sat in the middle of a small lot. In the steeple, I could see the bells, glistening in the morning sun. There were stained-glass windows on one side of the church depicting what I assumed were various scenes from the Bible. I had spent less than ten hours inside a church in my entire life. I barely thought about the deeper questions of life. So long as there were food on my plate and my bills were paid, I was content. Despite my unfamiliarity with church, the building was welcoming in a way I could not describe.

The church was packed. I figured at least half the town was there. They were all dressed to the nines.

Cletus led me to the front pew and had me sit down. It was almost dream-like; I could feel the weighty stares of the town on the back of my neck as I sat in the same spot John sat every Sunday. In front, a small wood box was sitting on a pedestal.

Cletus whispered to me that John Lincoln wanted to be cremated and to have his ashes spread along the cave entrance. The small box was delicately carved with inlays of knights fighting dragons under the watchful eyes of a cross. It seemed totally out of place in this farming community; I wondered if John Lincoln had a hobby that had something to do with the knights.

Dean quietly slipped in and sat next to me, nodding once as a greeting. His eyes were red and teary. He had been crying, which was strange since Dean did not seem to be the kind of guy that cried. Next to him sat a woman wearing a long black veil. She was sobbing. A young pastor emerged when the music softly started. He was probably in his mid-thirties and was very comfortable in the pulpit. The congregation got real quiet when he stood. Solemn southern hymns played lowly in the background, only interrupted by the occasional sob.

It was hard to understand how the death of such a strange man evoked such sorrow. Here was a man who lived in this town for most of his life and people were actually going to miss him. It was humbling to think of someone who had touched so many lives. I wondered whether anyone in the church was here because they were glad he had died. My headache subsided

"Friends, Brothers and Sisters in Christ, we are here today to mourn the passing of a great man." Even the pastor had been crying and his voice was some-what hoarse.

"But we are not really here to just mourn. Rather, we are here to celebrate John Henry Lincoln's new place in heaven. Right now he is gazing upon the face of Jesus, and walks proudly with him in the cool of the day; much like Adam did before the fall.

"To have that awesome privilege would be magnificent. For many of you, I do not need to tell you just how great John was. But for those who don't know a lot about John," he glanced at me as he spoke. "I would like to say just a few words. Not as your pastor, but as a John's friend.

"John's had been coming to this church since before I was born. He has seen most of you get married and have kids. He buried many a friend here, too. He sat, faithfully, in the front pew and thoughtfully listened to thousands of sermons. Barely ever dozed off," he joked, getting a few low chuckles.

"Now, John's faith was not simple, but it was founded on one simple belief. That Jesus was his Lord and savior. Beyond that, John had a lot of questions. Every once in a while, he'd approach me after the sermon and we would discuss those questions.

"Most of the time, his questions ended with me being more confused than John. But he always came, sat and listened."

The pastor stopped, trying hard to maintain his composure. Then he continued, "John was a true soldier of the cross. Many in this very room would benefit from John's example. Despite the heavy burdens placed on John, he was the first to volunteer when someone needed a hand. He was always the last one to leave when the work needed doing. Just last year he painted the whole church in two days. Of course he had help, but John was here at six in the morning and did not put his brush down until it was too dark to continue.

"John was a friend to the low and broken, a champion for those who needed one, and, well, I'd guess about the most giving man I've ever met. Stillwater has lost a great man, one this community will never be able to replace. At this time, I would like allow anybody who wishes to say a few words about John to come forward"

The silence echoed off the walls of the church. Everyone, including myself, was not sure how to react. Slowly, a young man stepped up to the front and related a story about how John helped his family out when he had been hurt at work, and was laid off. For the next hour and a half, I heard many stories of how John came alongside those in need and helped them out. Sometimes he would give money, sometimes labor, still other times, a simple kind word.

"Folks, I hate to interrupt, but John wouldn't have wanted this to take all day, but he once told me that he wanted to make sure you felt free to leave, or stay, if you wanted. His wishes were that music played until the sun sets. You are all welcome to stay or leave."

A line began to form and people slowly walked by the small box up front. A few people remained in the pews crying and praying. I stayed where I was, unsure about the whole thing. It was the strangest funeral I had attended. I also had a lot to think about. After hearing what everybody had said about John it was impossible to consider him a serial killer. After everyone but Dean, Cletus, the woman in black, and I had left, Cletus said, "Well, I suppose we should finish this, let's head back to my office and get the will read."

"No, wait," I said, driven by curiosity. "I'd like to talk with the pastor first."

A surprised look crossed Cletus's face and he and Dean exchanged knowing glances.

"OK. When you're done, Dean and I will be waiting at my office."

Chapter Four
Character Sketches

There is no character, howsoever good and fine, but it can be destroyed by ridicule, howsoever poor and witless. Observe the ass, for instance: his character is about perfect, he is the choicest spirit among all the humbler animals, yet see what ridicule has brought him to. Instead of feeling complimented when we are called an ass, we are left in doubt.
Pudd'nhead Wilson and Those Extraordinary Twins

I found the Pastor outside, standing in the shade of a tree talking with a young family, trying to console them about the loss of John Lincoln. He saw I was waiting for him, and nodded. The young family saw me, their eyes widened, almost in unison. Then they quickly left. I wondered what they had heard about me.

"I'm Bernard Devlin, John's nephew." By now, my headache had disappeared, leaving me more tired than irritable. The anger that had consumed me earlier was entirely gone.

"I know. My name's Mike, what can I do for you?" he asked gently, as he wiped tears away from his eyes. "I'm sorry, it's just that John was a very close friend of mine. You cannot imagine what his death means to this community."

The Pastor was well cut, his clothes crisp and put together. I guessed his wife picked out his clothes for him. He was average height and had dark hair styled in a slight spike. Not exactly what I considered "normal" for the Bible belt.

"It's OK. I just want to know more about John. I didn't even now that I had a great uncle. What can you tell me about him?"

"Well, it depends." replied the pastor. "You see, John was very stubborn. And he made quite a few enemies in this town."

"That's hard to believe, in light of what was said in the funeral."

"I know. John had a lot of people that really cared for him. But there was a certain part of this town that hated him."

I did not say anything, but hoped he would go on.

"Perhaps we should go to my office to talk about John." He glanced over his shoulder in the same way that Cletus had. Paranoia was apparently a town trait. He led me back into the church and into a cozy office, cluttered with paperwork and books. "Who'd have thought that a shepherd of a flock would be burdened with so much paperwork. Please, have a seat. Would you like some coffee? Water?"

"I'm good, thanks."

"I think I'll have some coffee." A pot of coffee sat at the ready on the credenza behind him. I sensed he was not sure where to start, or whether he wanted to tell me all that he knew. The worry lines on his face conveyed his belief that I was an OK guy, but that he was fearful. I could not fathom what there was to be afraid of. I certainly was not intimidating. "Please, have a seat."

"Tell me about John," I asked quietly as I sat in a chair right out of the 1970s.

"First, John was a good man. He may have ruffled feathers around town, but, all in all, he was a good man." The more he said it, the more I could tell he was sincere. "You see, John was," he paused, searching for the right word, "eccentric, maybe strange, at times. But most of us wrote it off on account of his age."

"How old was he?"

"I'm not quite sure. He told me once, that he came to this town back in 1916 where he worked as a sharecropper. He saved his money and went over to the local casino, back before they were banned, and won title to the land and the caves. Seems the man he won it from figured it wasn't worth all that much since the ground was not able to support crops on account of the caves.

"So John went out and built a small house on the edge of the property where he lived for many years on a small garden and doing odd-jobs for folks in town. Seemed like John could fix just about anything. Why, just last year he came and fixed the altar where it had split. He was really good a fixing things.

"Anyway, John told me that after a while, he had saved up enough to buy the neighboring property, which was where he figured the caves extended to. So he did. He continued to do odd jobs, but with less frequency. There was a lot of talk about where John could have gotten his money. He never told me, but I figured he must have earned it. John wasn't the type to steal his money.

"John was a fixture in this town. He spent his days and nights working out on his property. He raised his own food and was pretty much self-sufficient for many years. Then he met Ethel."

"Ethel?"

"Ethel was his wife. They married back in the early forties, I guess it would be. I never met her, but people say she was the one thing that turned John from being a life-long hermit. People figured that, without her, John would simply have remained on his small farm in his house, and eventually, stop coming into town at all."

"No kids?"

"Not to my knowledge. Ethel passed away about eight years after they married. John threw himself into civic activities after she was gone. That was when he ran for city council. Funny part was, he won by a landslide, simply because he knew everybody."

"So John ran the town for ten years or so. He did the best he could, but, of course, you tend to make people mad when you are in power. I think that was the start of it. John was fairly protective of the areas surrounding his caverns—you know, refusing to issue building permits, that kind of stuff.

"Over the years, John quietly began to purchase the land adjacent to his property until he had a substantial number of acres of land."

"Why did he do that?"

"I don't know. There was talk about him wanting to exploit the mineral rights of the cave. But, as far as I know, he never took any steps to do anything with it. Oh, well, he explored it. He really enjoyed it, I think. It was kind of his personal Mecca. I'd bet he would go in those caves just to sit by himself and think.

"Anyway, that's John, in a nutshell." He paused, like he wanted to tell me more. "How are you holding up?"

"Well, until Cletus called me, I didn't know John even existed. He was kind of the black sheep of the family, I guess."

"I can see that. John really did march to his own drummer."

"Can you tell me anything else about John. Or about the caves?"

"Well, I'm not sure anyone could tell you about those caves. John was really protective of the caves. As far as I know, John never let anybody near them.

"As for more about John, let me think about it. You're going to be in town till the end of the week, right? Stop by for dinner on Thursday, and my wife and I will entertain you with more stories about John than you can shake a stick at."

"I'll see if I can make it on Thursday. Thank you for taking the time to talk with me. This whole thing, well, it's complicated, and John is a hard guy to get a handle on."

"Not a problem. Give me a call if you need to talk." He handed me a slip of paper with his name and number on it.

"Thanks again." I left his office and saw that there were a few people that decided to come back to pay their respects to John.

As I left the church, I noticed that Sheriff Jones was sitting across from Cletus' office in his car, watching me. Even if John was a killer, the Sheriff's actions were inexcusable. I would rather risk harassment from him than help him. The sun had come back up, and I could feel its warm rays slowly searing the back of my neck. Sweat began to run down the back of my shirt and my headache returned.

I walked slowly towards Cletus' office, trying to get a hold on what was bothering me about this whole thing. Here I was, 2,000 miles from Miami, in a very small town, to collect an inheritance from a long-lost, and until recently, unknown, relation. It was almost too good to be true. Maybe, that was what was bothering me. I mean, I was no one special; my family was just an ordinary family—not wealthy, not poor. But somehow, John Lincoln, this recluse that liked caving, had amassed a fortune in this small town in the middle of nowhere. Now it was mine.

Or rather, almost mine. There still was the possibility that John was going to leave me nothing. After all, it is not as if the family had anything to do with him. Part of me hoped that was true. Then, at least, I would not have to carry the burden of the money. On the other hand, I knew I could get used to such a burden. I could not shake off the feeling that something was not right about the whole thing.

I quickened my pace to get to Cletus's office. There, maybe, I would get some answers. By the time I made it to Cletus's, I was a wreck. The headache had taken on a life of its own, sending bolts of pain into the very center of my brain.

I entered his office and was immediately met with a blast of cold air, sending a shiver down my spine. Air conditioning at full throttle every time you went into a building was something new to me.

Cletus immediately emerged from his office and quickly ushered me into his office. "Come in, come in, son. Have a seat." He gestured towards the only available chair. Dean was sitting the chair by the window, staring at Sheriff Jones across the street.

"I saw him," I said quietly.

"He's been there since we got back from the funeral. I'm guessing that he'll try to stop you on your way out there to let him have access to the caves."

"Not gonna happen." My response was full of venom and malice.

Dean looked at me, surprised by the strong conviction in my voice. "Really?"

"Well, let's just say that I want to take a look around to begin with. It doesn't seem right to allow him access until I figure out why John didn't allow anyone there."

Dean smiled. I could tell that I had taken a small step towards earning his respect.

"Well, son, now here's the part where I get out the will and read it to you. Are you ready?"

"I guess." I replied as I sat down.

Cletus solemnly took out a large envelope, ripped down the top and pulled out a thick stack of documents.

"I, John Henry Lincoln, being of sound mind and body, hereby, devise and bequeath my estate as follows:

"I declare that I am a widower. My wife's name was Ethel Lincoln nee Goodwin. I have no children. I have no other living children, biological or adopted, at the time of executing this, my Last Will and Testament. I have no children who predeceased me leaving issue surviving.

"I plan to prepare a list designating that certain items of personal property shall be given to specific persons. I understand that I must sign this list in order for it to be effective. I also understand that this list may be changed at any time and still be effective. This list shall be placed with my Last Will and Testament. I intend to send a copy of the list to my attorney.

"My entire Estate, including the rest, residue and remainder, is hereby devised and bequeathed to Bernard Devlin so long as he permanently blocks access to the caverns appurtenant to the real property contained in my Estate.

"I hereby nominate and appoint Dean Goodwin as the Personal Representative of this my Last Will and Testament, to act without bond or intervention of the Court. In the event that Dean Goodwin is for any reason unable or unwilling to act as Personal Representative hereof, then I nominate and appoint Cletus T. Montgomery III as the First Alternate Personal Representative, to serve without bond or intervention of the Court.

"I direct that my Estate be settled without the intervention of the Court, except to the extent required by law, and as required to assure compliance with the terms and conditions of this Will, and that my Personal Representative settle my Estate in such a manner as shall seem best and most convenient to him or her. I hereby empower my Personal Representative to mortgage, lease, sell, exchange and convey the real and personal property of my Estate for that purpose and without notice, approval or confirmation and in all other respects to administer and settle my Estate.

"All references to children and descendants shall include adopted persons. Unless some other meaning and intent is apparent from the context, the plural shall include the singular and vice-versa, masculine, feminine and neuter words shall be used inter-changeably.

"That's the end of the will. Here is the personal property list:

"As for my personal property, I hereby give, devise and bequeath the following to Dean Goodwin, (1) the antique radio with all accessories thereto, (2) the safe, and the contents therein, located in the guest bedroom, and (3) the library of LPs and records in the basement.

"I hereby give, devise and bequeath the following to Jessica Montgomery, (1) all of Ethel's sewing mach-ines, fabric, and all other sewing materials, (2) all furniture in the "sewing room," and (3) the safe, and the contents therein, located in the "sewing room."

"I hereby give, devise and bequeath the following to Zeke Loenbrough, (1) all contents of the hunting cabin, (2) all pelts, skins and trophies from the hunting cabin, and (3) the safe, and the contents therein, located in the hunting cabin."

"There." Cletus paused, "That's all. It was a simple will. As for what it really means to you," he looked directly at me, "you have inherited approximately $35 million in cash and stocks. You also have inherited about $1,000,000 worth of real estate. The residue of the estate is, I'd guess, about $5,000,000."

Dean and I sat in stunned silence. It seemed like such a short will for such a large estate. Those were big numbers.

So there it was. I was officially a millionaire. I did not really feel any different, any richer, any, well, any-thing. It was just that I now had enough money that work was now an option. Somehow, I was not elated, like I thought I would be. I could feel the money creep-ing its way into every relationship, every decision, and every part of my life. It was almost like I had just been

The Caverns of Stillwater

married to the money—everything I did from now, until I died, would have my wealth enveloped in it. I was never really good with my simple check book—I had credit card debt, too. I realized suddenly, that the money was not freedom, but just a different type of chain from debt. I could feel the weight of it starting to push on my shoulders.

"Of course," Cletus drawled, "you do have to prevent people from entering the caverns in order to inherit the estate."

"Huh?"

"There's a condition on the will. It's that you block the entrance to the mines."

"How am I going to do that?"

"I don't know. But, frankly, son, no one is going to care if you simply board up the entrance. That's what I'd do."

"What happens if someone goes into the caves?"

"Well, it would depend. Could be that the Court would make you give all the money back. Then it'd go to the state. Or at least most of it. As owner of the caves, however, you might be liable for any injuries."

"I see." I looked over at Dean, but he was still staring out the window at the Sheriff. "What was the deal about the safes?"

Dean turned back towards me, "John did not care for the government, all that much. So, I'm speculating that the safes contain some sort of money, likely cash. He left the safes with cash in them so that the value of the safe was all we'd have to declare on our income tax."

"Does that work?" I asked incredulously.

"Well, that's a grey area of the law," said Cletus. "And besides, I never told John that he should, or even could, do that."

I could tell he was lying, but, being no fan of the government myself, I kept my mouth shut. We sat around for a short while discussing the minor details of the estate and how Dean was going to act as personal representative. Eventually, we turned our attention back to the Sheriff.

"Well, how do you suppose we'll be able to get out of here without him knowing?" Dean asked. He was irritated with the Sheriff, but I had no idea why. After all, the Sheriff wanted access to the cave from me.

"Well, I guess I could go out there, tell him to stuff it, and get it over with." I suggested. Dean was not the only one mad at the Sheriff for how he treated me.

"Now wait, son," said Cletus. "There's no real need to tell the Sheriff anything. Even though I don't care for the fellah, confrontation is not the best way to deal with him—it'll just cause more unpleasantness, like your car. If you go and piss him off, he'll just work twice as hard to get into those caves."

"Perhaps a little deception is in order." I suggested.

"Deception?"

"Well, maybe deception is too strong a word. A little spin, how about that? You see, no one but us know the contents of John's will, right?"

"Yeah," Dean was nodding.

"So, if the Sheriff asks, I'll just tell him that John put some conditions on the inheritance and, because of that, you do not have the right to give him access to the caves."

"What if he asks for more information?"

"Send him over to me." Cletus smiled. "Tell him that you don't understand all of it, but that I could explain it to him. The Sheriff is long on talk and short on brains, if you know what I mean. I'm pretty sure a few minutes of legalese, sprinkled with a lot of wherefores, whatnots, and heretos, will persuade him you're not lying. Besides, I'd kind of enjoy it."

We all chuckled at that. "OK," I agreed. It made some sense to me to play dumb. The Sheriff already thought I was a little slow, and it would give me a chance to go take a look at the house and the caves without any interference from the Sheriff.

"Besides, the Sheriff will probably sit there all day waiting for us to come out." Cletus paused, "of course, we'll all be long gone by the time he realizes that you're not here anymore."

Cletus got up from his leather chair and ambled over to the door to his office. "You see, son, I used to do a lot of criminal law and family law. My clients expect some privacy, especially in this small town. So, I installed a backdoor to my office. Go down the hall towards the bathrooms and there's a door on the left. Down the steps and you'll be put out in the alley. If you head to your right you will end up half a block from The Landing. Go there now. In about half an hour Dean's gonna leave here in a hurry, as if he's really mad. He'll speed off away from town. Maybe Sheriff Jones will follow him, maybe not. Regardless, he'll think you and Dean are not friends due to the inheritance. That might come in handy later. Then, he'll come back to pick you up and take you out to the house.

"It'll buy you some more time, too. And if the Sheriff figures out what happened, just tell him you were not feeling well and went back to your room. You must have fallen asleep and not heard the phone or his knocking."

I thanked both Dean and Cletus. They had been so nice to me, and I really appreciated it. After all, here I was, an outsider from a large city that came in and inherited a huge amount of money from one of their closest friends. If our situations were reversed I was pretty sure I would not be so kind.

Naturally, I was suspicious. Dean and Jessica were, apparently John's closest friends. All he left them were safes. Of course, there was no telling exactly what was in those safes. Still, I doubted millions of dollars could be in them. So why were they being so nice? Maybe this was all a ruse to get me to agree to not take the money—or maybe they would ensure that the caves were accessed, and challenge my right to have my money.

That thought sent a chill right down my spine—I was already calling it *my* money. It had already taken possession of part of my heart. Regardless, I was certain that I was not going to give up on all that money. I figured that, if I had to, I could dynamite the cave entrance, take the money and run. Another part of me wanted to stick around and explore the caves. There had to be a reason why John was so protective of the caves.

I made it back to The Landing without any incident and went up to my room. When I got there, I noticed that something was different. I thought I had left my suitcase on the bed, but it was back on the floor of the closet. I got the suitcase out and opened it. Inside all my clothes had been messed with. Someone had gone through my clothes, then just put them back. They were not in the right place. Someone searched the room. It could have been the Sheriff. He had the time since he did not show until after John's funeral. Dean could have done it when he left the funeral, but before I made it back to Cletus's office. Even Jessica could have done it—it was, after all, her hotel, and she had not even been at Cletus's office. The Sheriff was the most likely suspect in my mind.

What could they have been looking for? I was simply a long-lost relative of John's. Maybe it was just background snooping, to make sure I was normal. I figured I would tell Dean about it, blame it on the Sheriff, and then see what Dean's reaction was. I still had about fifteen minutes to kill before Dean was coming to pick me up, so I started to refold my stuff. It helped ease my headache. I then realized John's will called me out by name. Which meant John knew about me.

I did not know anything about John. It did not

make any sense. Cletus had not said anything about John knowing about me. I had to wonder why he would wait until he died to contact me. If I were going to leave a fortune to a long, lost relative, I would find actually want to meet him. Kick the tires, so to speak. Everything that had happened since the call had been weird. Since then, everything in my life had been off. I hoped I would survive until the end of the week, when I got to go home. This small town was too weird for me. I just wanted to leave with my money.

Chapter Five
Homestead

Now, however, she knew the house was empty. Everybody had gone out of it; and there is something fearful to a little, lonely body in the possibilities of a great, empty house.
Poganuc People

Dean picked me up a few minutes later out front. By then my headache had decreased to a dull roar. He was driving a lime green Ford pickup. It certainly had seen better days, but it still rode well. Dean and I did not talk on our way out to the house. Between the heat rising in the day and John's funeral, neither one of us had much to say. I stared off into the auburn horizon. Each mile that we passed helped my headache. We passed acres of fields roasting under the hot summer sun.

Off and on, I could see a farm house off in the distance, usually on a slight hill, as if the owners wanted to be above fields and not just a part of them. The roofs were worn and dull. Next to the small houses would be large barns built a hundred years ago. It was a different, but somehow better, way to live. Alone with the crops that grew outside.

Breaking the silence, Dean asked, "Looks lonely, doesn't it?"

"I suppose it could be, that's for sure." I agreed. I liked being alone—at least most of the time. I lived in a building with over 100 units in it—but I did not really know anyone. Sure, I knew the girl down the hall because she always wore short skirts, but that was the extent of my knowledge about her. And the manager,

I knew him because, every month I paid him the condo dues. Other than that, I might as well have lived on a remote tropical island.

We passed another unmarked gravel road. "You should see it at night," said Dean, smiling, "this road's so dark and there's nothing but darkness with the occasional porch light out here. And the stars, they're something else. I think that's why John liked it so much. He'd say, 'Out here, there's quiet enough to think.' I never could figure out what John had to think so hard about, but, he should would."

"What do you mean?"

"John was a quiet man, in large part. I wouldn't say serious or somber, but, more like he was always think-ing about somethin'. He was sometimes distracted by his thoughts. You know, you'd see him in the store, staring at the stuff on the shelves. You'd come up to him, say hi, and he'd not even hear you. Though, as he got older, most folks attributed it to a hearin' loss, or something. Old age. But I'm not so sure."

"No idea what he was thinking about?" I asked.

"Not really. It wasn't no secret, him bein' wealthy. I figure it money wasn't somethin' he'd worry about. And, he never cared about the news, or politics, or anything like that. I accounted it to his faith. I figured he was on good terms with God and such. But that's just a guess. He talked to Pastor Mike a lot." He paused, and I could tell he was uncomfortable with talking about John's religion with me. "Well, here, we are," he said, as we pulled into a gravel drive. There was nothing around and we continued down the road. "The driveway's like a quarter mile long."

We bounced down the gravel drive and then the small house came into view. It sat, like most of the others, on a slight rise, but behind a wind break. Painted a pale yellow, the house was a modest size. The front door stood at the top of six concrete steps. On either side of the door were two windows. There was a detached garage in the back. The house had one dormer above the front door, which, I guessed, looked out from the attic. I could see two small windows in the foundation, which meant there was a basement. Behind another row of wind break trees, I could just make out a barn that had been recently painted.

Dean parked in front of the garage door, "Get out," he said, "wait 'til you see this."

I got out as Dean walked to the garage door, took out a key, unlocked to padlock on it, and opened the door. As the sun cascaded into the garage, I saw a car tarp that must have had half an inch of dust on it. Dean grabbed it gave it one good yank and sent the dust flying. As the dust settled, I couldn't believe my eyes. It was a burgundy-red Packard—in excellent condition.

"What is this?" I asked dumbfounded.

"This," Dean paused for dramatic effect, "was John's car. It runs perfect. He kept it up after he stopped driving. You like it?" asked Dean, again a big Midwest smile on his face.

"It's awesome." I stammered. I was never a big car guy, but, even I, neophyte that I am, could appreciate this car. "And you say it still runs?"

"Better than ever. John had the whole thing overhauled a while back—it's got a newer engine and just purrs."

"I guess I don't need to worry about the rental, huh?"

"Guess not," Dean said, laughing. It seemed like just being out here lifted Dean's spirits. He turned serious. "He did a number on your rental, didn't he?"

"He?" I asked, slightly suspicious.

"Sheriff Jones. Least that who I think it was." He changed the subject abruptly. "OK. Jessica made these for you," he said, "Each key is labeled—but there are some that aren't cuz they were keys John had, but we never saw him use them. We figure there must be some safes, file cabinets, gun safes, stuff like that, in there." He handed me the key ring.

"Do you want to show me around?" I asked. After all, for me it was like entering a complete stranger's house.

"Well, I've got about ten minutes before I've got to head back to town and give Jessica a hand, but I can walk you through the house. I'd save the barn for later."

"I'll take what I can get."

As Dean and I approached the front door, Dean said, "You know, it'll be really weird for me to go in here. I haven't been inside since before he died."

"If you don't want to..."

"Nah. It's alright. Just, it's gonna be weird."

"Well, I appreciate your help on this."

"No problem. That's what John would have wanted."

He opened the screen door, and it emitted an ear-piercing screech that sounded like a cat dying. Dean smiled when I jumped. "I told him I'd fix that, but I never got around to it. All it needs is a little oil on the bottom hinge."

Dean unlocked the door and opened it. Immediately, hot air rushed out of the room, like we opened a tomb. The smell of the house enveloped us. It was not a bad smell, but it did have a distinctive "old person" smell mixed with something I could not put my finger on, a cross between dust, time, and manure.

The door entered onto a small patch of linoleum, which turned into a textured carpet and opened into the main room of the house. Along one wall was a sofa with a framed picture above it. Next to it was a doorway through to a kitchen. Next to the door way was an easy chair that had been well loved. Next to it sat short table with a book and a pair of reading glasses on top of it. In the corner there was an old vintage radio—it looked like it only got AM. On the other side of the table was a less used, but just as old easy chair. Along the wall across from the sofa was a window that looked out onto the garage. The front wall had another short table, filled with books, magazines, and newspapers placed in front of it. Above it was the window that was next to the front door.

The walls had antique wallpaper on it; blue flowers on a field of off-white. I guessed Ethel had picked it out.

"This was where John spent most of his time when he was inside. He'd sit in that chair right there, listen to the radio and read. John must have read a million books over his lifetime. There are boxes of them out in the barn, combined with what you find in here."

As we moved on through the door and into the kitchen. The kitchen was a throwback to the past. The oval table was a green Formica relic, it even had aluminum trim with three matching aluminum chairs. The countertops were a blonde tile on top of dark oak cabinets. There was a modern refrigerator and stove, but the sink looked like it was original. Above the sink there was a window that looked out behind the garage.

At the far end of the kitchen a door led out onto a porch that had been screened in. It had a bunch of potted plants on it. They were still perky and green, despite the heat—I guessed Jessica had been taking care of them since John's death. To the right was a short hallway.

"Jessica cleaned out the fridge so that the food wouldn't spoil. There's still soda and ice in it, if you get thirsty.

"Down this way is the guest bedroom," he said pointing through a door in the hall. Straight ahead is the bathroom, and here," he stopped. "This was John's bedroom."

We both left the door closed.

Dean turned and pointed to a telephone on a small wooden counter in the hallway, "This is the only phone in the house. Jessica and my numbers are here," he gestured at a chalkboard hung above the phone. As he passed the thermostat, he turned the air conditioning on and the whole house shuddered to life.

"John had the A/C installed about five years ago. He'd said he'd been hot long enough in this lifetime; he figured the least he could do was be comfortable while he sat in his own house."

The cool air began to fight off the oppressive heat, making the small house more liveable.

"Any questions?"

"Where should I start?"

"Well, it depends. When my aunt died, I helped my mom pack up her things. Mom packed up her clothes first and donated them to the Church. After that, she let the family come in and take what they wanted. The rest, she hired Will Kindle, the town auctioneer, to sell." I could tell Dean would really hate to see John's stuff sold to the highest bidder.

"Actually," I said, "I'm thinking I don't want to sell John's stuff off at auction. Maybe just keep it as it is for a while. I'd like to come back from time to time— maybe go exploring in the caves."

"Well, I'm glad to hear that. I really wouldn't want all of this to be sold to some megafarm or mining company. John had lots of offers, but never accepted."

"Really?"

"Well, John refused several offers a couple of years ago to buy the property. One was some company out of Ohio who's been trying to buy into Stillwater to stop local farms from making as much money. The other offer was some mining company out of Idaho. Apparently they think there's silver in the caves."

"Could this be a viable farm?"

"It could be. John's got enough arable land that would support soybean or cotton. He chose not to."

"I see."

"Well," Dean looked at his watch, "I gotta get back

to town. Give me a call when you're ready to come back. Tomorrow, I'll give you a tour of town so's you can get around on your own."

"Sounds great to me. Thanks."

"No problem. I'll lock the garage down on my way out. And keep an eye out for the Sheriff." He stopped and looked me in the eye. "If you're here after dark, I'd suggest you stay inside until you see my truck. It's... not safe."

A dark chill shot down my spine. "I will." This was the second time someone had told me how unsafe it was after dark. As Dean left, I locked the door behind him. It was a city habit, I knew. After all, out here I doubted it was necessary. Better safe than sorry.

I plopped down on the worn couch. I was tired. Even though it was only one-thirty, it sure had been a long day. The house was nearing comfortable and the air conditioning chased the hot air out of each room. I could hear the pops and snaps as the hot wood reacted to the cool air. I sat up and reviewed the rows of book on the shelves. They were in a random order, Maturin, Dickens, Tolstoy, Goethe, King, Lewis. It was clear to me that John's tastes ranged wildly. I had to wonder what books were hidden away in the barn.

I went over to the radio and turned it on. Immediately country music coursed through the old radio and filled the room. I smiled; it was the same station I had listened to on my drive to town. I sat down in the lesser worn chair and perused through the stack of books under John's reading glasses. Again, a random mix of literature, popular fiction and even biography.

I sat back in the recliner and looked out the window at the lush emptiness. From this chair, John could see the driveway and the grassland around him. It was a mixed palate of greens and browns, framed by a blue clear sky. It was the first time I was all alone in the wilderness. In a sense, I felt the solitude that Dean had alluded to. I actually enjoyed it. My headache was completely gone and I felt refreshed. The sense of being alone permeated the air and I deeply inhaled it, relishing the intoxicating sensation of simply being alone. I understood why John lived here. John did not hate people. He was not running from something. It was the rare chance to be truly alone. It was exhilarating. I wondered whether John got used to it or whether each day he relished the opportunity to be himself, by himself. He was able to withdraw from everything and everyone and just be.

I shook off my reverie and decided to take a look at the rest of the house and see if I could get a better idea of who John was. I turned the radio off and went into the kitchen. I decided on a methodological approach and began on the lower cabinets closest to the fridge. Inside were cast iron pots and pans—nothing remarkable except for their age. In the overhead cabinet faded china sat chipped and worn, relics from John's past.

Next, I found some of John's food. The Boxed dinners of Macaroni and Cheese and Rice-a-Roni reminded me of my cupboards. On the bottom, I found an electric skillet older than me. In the very back of the cabinet a Sanka brand coffee can sat, out of place and out of time. I grabbed it; the can was so light that I hit my hand on the shelf above it. It rattled, so I something was hiding inside.

I opened the tin lid and was so stunned I almost fell over—bullets. Not the unused kind. They were smashed and deformed—like the kind you see them take out of dead bodies. Along with the bullets were their casings. There were more casings than bullets. Some of the bullets were covered in something that looked like dried blood. I counted fifteen bullets and, at least, twenty casings. I had no idea why anyone would keep used bullets—except to hide them from someone else. Until I knew more, I wanted to hide them, too. I dropped them into John's sugar sack, shaking it until they disappeared under the granules.

I put the sack back into the dark recesses of the cabinets. I knew where they were, and that was good enough for me. John looked more suspicious now. Maybe he was the killer—that thought gave me the chills.

I shook it off and continued my search of the kitchen. I did not find anything else too creepy, except for the huge selection of hot sauces John kept. I took Dean's suggestion and went to pack John's clothes up to donate. As I went down the short hallway I heard a car pull up on the drive. Instantly my heart began to race. I quickly turned the A/C off so I could better hear what was going on. I tried to open the door to John's room, but it was locked. I needed to find a window to look out to see who it was. None of the windows had shades. If I moved from the hallway, I would be seen. So, instead, I decided to stay put.

I heard someone stomp to the front door. Then the doorbell rang, followed closely by pounding on the door. The screen door screamed as it was yanked open. I was about to go see who it was, when I heard the doorknob rattle. Whoever it was, they wanted in badly. They were not waiting to see if anyone was here.

"Bern-ard!" a voice hollered, drawing out my name. "It's Sheriff Jones. I know you're in there! Open up!" Again he banged on the door. "Open up!"

I stayed where I was. He could not know I was there. Heavy stomps echoed through the house as he left the front porch. His shadow betrayed his feeble attempt to peek though the front windows. The Sheriff was not one to give up easily. The shadow passed and I could hear the crunch of boots on the gravel driveway. His engine roared and he peeled out, sending gravel to hit the side of the house.

I took a deep breath and tried to calm down. My dull headache returned. I hoped it would stay away long enough for me to complete my search. I tried John's bedroom, but the door was locked. The modest house was eerily quiet in the summer sun. Aside form the air conditioning, and my breathing, it was silent like a tomb. The faded wallpaper that hung hinted at a rural and unremarkable life. The linoleum and carpet floors were old, but clean. The place was tidy, but lived in. There was just enough disorder to show that someone actually had lived here. I wondered whether John even saw the decorations when he was here alone.

I imagined John's solitary existence had devolved into a routine. He would get up, eat breakfast, maybe watch the morning news. Then he might shuffle over to his chair and read until he fell asleep. He would wake at lunchtime, only to return to the chair until it was time to go to bed. However, he did not live such a domesticated lifestyle. The used bullets spoke volumes about John's daily routine.

Nothing in the house led me to believe he was doing anything illegal. I had not even run across any alcohol, and I doubted the basement would hold a pot farm that would make millions. There were no guns, no signs that he was anything other than an elderly man. This meant that getting into his room was so much more important now. None of the keys on my keyring worked on the damn lock. So I decided to do the next best thing to finding the key was to break the door down. I took a short run at the door, and tried to push my shoulder through it. Pain blossomed all down my arm, and my headache flared dangerously to a higher amount. Once I regained my senses and recovered, I stood back up. As I stood, I leaned against the telephone stand in the hallway. Unfortunately, the stand was less than stable, and I ended up back on the floor, this time tangled in the telephone wire. Had this happened yesterday, My rage would have caused me to damn everything to hell. Instead, I found myself laughing. I kept laughing until tears came, which seemed to wash the headache away. I untangled myself from the phone and started to put it back, along with the wooden top. I saw a cubby hole underneath. And in that hole was another set of keys. These keys looked remarkably older than the set I had been given earlier. The last key on the ring worked and I entered John's room.

I half expected to find John's secret base of operations. Maybe a money printing machine, or a control room full of monitors and computers that ran his criminal enterprise. Either that or a collection of decaying corpses hanging from meat hooks attached to the ceiling. Instead, the room appeared to be, well, an old man's bedroom. A bed, a dresser, a small closet and more damnable books. John must have done nothing but read—I got the impression he would be lucky if he remembered to eat and bathe. Next to the bed a stack of books on serial killers was leaning precipitously to one side. They were an odd collection to find. These books were not the paperbacks from the true crime section. There were treatises and scholarly works that were used by professionals in the field. I picked one up and leafed through out and saw where someone had highlighted various sentences. I tossed it down on top of the bed and went over to the dresser. On top of the dresser were John's wallet and watch. I picked up the wallet and quickly leafed through it—nothing of any import, some money, credit cards, and his driver's license. I thought it was weird that he did not have any photos in his wallet. Neither did I, so, I guessed I should not judge.

I went back into the kitchen and located a trash bag to put John's clothes in. I figured Dean and I would drop them off at the church as a donation. I just threw his clothing into the bag—I didn't really pay much attention to it, after all these were John's socks and underwear. In the bottom drawer of the dresser I found an old, worn out book. It had a cracked black leather cover on it, but no title. As I opened the book,

I realized it was a journal. The writing was feminine and the pages were faded with time. It must have been his wife's journal. I wondered if John had even known the journal was there. I flipped through, but most of it was small town gossip and self-reflections about life in general. I felt like I was intruding, so I closed the book and planned on burning it so no one else could read it. It was way too personal for it to just be floating around.

Once I had the dresser cleaned out, I moved to the closet. Aside from the normal jeans and shirts, I found John's overalls. They were old and worn, and it was obvious John has worn them quite a bit. They were stained. I could not tell if it was blood, oil, wood stain, or paint, but it did have a faintly metal scent to it. I could burn those too. I might as well protect John's reputation and get rid of it. I search through the pockets and found a key. It was very small, like a suitcase lock key. I wondered what it went to. I put the key into my wallet, hoping I would find a lock somewhere it would fit into.

In the bottom of the closet was a fire safe. I tried the key I had found in the overalls, but it wasn't the right kind. I searched the keys on the key ring but none of them fit either. So now I had to find another key. John seemed to be a very secretive guy. His secrets seemed to stay hidden from me, no matter how hard I tried to get at them.

I spent another half hour in John's room, and then I moved on to the guest bedroom. There I only found another fire safe, some old shoes, and some blankets. By now, it was getting dark, and I was tired and somewhat frustrated—I had spent the better part of a day going through John's home, but did not find anything that would help figure him out. Thankfully, I had not found anything that point to him being the killer that Sheriff Jones desperately wanted him to be.

His secrets must lie somewhere else in the house.

I would hide secrets in the basement, away from the light and from the prying eyes of casual visitors. The basement door was unlocked. Outside, the sun was setting, turning the entire horizon a crimson-orange that reminded me of blood. In the distance I thought I saw some wild foxes running through the fields. I shuddered, remembering Cletus's warnings about the beasts. A rickety flight of steps led down into the dark. I fumbled around until I found an old-style push-button light switch. The light came on and I took a deep breath and descended. Each step caused the entire staircase to vibrate as if it wanted to shake me off and resume its darkened slumber. My fears were unjustified once my feet finally met the cement floor. The basement was actually well furnished. At the top of the walls there were small windows to the outside, allowing in the dusky light. In a room to my left was a workshop with a bunch of antique hand tools handing from peg board. To my right a pantry, stocked with canned vegetables, held the washing machine and dryer. Another section of the basement had full book-cases lining the walls with a chair and end table sitting among them. I was amazed at the sheer quantity of books John seemed to have. They were everywhere. I wondered if John had gone insane and the books were the palette from which his madness drew its colors.

I went over to the books and began to look at the various titles. John's tastes were just as eclectic as the upstairs book case suggested. Everything from classics, by Jack London and Dante, to best sellers. I took several books I had never heard of off the shelf and sat in the chair and leaved through them. The first was a book called "Melmoth the Wanderer." I read the preface and was just about to start Chapter One when I heard it.

Someone was outside. I briefly wondered whether Sheriff Jones had returned. Whoever it was had a stick and scraped it along the side of the house. My heart thudded loudly in my chest as I struggled to breathe. Without moving, for fear of being seen, I peered out the small windows into the dusk, but I could not see anything. Still the scraping continued. A shadow moved slowly across the window. Something stirred the dust, forming a small brown puff of dirt. I could not tell what, exactly, it was. I could hear deep breathing. A heavy, wet inhale, followed by a hearty exhale emphasized labored breathing. I sat as still as death, reminding myself to breathe. My eyes focused on the dusty window. A formless shadow blotted out the sunlight streaming through the window. The scraping had stopped, only to be replaced by guttural grunting and snorting. I heard a piercing animalistic scream, then, as if it had never been there, it disappeared.

My hand and trembled slightly, still holding the book with an iron grip. I tried to reconcile what I had just heard with what little I knew about wildlife. Either it was a very sick animal, or something else. I had so little experience I wondered if I had let me imagination run away with me.

The doorbell rang and I just about fell out of the chair. I raced up the rickety stairs and went to the front door. It was Dean.

"You OK?" he asked. "You look like you've seen a ghost or something."

I was not ready to admit to Dean that I had just had the piss scared out of me by a noisy shadow, I lied. "Oh, I fell asleep in the basement and the door bell scared me awake."

"I'm sorry about that," smiled Dean. "I figured it was time to get you back to the hotel. How about dinner?"

"You know, I'm not really hungry—I really didn't do that much today—just looked through some stuff. I guess tomorrow, I'll have to be more serious about going through his stuff. I've got some clothes to give to the church." I grabbed two of the trash bags.

"Find anything interesting?" Dean asked, taking the other two bags.

"Not really." Another lie. "Just some stained over-alls and a bunch of books. I take it John really enjoyed reading?"

Dean laughed. "The guy loved to read. When you could start ordering books off the internet and have them delivered, he was in heaven. I bet there are still some packages on their way. He would read anything. I swear, if he didn't have a book handy, he'd likely read the telephone book. There was just something about books that he couldn't resist."

As we walked back to Dean's car, I thought I could hear the strange grunting noise again and quickened my pace. Dean did too, although I could not be sure he had heard it. He continued to tell me about John's reading habits.

"Once, John and I went to a farm sale a couple of counties over, I was looking for a new combine, and he must have bought ten-twelve boxes of books from the estate. John would read fast, too. I think he'd finished reading the entire lot in a month or so. Definitely a fast reader."

As we drove out of John's driveway, I thought I saw something moving in the weeds, but never got a good glance at it.

"What's a matter, you see something?" Dean asked.

"I thought I saw something in those bushes, there" I said, pointing at the edge of an overgrown field.

"It was probably a rabbit, or something," Dean replied, "John used to complain about them eating his garden."

We drove in silence for a while, then I decided to invite Dean to dinner. "You know, I am getting hungry, how about I treat you to dinner—after all you've gone to all the trouble of ferrying me around."

"OK," Dean replied, smiling. "Sounds like a plan. How about the Shoney's off of I-13?"

"I've never been to a Shoney's, but if you recommend it, I'm sure it'll be great."

Chapter Six
Relationships

Your mind now, moldering like wedding-cake, heavy with useless experience, rich with suspicion, rumor, fantasy, crumbling to pieces under the knife-edge of mere fact. In the prime of your life.
Snapshots of a Daughter-in-Law.

Shoney's turned out to be a greasy spoon with an all you could eat buffet just on the edge of town. The parking lot was filled with semi-trucks since the place was just off the highway. We found a parking space around the side. The place had an old jukebox blaring hillbilly rock at a level that almost brought tears to your eyes it was so loud. The diners had to virtually yell over the music to be heard. The blaring buzz of the music, accompanied by the yelling patrons was almost too much for me. I could feel the oppressive air attacking me. Dean led me through the crown to a room separated from the din of the dining room by a short hallway. Thankfully, the smaller room was so much quieter that my ears sighed with relief.

The smaller room had several couples and families seated at booths and tables strewn throughout the room. We chose a booth that looked out the window at Dean's old truck.

"This is where the locals sit," Dean explained.

As we sat down, I could hear the people in the booth immediately behind me.

"It's him! John's nephew from Miami," said a woman with dyed-blonde hair excitedly—like she'd seen some sort of celebrity.

"He's a lot younger than I'd figured" replied a deep

male voice.

I smiled; I knew this could be a very interesting dinner. they had no idea I could hear them.

Dean must have seen me smile, and he grinned back. "Thought I'd bring you here to show you off to the locals. You know, give them something to talk about."

"I don't mind," I replied, grateful for any information I could glean from the townsfolk. "You never know, I just might learn something."

"Learn something?" Dean asked, "Like what?"

"The town. John. I don't know. Something, anything."

The waitress came up and took our drink orders—the only thing on the menu, other than drinks, was the buffet.

As she walked away Dean again asked, "So, did you find anything of interest at the house?" I wondered what he knew, or thought he knew, about John.

I had to think about how best to answer that—the last thing I wanted was to tip my hand too early. I liked Dean, and wanted to believe he was a good guy; but I still unsure if I could trust him. Especially about things like bullets in coffee cans. No doubt he would think I was nuts if I told him about the shadow I saw. He would think I was a coward for not going over to the window to see what it was.

"No not really," I replied. "I went through his room, the main room, the kitchen, and I went into the basement. I still can't believe John had all those books."

The waitress came up, gave us our sodas and two humongous plates. As we headed to the buffet, I could hear the whispers of the other diners. After piling our plates with way too much food, we made our way back to the table. As we dug into our food, the conversation naturally lagged, and I began to eavesdrop on the couple behind me.

"It's a shame about John, isn't it?"

76

"Yeah. I never figured he was so twisted."

"He was a nice guy, but you know what they say about serial killers; they're always the people you'd least suspect."

"And he was a church-going fellow, too. Doesn't say much for *that* church does it?"

"Nope. That's for sure."

"I wonder if the families will sue. After all, they should get something seeing as he killed them all."

"I hear he had a ton of money."

"A ton?"

"Yeah. Like over $500,000."

"You don't say? He lived like he was destitute. I mean, I never saw him beg or nothin' like that, but that house is ancient. And when was the last time you saw him drive his old truck?"

"And he never ate out—he only came to town to buy groceries. I wonder where I got it?"

"I hear he was into something illegal when he was younger—you know prohibition and all that. Probably got a taste of crime then, and, when he got old, he must have wanted to relive his glory days in the mob."

"I wonder what he did with them; the bodies, I mean."

"The paper said that all that was left were them bones. Probably ate them, I'd guess."

"Ate them?"

"Sure, why not? Either that or his freezer will be full of various body parts. Who knows what sort of sick and twisted things he used the flesh for."

"But eating them? Come on, that's just gross."

"No kidding. I wonder if it's genetic—maybe the nephew from Miami is psycho too."

"Don't know. Did you see his rental car? It was parked outside Cletus's office—Somebody took a dislike to him and did some serious damage to it."

"I never seen it, but I heard. I wonder who would've done it?"

"Probably Ricky Larsen. You know how he'd hated John."

"Yeah, but why take it out on the nephew? It's not like he done anything to Ricky."

"Guess it'd be the only way to get back at John—or at least his kin."

"Could be. Guess it could also be the Sheriff. Maybe trying to intimidate the nephew into access to the house and stuff. He's been itchin' to get into the house and caves for forever."

"Bet he finds some sort of Satanic alter or something. John must have been real bent to kill all those folks."

"Hard to say. Up 'til now, I figured John just didn't like the sheriff on account of their politics and he just wanted to piss the guy off by blocking him from gettin' into the caves. Now, I don't know. Maybe it was his killing fields, so to speak. I never liked Sheriff Jones anyway. Not since he waited until I drove off to get me for expired tabs instead of just walkin' up and letting me know."

I realized that Dean had just asked me a question, and I totally missed it. "I'm sorry, what'd you say?"

"It's OK, I asked if you had heard anything interesting."

"Just talk about how evil John was and how horrible it is that he'd killed all those people."

Dean's face hardened; to him John was not a killer.

"Who's Ricky Larsen?" I asked, hoping to catch him off-guard—it worked.

"So you've heard about him, huh?"

"It's been said he's the one that vandalized my car."

"I kind of doubt it. See, Ricky Larsen's been in the lock up since last Friday. He beats his wife."

"Oh. Wow."

"Yeah. But Ricky did have a history with John. If he'd been out, sure, I could see him screwing around with your car."

"How's that?"

"Well, I'd say it goes back, three, four years, maybe. Ricky's wife, Sue, had joined John's church. She spent a lot of time there—at the time we didn't know Ricky was beating her. So anyway, she helped John with some work, I'm not really sure what, and John and she got to be good friends.

"He was the first to realize what was happening at her home. I'm not sure how it come about, but he knew. And John was the kind of guy that, if he saw something like that, he wouldn't just let it go. And I'm sure he told Sheriff Jones. But Jones was up for election that year, and, well, he felt arresting Ricky would be bad press."

"Bad press, but the guy-"

Dean held up his hand. "I forgot to mention, Ricky is the son of the County Transportation Commissioner. Arresting him would not be good news, even if it was to stop him from beating on Sue. So anyway, John waited awhile to see if Sheriff Jones would do anything. And, of course, he didn't. John then went to visit Sue. It was a Friday afternoon, if I recall. He and Sue had some iced tea and talked the whole thing over. And then Ricky came home.

"Sue left immediately. John had helped her pack her suitcase and she came down to The Landing and Jessica gave her the room.

"Needless to say, Ricky was not real happy that John had butted in. Some words were exchanged and I guess the two got into it."

"Got into it?" I asked incredulously, "John was what, eighty-nine, ninety at the time?"

"Somewhere around there, I'd guess. Anyways, by the time it was through, Ricky spent the weekend in the hospital; John spent the weekend in the jail. Sheriff Jones loved that. In fact, he'd bring it up, from time to time, trying to get to John. But John was proud of that arrest. He knew what he'd done was the right thing. That evening, I visited John in the jail and that's what he told me—he was never charged with anything, and everybody considered him a hero"

"What happened after that?"

"Well, Sue did what most people do—she tried life without Ricky for a while, but Ricky had a job, she didn't, I guess she decided she'd rather go back to him and hoped he changed. But he didn't."

"Damn."

"Yeah. It's a bad deal. Since then, Ricky's had it out for John."

"Enough to kill him?" I asked quietly.

"Kill him? John was killed by a cougar or something like that." Dean said.

"Are you sure?"

"What are you getting at?"

"Well, I've been thinking. What if John didn't die of an accident with some wild animal? What if he was killed by a person?"

"Who would do that? Surely you don't think Ricky could have done it?"

"No, nothing like that. What if John had figured out who the killer was? What if John confronted him? And lost?"

Dean sat there, staring at his plate, trying to keep up with all my 'what ifs.' "I suppose is possible, but wouldn't you think that the killing would have been like the others? And if John knew who the killer was, why didn't he go to Sheriff Jones?"

"Would you go to Sheriff Jones to say you knew who was killing people around here if Sheriff Jones thought you were the killer? And, you just said, John wasn't the kind of guy who would allow something like that to go on, if he thought he could stop it."

"So, you think John had figured out who was killing these people, and was killed because of it?"

"Sure, why not?"

Dean did not have an answer to that question, so

we sat in silence for a few minutes. I could seek Dean working through my theory in his head. He was probably taking into account his experiences with John, trying to see if my theories fit. The waitress came up and I paid for dinner, leaving a generous tip. As we went out to Dean's truck, he said, "You could be right, you know? It's just, how do you prove something like that? I mean, with John gone, maybe he took his secret to the grave."

"I'm betting I'll find something in his house that will give us something to go on. After all, I've barely scratched the surface. It would explain why John had a bunch of books on serial killers and psychology in his bedroom."

"That it would," Dean replied. I could tell my theory had shaken him. Up until now, he figured John had died at the hands of a wild animal; now Dean was wrestling with the idea that a human animal had killed John. "Course it'd been years since he'd read that stuff. Right before he died, he was into biology of animals, anatomy, more scientific stuff."

As we headed back to The Landing, I asked if we could stop somewhere to get some supplies that would help me go through the house—boxes, tape, things like that. I also wanted to pick up some paper and a few pens. I have always found that writing things down helped me think. We stopped off at the Wal-Mart and I bought a bunch of stuff to pack up the house. I also bought a pack of legal pads, a pack of graph paper, and a set of pens. While I was at it, I figured an inventory of John's stuff might be helpful. Dean did not say much as he processed my theories. He said he would stop by tomorrow morning to take me to the house. He was not sure he would be able to pick me up tomorrow afternoon.

I told him it wasn't a problem—I wanted to stay out at the house and get as much done as possible.

As he drove off, I began to doubt my sanity for

wanting to stay at the house. If that thing was a wild animal, I would not be prepared if it got inside the house. I shook off my unease, the chances of something actually getting into the house were very small, especially if I kept the doors closed and locked. As I sat on the bed, I opened the legal pads and the pen set. I started writing down theories.

First, that John was the killer. This theory was supported by the bloody overalls and the bullets in the can in his kitchen. Also, the Sheriff seemed to think he had done it. Next, John was somewhat of a recluse, which gave him the freedom to kill without too many interruptions. Further, many people seemed to think John had done it. Finally, the dust on the bones was consistent with the caves.

My next theory was that John was not a killer. First, there was no direct evidence tying John to the murders—it was all circumstantial. Next, the bloody overalls could be due to hunting trips he had taken with Zeke. Also, the bullets may have been from his hunting trips and not the human victims. John did not seem to be the kind of guy that would have killed people—he was generous with both his time and money. Nothing in the house led me to believe that John was a killer—i.e. there were no body parts, bones, trophies, things like that. At least none that I had discovered. Unless you count the bullets or the serial killer books.

The third theory was that John was not the killer, but knew who was. The only thing that really supported this theory was the serial killer books I found in his bedroom. Also, it just felt right to me. In my gut, I sensed that this was the most likely theory.

After staring at these lists for a while, and trying to figure out other things to put on the various lists, I gave up. It was about 8:00 pm. I turned on the TV and watched a mindless sitcom for a while, then grabbed another legal pad and listed out the various tasks I thought I would need to accomplish if I was going to be able to leave by the end of the week. I was surprised how hard the decision to go back was for me to make. Now that I was here, it seemed that *here* was where I was supposed to be. I could see why John Lincoln had decided to stay here. It was beautiful country, bursting with wheat, corn, and cotton. Dean and Cletus had been nothing but nice to me, and even though I was an 'outsider,' nobody had been overly hostile to me— that is except whomever vandalized that rental car. I figured I might actually *like* it here. I knew Dean and some of the locals would turn into friends. Also, I was kind of a loner, so John's home, or I guess my home now, appealed to me. The solitude calmed me; it made me feel like I was truly alive. I felt more alive there— like each breath I took was slowly revitalizing me. I began to notice things like the colors in the sunset, or the simple pleasure of sitting in the sun allowing it to slowly warm you into a sleepy fog, which I had long ago stopped seeing.

These thoughts kept spinning in my head as I fell asleep to a laugh track of an obnoxious sitcom. The next morning, I woke up with the idea that I should try to make the home easier to come back to. After Dean dropped me off, I went into John's bedroom and immediately stripped the sheets from the bed. I struggled with the mattress and box springs until they sat in the corner of the basement. While I was down there I grabbed a screwdriver, went back up and took the bed frame apart too. After the frame was apart and stowed next to the mattress in the basement I went back up to move the rest of the furniture out of the room. I did not want to get rid of John, or his character, but I was just kind of spooked about being in the room.

Half an hour later, the room was empty. It was then that I noticed a faded square in the carpet in one corner of the room. The sculpted carpet hid the outline pretty well. I felt along the edges and found a small fabric tag on the one edge. I took a deep breath before I pulled the carpet back. Doubts attacked my mind— would I find John's trophies from the kill—Or something worse? I really didn't know what to expect. After all, if John was the killer, God only knew how the town would react to the news. I exhaled, tossing my fear to the fates and pulled the carpet back to reveal a small, hinged door built into the subfloor. I took another deep breath and opened it.

Inside the two-foot box were three worn and faded journals tied with gray twine. Next to the journals was a faded map with a post-it stuck on tap. I took the journals and the map out and discovered, underneath, a worn John Deere baseball cap with stains on it. I decided to leave the cap in the hidden cache—I did not want my DNA anyway near that cap. I hoped the journals would have a reasonable explanation in them. I carefully replaced the carpet to hide the box. I took the journals and the map to the kitchen table, and then went to find a nightstand to place over the carpet. No one else needed to find that cache until I had a chance to get to the bottom of this mystery.

After moving a nightstand into the room, I realized that, now, it looked out of place in the vacant room. John's journals would have to wait until the room was back in some semblance of order. I reluctantly took the journals and maps and hid them behind the refrigerator. I was alone, but still, it seemed too risky to simply leave John's secrets out in the open.

Forty-five minutes later, the room had been rearranged. The guest bed was in the room, along with an old chest of drawers. As I stood, looking at my handiwork, I realized that I had forgotten to take the four pictures off the wall. They were typical mid-west art—landscapes of barns and fields of grain. I liked them and I figured that the pictures would actually look better in the main room.

I took the first three off the walls without incident. The fourth picture, however, held another secret; a wall safe. I did not have the combination, but I tried to open it anyway. Of course, I had no luck. Why would John have hidden the journals in the floor, when there was a wall safe? What would John need both a safe and a hidden compartment for? John's life just kept getting more and more complex. I wondered whether the safe and compartment were part of John's paranoia, or if he actually needed two places to hide his secrets. I replaced the picture on the wall to hide the wall safe—I hoped I could find the combination in John's stuff.

The rest of the morning I spent going through the various stuff that John had accumulated throughout his life. There were a lot of books, receipts, instruction manuals, and paperwork that, basically, littered the home. I also managed to get the rest of his clothes packed up for donation.

At lunchtime, I went back into the kitchen and went through the fridge to make lunch. Looking outside, the heat was everywhere, soaking the land with its powerful rays. I thought it might not be a bad idea to eat outside on the front stoop. I still was not used to the heat smacking you every time you opened the door, but I took a deep breath and sat down next to the daily paper. I felt bad for the poor paperboy who had to drop off the paper—it was quite a ways from the main road to John's stoop. The paper had nothing new on the murders, which, I figured, was a good sign. I decided to continue disassembling John's home so it could remain in storage until I could decide what I wanted to do with it. The next hour or so was spent boxing up stuff, storing various things, and, generally, cleaning the place up. By the time the afternoon was in full swing, I was totally exhausted.

I wanted to get back to town, so I could take a shower and get some rest. While my body labored on various projects, my mind spent the afternoon working on John. I still had no answers. There was one really important thing I wanted to do all day. but I had to make it look like I worked on the home. That way I had plausible deniability when they asked me if I went to the caves. That was exactly where I planned to go. I had to know why John had been so dead set on prohibiting anyone access to the caves.

After half an hour I had everything I thought I needed to go spelunking—a back pack with a flashlight, extra batteries, bottles of water, rope, and an old oil lantern. I slung the pack over my shoulder and headed out. I locked the back door behind me. No more surprise visits from the Sheriff. The heat was still amazing oppressive. When you live in a more temperate climate the heat is a welcome distraction from the seasonal mildness. Here, it was everywhere. It was like the heat lived inside every living thing. The grass seemed to radiate the heat back into the day. The sky was a clear blue that magnified the heat tenfold. Even the birds remained still and quiet out of respect for the sun. I walked along a well-worm dirt path to where the caves should be. Each step created a small cloud of dust that floated for several seconds before returning to the surface to rest. I could feel the sweat accumulate at the base of my back where the backpack sat.

Ten minutes later I was there. The entrance to John's caves was inauspicious at best. It basically was a small hole in a rock wall. I had to get on my knees to crawl through it. Once inside, the cold, moist air licked at my sweaty face, giving me a slight chill. My breathing became slower due to the wet thickness of the air. The small of my back, where the sweat had pooled during my hike to the cave rapidly cooled, sending another shiver through my body. I should have brought a jacket. A sweet musty smell permeated the air. Squeaks echoed throughout the room, but had no apparent source. I figured it must be field mice that used the cave as a shelter. I stood up and brushed my sleeves and pants off. Under my feet, the floor felt spongier than I had expected. I figured it must be moss or mold.

I flicked on my flashlight to reveal a small cave, slightly larger than a standard bedroom. The walls were chipped smooth, as if someone had taken a chisel and tried to remove all hints that this was a natural formation. When the light turned on the squeaking diminished slightly. It was then that watching all those educational programs on cable came in handy. I slowly sent the light up towards the ceiling to reveal a coven of bats. I realized that the spongey floor was guano. I hoped I avoided contracting some strange bat-shit disease. I do my best to avoid rodents and their droppings in my day to day life. Bats are flying rodents. I pushed the unpleasantness of being covered in bat-shit from the front of my mind and tried to focus on the cave itself.

The ground looked like it had been worked over—like John has spent a lot of time and energy trying to make the cave less, well, cave-like. At the far end of the cave was an opening that I figured must lead to the next cave. So I squished my way through the bat shit and into the opening. I hoped that the next cave would not be inhabited by the filthy creatures too.

Fortunately, the next cave was bare of all bats. Just like the bat cave, as I had nominated it, the walls, floor and ceiling had been modified to look more like a man-made cave than anything else. This cave was about the same size as the bat-cave, but it had three new openings to go through, and, of course, the one I already passed through. In one corner an old wooden crate stood with picks, shovels, and other hand tools piled into it. The handles were shiny with the oils left on them from the many years they had been wielded.

I was trying to decide which path to follow when it occurred to me that I might never find my way back. If all the caves had been remanufactured, they would all start to look alike. Getting lost in the caves was not something that would win friends and influence people. Especially since no one knew I was here. I took a second look at the pile of old tools that sat, collecting dust, in the corner of the cave.

I pulled out the pick and hefted it. I tried scratching at the floor first. With minimal effort, I noisily scratched a primitive arrow on the ground. I laughed as I wondered if, in 100 years, when someone was exploring this cave they would wonder at the Neanderthal that carves these strange marking on the floor. I checked my watch before I decided to move on to the next room. I figured I had another couple of hours to explore before I had to head back. So long as my flashlight and lantern held out, I could keep going. I decided to take the opening on the far left of the three.

The next cave was radically different from the terraformed caves I just passed through. Here, stalactites and stalagmites littered the cave. Some formed columns in the middle of the room, while others dangled from the ceiling like strange alien chandeliers. They were almost all a pale white color that seemed to glow when the flashlight beam swept over them. Carefully, I scratched another arrow into the floor before I picked my way through the strange points that rose from the floor to get the other side of the cave. There two more openings greeted me. I could hear the drips of water that fell off the stalactites and hit the floor, echoing throughout the room. I began to wonder exactly how far into the earth the caves went. If John had managed to explore them all before his untimely demise. I wondered if he had mapped the caves. I wondered how he found his way through these caves; no other markings were around that John used as guides.

Picking one, I, again, chose the far left opening. The next cave was just like the last one, only slightly larger. The geologic formations were spectacular. I wondered if John was afraid visitors would ruin the natural beauty of the cavies. On my way to the back of the cave, I tripped headlong into one of the stalagmites. I shined my flashlight back where I had tripped and, almost at the same time, felt the cold water seep into my socks. There was a small pool of water, no more than six inches deep.

In falling, I managed to drop the lantern which shattered against the cold, hard floor. I was glad it had shattered and not my kneecap. I stood up and found that I was still in pretty good shape; I hadn't twisted my ankle or done any permanent damage. A large bruise would form on my forearm, where I broke my fall, but other than that, I was OK. My left foot was wet.

I moved onwards through the caves, exploring as I went. The caves all started to look alike after a while— they were still beautiful and majestic, but a rock room with a bunch of spikes coming from the ground up and the ceiling down gets old after a while. A few hours later I knew it was time to go back to John's house, otherwise, I might miss my ride back to the hotel. As I scratched my last arrow, suddenly I heard it. The same scraping noise from the house, but this time it was fainter, but even more terrifying. The huffing breath echoed throughout the caves. I could hear whimpers and wheezes, but had no idea from where they were coming. I immediately shut off my flashlight and stood in total darkness. The darkness swam around me, sending my imagination into overdrive. In the darkness, the drops of water that fell from the ceiling became footfalls of the beast that lived in the cave. The damp air seemed to wrap itself around my throat, squeezing tightly, making me gasp for air. Dark shadows twisted in the ink black in front of my eyes. My heart thudded loudly in my chest, and I tried to control my fear.

The scraping noise seemed to go on forever. My mind filled in panicked details of someone using a bone to drag along the rock walls of the cave. Or maybe grinding the bond into a fine powder, while twisting it against the stone. This time, instead of a scream, a wail punctuated the darkness of the cave. I held my breath, trying hard not to panic. Then the sound receded and, eventually disappeared. Even after the noise was gone, I sat in the corner of the dark cave and dared not move. Every fiber of my body was straining to run. My mind filled in images of diseased and rabid animals waiting for me to move to strike. After five minutes or so, I could barely force my finger to turn on the flashlight. I was sure that it would reveal the monster haunting these caves right in front of me. I flicked on the light, flinching from the light, and saw the cave exactly like it was when I had hid. Only this time, every shadow seemed fraught with danger or death. Despite my fear, I knew I needed to get out of there. So I pushed on as quickly, and as quietly, as I could, back through the caves. I realized that, throughout my exploration I had been descending. It was a slight incline, but on the way back, it seemed like it was uphill. Despite the natural coolness of the caves, I began to sweat as I worked harder and harder to climb my way out of the depths.

I finally made it back to the second man-made room and stopped, taking in deep lungfulls of moist cave air. I looked at my watch, my terror had taken its toll. I was exhausted and it had taken a lot longer to leave the caves than going into them. I sat on the edge of the crate of tools to catch my breath. As I sat there, I noticed that the arrow I scratched into the ground had changed. Something had walked over it, causing dust and dirt to cover part of it. I shook off my irrational fear—I had survived, after all, and had to continue back to John's house. After squeezing through the cave's opening, I made it outside. The sun was just dropping below the horizon, sending long shadows across the fields.

As I stumbled along the worn dirt path back towards John's home, glancing behind me every other step. My muscles dully ached and I knew that to-morrow, I would be sore. My ankle throbbed, and the adrenaline fix was starting to wear off. It was clear out, and the full moon shone brightly, casting dark and fearsome shadows around the fields. The evening air still had a hint of the day's scorching heat, but it was cooling rapidly.

I tripped on my own two feet and nearly went sprawling into the dust. Seemingly out of nowhere I was grabbed by a vice-like grip of an old man's hand and yanked upright. Too afraid to scream, I jerked my arm away and took a few steps back, fully expecting a beast to bear its ugly fangs at me and sink its teeth into my tender neck. Instead, blending into in the tall grass an old man with a long white beard stood silently. The beard would have reached his waist, but for the immense stomach that strained at the worm denim overalls. Tobacco stains yellowed the corners of the old man's mouth and chin. His dark eyes were recessed behind white, bushy eyebrows. He looked at me with a mixed expression of disgust and pity. He just stood there, silent in the cooling night air. His right hand carried a rifle, the barrel pointing towards the full moon. A hunting knife, with a worn wooden handle, dangled off his left hip. I supposed he could have been the one making those sounds. Maybe it was some sort of mental torture, designed to harass and weary his prey. I wondered if I would be the next pile of bones to be found—just another outsider who went missing in the dark hills of the Ozarks. I swallowed hard and regained my voice, but was still working on regaining my courage.

"What the hell? Where'd you come from?"

The old man jerked his head behind him, never

taking his sharp and hard eyes off of me, indicating he'd come from the hills behind him.

"Who are you?"

"Name's Zeke. John and I was friends."

The pieces fell into place; I could see John and Zeke hunting in these woods together. "You were his hunting buddy, right?" I relaxed slightly; all I had to worry about was the demon in the caves. "Come on," I urged. "Let's head to the house, we can talk."

He replied icily. "You ain't got to worry, it won't come out after ya."

I was speechless.

"We hunted, sure," Zeke said noncommittally, changing the subject.

"But what is—"

"Boy, you'd best not talk about such things round here—people think you crazy."

"But-"

He gave me a glare that shut me up, and right quick.

"So you knew John?"

"Yup."

"OK." I paused, if he was not going to talk, he had no reason to be here. He must want to say something, otherwise, he would have left me to fall. "Was John killed by that-"

A wild look in his eyes made me stop mid-sentence, so I rephrased the question. "They told me John was killed by some wild animal. Do you believe that?"

A stream of tobacco-laced spit shot out of the old man's mouth and landed with a muted thud on the path. "Nah."

The eyes flicked quickly from pity to scorn. "John was killed, then left for the scavengers. It's a shame too. Good man, John was."

"Murdered, you mean?"

"Killed. He was dead."

"OK," Zeke's one-track mind was hard to follow.

Unperturbed, I continued trying to pull information out of this strange old man. "Were those other people killed... the same way?"

"Yup. Pro'ly."

"Who?" I was not as optimistic about getting a straight answer out of Zeke as I had been just a few minutes ago.

"Don't matter," this time he spit towards his left. "Soon enough, killer'll be judged. Least that's what Pastor Mike say."

My frustration started to tighten in my chest and my anger began to rise in my throat. Before I could bark at Zeke, he said, "You should go on home." As plainly stated as his prior threat, but still as jarring, I closed my mouth. "You'll pro'ly end up hurt."

"Was that a threat?" I asked, my hands balling into tight fists. I started calculating the odds in a fist fight with this old man. They were not good. The creature in the cave had made me feel powerless.

He spat between his boots and sighed, as if in boredom. He did not answer my question; he just stared at me through those impenetrable jet-black eyes.

"Figured I owed it to John to warn ya." He said, turning back towards the woodland behind him. Almost silently he pushed his aged frame through the grass.

"Wait," I said with as much conviction as I could muster. "I'd like to talk to you about John, you know, find out what kind of man he was."

Over his left shoulder he said, "Like I said, John was a goodun. Watch yo'self—you don't wanna end up like John."

This time I could detect hostility in his statement to me, but that might have been my paranoia. Even if it had not been a threat, I would hate to meet Zeke again in the dark. The man was just plain scary. Despite what he had said, I was still afraid of whatever was in the caves, so I hurried the rest of the way to

John's house, I tried to analyze our conversation. I realized I had done most of the talking, but Zeke had told me a lot in the few words he bothered to share with me. Zeke was not the kind of guy that wasted his words, especially on cityfolks.

I kept repeating his words, each time trying to place the emphasis exactly where he did, figuring I might be able to capture his intent, but I never could get it quite right. The way he had talked was almost too mono-tone, like he had no affect. The undercurrent of his statements was that he knew more than he was telling me. How much more, though, was anyone's guess. A guy that could walk as silently as he had along the trail probably saw quite a bit without anybody realizing he was there. I wondered if he had seen John get killed. How much he know of what was going on in the cave. The rational part of my brain started to reassert itself and I wondered if Zeke was the one in the caves, making those noises just to freak me out. Then my mind took an involuntary side-step. Zeke could have killed John. Especially since Zeke was sure John could have taken care of himself if he confronted a wild animal. Could he handle Zeke? If Zeke was the murderer, then it would be in his interest to point the blame at the townsfolk, even if he did not specifically finger anyone in particular. I had little doubt that Zeke was easily capable of killing someone. He also inferred he knew an awful lot about John's death; and maybe his guilt was the something I knew he was holding back. Which made the cave encounter much easier to accept. No animals or monsters lurked there. I was just a crazy backwoods country redneck who had taken great pains to scare the city boy. I felt like a rube.

Climbing the steps back into John's house, I had a new suspect. Zeke was certainly the 'right' kind of person to kill outsiders to the town. He was loner. I doubted people ever even saw him; sure everybody knew him, but nobody would have noticed him. Not to mention he had intimate knowledge of the back country. I bet he was quite handy with that hunting knife. Taped to the door was another note. Maybe this one would be signed from the killer. That would put a short end to this strange journey. It was not a confession, just a note from Dean giving me directions to town and telling me that John kept an old run-about Ford in the barn.

I began to wonder, exactly, how much danger I was really in. My rental car had already been trashed. How badly did the killer really want me out of his town? I doubted I would be in real physical danger since that would be too overt, too risky for someone who liked to kill in private. Zeke's warnings lingered in the forefront of my mind. I could not figure out why the killer would be threatened by me. If he chased me away, the money would still be mine, but John's caves would be more vulnerable then. I had to admit that the caves were spectacular, but nothing worth killing over.

It was time for me to go back to the Landing, get a nice, hot shower, and think about everything. I was reluctant to drive around in John's truck after what had happened to my rental, but I knew I did not want to spend the night in a home where no one could hear me scream if the killer came after me. So I ventured into the rapidly cooling night air and into the barn.

Under an old army tarp, a red Ford truck sat, its keys dangling in the ignition and, remarkably, a full tank of gas. Clearly, the truck had seen better days; the paint was faded and chipped in several places. Dents peppered the passenger side, like someone had taken a baseball bat to the side. Long scratches ran along the bed. I could sympathize. I wondered who had hated John enough to beat his truck up. I made a mental note to ask Dean about that.

The engine started up immediately. I could feel the powerful engine come to life and idle like a hulking beast, just waiting to be unleashed. After a few jerky starts and stops, I got the feel of driving the machine and edged out to the end of John's driveway. Dean's directions said to start out heading east, then take a quick right onto a two-lane road about a mile and a half down the road.

So, off I went into the night. After about a mile, I slowed down, hoping to see the road Dean told me to turn on. I could not see it. Two miles went by. Then three passed. By the time I reached six, I figured I must have missed it and made a U-turn—well actually, it was more like a ten-point turn since the truck was so big and the road so small—and headed back. The headlights were of little help to me as each side of the road was flanked by windbreaks.

Over the road noise, I heard another hoarse bark, just like I had heard in the caves. My pulse quickened, thudding deep in my chest. I tried to calm myself by taking deep breaths. After all, this was real life, not some B-grade novel where the hero is attacked. I figured I must have imagined it, an echo of the fear that had momentarily overtaken me. I started looking in earnest for my turn.

Out of the inky darkness, a solid form slammed into the back of the truck. I was violently thrown forward and my head hit the steering wheel, causing me to see stars. A second gut-wrenching impact came from the passenger side. The truck swerved all over the road and the rear of the truck skidded from side to side. The mirrors gave small peeks at something trying to destroy the truck I wrestled with the steering wheel, using brute force to pull the truck under my control again. Involuntarily, I stepped on it, hoping the engine had enough power to outrun whatever it was that was hunting me. Zeke's advise that it would not come after me, whispered bitterly in my head.

The rear passenger side of the truck was nudged by my assailant. Then I was spinning again, this time, my tires left the road, throwing gravel everywhere. As the truck flipped over on the driver's side, I knew all was lost. The impact caused the window to shatter, throwing glass all over the cab of the truck. The ride was not over—the truck continued rolling until we landed upside down in a corn field. Just before I lost consciousness, I saw a large deer with antlers looking at me menacingly. Briefly I wondered why a deer would come so close to an accident. Then the darkness of Stillwater took over.

Chapter Seven
Going Home

Home is so sad. It stays as it was left,
Shaped to the comfort of the last to go
As if to win them back.
"Home is so Sad" Philip Larkin

The next morning I woke up in a small medical clinic. I was surprised both by my surroundings and the fact that I had actually woken up. Next to my bed, Dean sat with a stunning girl. Her long auburn hair was pulled back into a ponytail and revealed dark brown eyes that penetrated into my semiconscious fog.

"It's OK," Dean said, interrupting my focus on the girl. "You're at Major's clinic. You're OK."

"What?" I mumbled, my throat dry. The headache was back.

"When you didn't make it back, we went out looking for you. We found the truck upside down in a ditch." Dean gave me a sip of water. "What happened?"

"Well, I was driving back to town and must have missed the turn. Then, out of nowhere, I—" I remembered Zeke telling me no one would believe me. "I think I may have hit a deer, or something."

"Really?" Dean asked.

"Yeah."

"Huh. I didn't see a deer, but-"

The doctor walked in and interrupted us. After giving me a quick once over, he concluded I had no major medical problems. He told me my headache would go away in a few hours, and I'd be sore for the next week or so. He smiled like it was good news. I left out my anxiety that someone was out there trying to kill me.

After the doctor left, I could smell Sheriff Jones coming down the hall. I had to wonder what he was trying to hide with that awful cologne. As he entered the room, he coughed, flexed his muscles and sat on the edge of my bed. With an overacted sorrowful look, he looked me up and down.

"Had a bad night, did you?" his slimy smile.

"You could say that," I replied.

"So, you been drinking?"

The throbbing in my head intensified. "No. Nothing like that. I hit a deer, I think."

"Are you sure? I mean, no deer was found."

"Not really," I said.

He frowned. "Well, I looked that scene over pretty good." He smiled again, this time trying to ingratiate himself to me, "I once supervised the accident reconstruction unit of the Arkansas police. I didn't see anything that indicated you hit anything. Sure you weren't drinkin'?"

"I don't drink."

He looked at me like I was lying. "Well, that's good. My opinion, based on my knowledge and experience, will be that you simply fell asleep at the wheel and dreamed the rest. Hell, you prob'ly had a deer come by while you were there waitin' to be rescued."

I looked at him. His too smooth face, along with perfectly groomed hair, sickened me. I tried to look behind his polished exterior and nearly blank eyes. There was nothing behind those eyes.

Sheriff Jones was quiet. Another tactic I used to my advantage from time to time. I have found people tend to hate uncomfortable silences. So they say more when you step in to break the silence. I wasn't biting. We sat in silence for half a minute.

"Well. I'll mail you a copy of the report. Should I

send it to John's old house?"

His real question was whether I was planning on staying in town. "No. Send it to my Miami address." I rattled off the address and Sheriff Jones left, leaving me with Dean and his female friend.

Dean's eyes were focused on the linoleum floor and his jaw as hard and set. He was angry.

"Hi," I said, introducing myself to the woman.

"Hi." She replied, a smile across her face. It somehow made her more beautiful. "I'm sorry. We haven't had a chance to be introduced. I'm Jessica. Call me Jessie."

"Hi. I'm Bernard. Most people just call me Berns."

"I'm sorry about the Sheriff. He's not very motivated to help, that's for sure."

"No kidding," Dean interjected. "Especially since he thinks John's a serial killer." He stood up. "Well, guys, I've got to get going. I'll leave you in Jessie's capable hands."

"Thanks."

As Dean left, I was nervous. I always get a little nervous around pretty girls. An awkward silence sat over us for a few seconds.

"Well, I'm glad to get some alone time with you." Jessie said as she went over to close the door to the room. "I think you need to know more about John."

"I'm not sure I can handle more; what little I know almost got me killed." I looked at the slightly open door. I remembered Cletus's admonition about small towns with large ears. "Is it safe to talk?"

Jessie laughed, sending chills through me. My headache was instantly better. "If we close the door, they'll say I took advantage of you. You know, since I'm over thirty and not married, I must be one of those loose girls. If we keep it open, all they'll hear is the same thing I've said since the day John passed." She choked back a small sob. "I've known John all my life. He was like a second father to me. He helped me out every time I needed it. Not to mention he taught me an awful lot about life along the way. When I had to take my parents up to Jeff City and take over the farm, John was the only person who thought I could do it. Most folks around here thought I'd sell it since running a farm is not women's work. Now I run one of the most successful farms in South Missouri.

"So, I suppose you could say I'm biased when it comes to John. But, even with that bias, I know he's not a killer." She stopped talking, the anger in her eyes flashing light lightning.

I decided to keep my mouth shut. I could tell she had more to say, just needed the time to say it.

"John couldn't have been the killer. It wasn't like him. He was strange about those caves. And with good reason. He told me that they cover almost 80 acres and are hard to navigate."

"So John would explore the caves?"

"Oh yeah. It was his hobby. He didn't want anybody to get lost in the caves."

"But, if he was so concerned about that, why didn't he let Sheriff Jones have access to the caves? You know, walk him through it?'

"Sheriff Jones and John's rivalry goes back almost fifteen years. When the Sheriff first came to town, he and John got into it at a town hall meeting. John never told me what the original argument was over, but he said it was a small thing. But the Sheriff never got over it. Then, when John and the Sheriff vied for the same position on the City Council, things got worse. Since then, the Sheriff has truly had it in for John."

"I see."

"Anyways, I hope you believe me." She looked down and stared at the floor, like she was ashamed.

"Well, everything you've told me is consistent with what I know about John. Not to mention my gut tells me that you're telling me the truth. Besides, I need you to help me. And since you knew John the best, I'll believe you."

"Help you?"

"I need some help getting John's place in order and figuring out what to keep and what to get rid of."

"Are you planning to stay in town for a while, then?"

"After this," I swallowed hard, "accident, I think I'll head back to Miami for a while. But I don't want to sell John's house or anything like that. I'm also hoping you'll keep an eye on the place while I'm gone."

"I could do that," she replied. I could tell that she was disappointed that I'd be leaving. I guess she thought I'd want to stick around and try to clear John's name.

Thankfully, the door opened and Pastor Mike poked his head in. "I'm sorry, am I interrupting?" he asked. Jessie gave me a knowing look.

"No, I was just leaving." She turned to me, "Give me a call once you're released, and I'll meet you at John's place."

"OK."

"You alright?" Pastor Mike asked. It was the first time I got to focus on Pastor Mike. His hairline was receding, but he was still young. His grey eyes seemed filled with compassion and concern. It was strange that so many people in this small town would be concerned about me.

"Oh, I'm fine. Just a few bumps and bruises," I replied. "They said I could leave in an hour or so."

"Sheriff Jones tells me that you fell asleep at the wheel last night?"

"That's the story." I was amazed that news traveled that fast in the town.

"Hm. You must have been working too hard at John's place, to fall asleep at the wheel like that. I saw pictures of the truck—it was pretty scratched up."

"Well, I'm just trying to get to know John. What brings you by today? I'm sure it's not just to check up on me."

"Well, I happened to be here visiting one of my flock and heard you were here. Thought I'd stop in."

"I appreciate the concern, Pastor. I'm fine. Just going to have some aches and pains as souvenirs."

"Souvenirs? You're going back to Miami, huh?"

The Pastor did not miss much. "It seems the only luck I have around here is bad. After what happened to the rental car, combined with my accident, it seems like Miami is a much safer place for me."

"Well, that's too bad." He scratched his head. "I was hoping you would stick around for a while. I guess this means you're not going to make dinner tomorrow?"

"Probably not. I figure I'm going to head back tomorrow morning."

I sensed he wanted to tell me something else, but held back. "Well, good luck." He left when another doctor came in to have me sign a bunch of forms.

As I got dressed, my muscles grumbled to me that they did not appreciate the abuse administered to them. I had to agree. Getting tumbled around in a pickup truck in the middle of the night was not conducive to a healthy lifestyle. The more I thought about it, the more I became scared. If I disappeared, like those hitchhikers, no one would report me missing. The folks in this town would assume I had gone back to Miami. With a gentile encouragement from Sheriff Jones, it would be likely that no one would ever know. Maybe I should stay in Miami and spent my fortune there. This town, with its very strange monsters, was very dangerous. As I left the clinic, which happened to be two blocks from the hotel, Miami kept repeating in my head. Home was well outside the zone of danger that seemed to follow me wherever I was in this town.

At the Landing, I plopped back on the hotel bed and stared at the ceiling. Despite my decision to go back to Miami, it gnawed at me. Had Zeke attacked me last night? How had he managed to crash my truck? I had not seen another car, but that only made sense. Again, the rational part of my brain was asserting its dominance over the fantastical theories of monsters that go bump in the night. Running away felt like I was abandoning John. I was leaving him to lose his good name from the grave. It left a sour taste in my mouth too. There were too many loose ends here. I was sure staying was not an option, not with Zeke trying to kill me.

As I packed my bag, I started getting angry at everything. Not only did my pants not fold right, but John deserved more than this. My headache had all but disappeared, which was a blessing. I could not justify staying around here and risk getting killed. At least not until I had a chance to get my mind right after the accident. It really rattled me. Combined with the death threat, it was too much. Sticking around was simply too risky.

I double checked to make sure I had not left anything, went out, and threw the suitcase into the back of my trashed rental. Thankfully, Cletus had arranged for the tires to be replaced. I drove out to John's house reversing the directions Dean had given me. As I passed the fields, I could not feel the same beauty I felt before. Now they were hostile and alien. Their whispers sound like the dry death rattles you read about in bad mystery novels. Despite the fact I did not have the air conditioning on, the hair on my arms stood up as a chill passed through me. Every dry field seemed to harbor a dangerous predator, waiting to attack.

Turning off the highway and back in to John's driveway, I got myself back under control. Getting run off the road had changed my perspective. Up until now I had lived a fairly peaceful life. Admittedly I had little reason to be a target, even when I was working as a private investigator. Unlike what is shown on television, most of the time I took videos and photographs of the subject and went away. They never knew who I was or what I had done.

I parked behind a newer Chevy Tahoe. I hoped it was Jessie's. As I made it to the top step the door opened and there she was. She was a stunning sight that took my breath away.

"Hey," I said. "I thought I was supposed to call you?"

"Hi. You were. But I came out anyways. How are you feeling?"

"Well, I'm gonna hurt for a few days, but all in all, I think I'll live."

She laughed, "That's good. So, what are you planning to do?"

"I'm not real sure."

We sat down on the chairs. The air conditioning hummed in the background, an ever-present reminder of the oppressive heat outside. "I think John was looking into the murders."

"He was." She replied matter-of-factly.

"You knew?"

"John and I were like father and daughter in some ways. He talked with me about it, but only when he was really tired. It was like he was trying to keep the unpleasantness from me."

"Had he reached any conclusions?"

"I know he had narrowed his list down. But I don't think he knew for sure." She was holding something back

"What aren't you telling me?" I pried, gently.

We sat in silence, the cold air-conditioned air swirling around us. She was trying to decide whether to tell me what she knew. I looked at her. She was quite attractive. Her auburn hair was shoulder length and her eyes sparkled in their depth. As she thought, she nibbled at her upper lip. "It sounds crazy, though."

I tried to smile charmingly, but failed. "Crazy is my specialty."

"He talked about dragons, worms, those kind of things, that were responsible for the killings." She blushed and looked at her lap. "I figured it was his old age and his love of books. He had been reading about dragons and such."

My interest was piqued—whatever I had heard in the caves, and what I figured had attacked my truck, could have been a dragon. Or a creature much like a dragon, at least. "But..." I goaded her, trying to draw out what she thought.

"But, I don't know. John was mauled by something. And he was the kind of man that would not be mauled by a wild animal. I mean, he'd have heard it long before it snuck up on him. But, I just don't know." She started to cry.

"Have you ever been in the caves?" I asked.

She looked startled. "No. John would never allow it. In fact, he would have killed me if I had disobeyed him. It was his one big rule. He was always real clear on that."

"Why? Everyone I've talked to have been unclear why he was so concerned about the caves. You have any ideas?"

"He told me once it was for my own good, not to go into the caves. When he said it, it seemed based in a concern over my safety. I guess I always figured it was because the caves were old, unstable, things like that. But as time went on, I wondered exactly what he had seen in the caves. Once I think he almost tried to tell me, but something held him back."

I let her sit quietly for a while, remembering her old friend John. "Hm. Well, we won't find anything sitting round here," she said as she got up and headed into the kitchen. I followed her, only to be confronted by a complete and total mess.

"What happened here?" I asked.

"What do you mean?"

"The place has been ransacked." The entire contents of the kitchen cabinets were spread across the table and floor. Silverware and pots were scattered all around the kitchen. I was thankful I had found the bullets and hid them somewhere else. The rage I had been feeling ever since I came to this God-forsaken town suddenly resurfaced violently, Without thinking, I grabbed the table and tipped it over, sending the debris across the floor.

"What are you doing?" Jessie asked in a shaking voice.

"I, uh, well..." I looked down at my shaking hands, tying to reel in the anger. I did not have an answer. It was like something had taken control of me, trying to push all the right triggers to push me over the edge. I took a few deep breaths. "I'm just am so mad," even the word caused my headache to worsen. "Who would do this? What could they possibly be looking for? John's dead. If he was the killer, then it's over. If he's not, what's the point?"

She reached out and gently patted my arm. Her touch soothed my headache, and calmed me even more. "I know, it's not right." She looked at the mess in the kitchen. "But, this town has been suffering for a long time. It's like there's a poison in the water. It turns the people bitter."

"Bitter, huh? Do you think Sheriff Jones did this? Was the door forced or anything?"

"Yeah, I do." She looked in my eyes. "It's sad to say. But he's had it out for John for years."

We quickly examined every window and door in the place, but it did not look like anyone had broken in. Returning to the kitchen, I found Jessie starting to put things back where they belonged.

I stooped down next to her. "I'm sorry about doing this, it came over me like-"

A knowing glance showed me she understood. "It's OK, really. It takes a while to get acclimated here. Like I said, bitterness is a town tradition."

"Bitterness?"

"We've struggled once the trains stopped coming to town. I've lived here my whole life and it feels like one long, hard fight. The farmers in town drive the town's success. When they have good years, everyone prospers. A bad year, and, well, it scars the people. My people wake up wishing they hadn't. Even my folks, who were moderately successful at farming, are happy to be gone. I've never seen them so happy since they left. They hardly fight. The people here, though, are different. You won't see too many real smiles."

She could read my face. "Oh, sure, there's folks that are pleasant. And Pastor Mike is always chipper. But in the honesty of their homes, they are mean, angry folk." She looked out the windows at the wilderness bathed in the sunlight. "We should be happy, or at least content. We live in a place that God has blessed. The ground grows food, the air is clean. There is hardly any crime here. All in all, it should be a great place to be." She turned away from the sunshine. "But it's not. There is something in this town that sucks at the very joy."

A deep sigh punctuated her thoughts. "I'm sorry, too. You don't need to hear any of this."

"It's OK," I replied. "It's good to have context for all of this." By now the kitchen was back to normal. The sugar sack was where I had left it, and I kept quiet about the bullets. Jessie seemed to have enough on her mind. "How about we divide and conquer? I'll take John's room, you take the guest room, and we'll meet in the hallway before we head downstairs?"

She weakly smiled at me. "OK. What's the plan?"

"Well, I just want to sort the wheat from the chaff—find things that we should get rid of, clothes, etc. and anything else that might help figure out what happened to John." I paused. "Or the other victims."

She looked at me hard, trying to gauge whether I thought John was the killer. She turned on her heel and entered the guest room. After another half hour, I had cleared out the rest of John's room and decided to check on Jessie. She had managed to make some progress, but was crying on the edge of the bed when I came in. I sat down next to her, put my arm around her. I decided to keep my mouth shut. I thought it would be better to let her simply know I was there, if she needed me. It was strange, putting my arm around her. After a few more sobs, she quietly apologized.

"It's OK," I whispered back. The rage bubbled up at the fact that this woman was hurt and crying.

"I miss him already." She sat up and looked through tear filled eyes at me. "I knew he was old, and I knew he was going to pass on soon. But to have him taken from me, it's just, hard."

In her eyes reflected a simmering fire of anger and hatred. I wondered if she realized just how much anger was bottled up inside her.

"I wish I had a chance to get to know him."

"He was a better man than everyone else in this town." Another sob escaped her body, "Hell, he was probable a better than anyone else in the world. He was generous to a fault, stood up for those who needed him, and, was always there for me." She angrily stood up. "And he was no killer."

"I know." I agreed.

"I can't do any more of this today, I'm sorry."

"I understand."

She gave me a hug and hurried out. The gravel crunched under her tires as she drove away and I turned back determined to find John's hidden investigation notes before I left for Miami. I made sure I locked the door behind me. One attempt on my life was enough. I stood in the living room and realized that I had been looking at John's house the wrong way. The main level was too clean and nondescript. He hadn't been using it regularly before he was killed, which meant he must have been spending his time somewhere else. I had been in the basement, and it was just as devoid of the clutter associated with daily life.

I must have been missed something. I went back to the hallway between the kitchen and John's room. The bathroom and the guest bedroom doors were open. There was a door that opened to a closet that I had discounted.

Opening the door, I hoped that John's secrets would be there. The rack was full of coats and overalls. I pulled them out, looking for the box, or safe, or something that would help explain this mystery. Nothing remarkable was in the closet. In disgust, I picked up one of John's boots and threw it against the back of the closet. Instead of a satisfying thump, the shoe slid down the wall and landed on the floor. I reached out to touch the back of the closet and found it was not a wall there. Instead, my hand touched a soft velvet sheet stretching from floor to ceiling. In the middle, my hand pushed through to the other side. I followed my hand through the false closet back and found myself at the bottom of a staircase.

"Unbelievable" I muttered. I climbed the stairs, grabbing on to the rail to guide me in the semi-darkness. At the top of the stairs a curtained window allowed in just enough light for me to find a light switch. Flipping the lights on, I realized I had found John's secret. Along one wall there was a huge bulletin board with photos of the victims and information posted on it. Along the other wall was a large desk covered in police reports, photographs, and note-books. The third wall was a map, showing where the remains had been found in relation to the caves. The fourth wall, the one with the window, was largely vacant, but it had the "lived in" look I had been expecting. There were candy bar wrappers, half-empty bottles of water, and used Kleenex. This was where John had spent his time. I sat in his chair and won-dered at the number of hours he must have spent up here trying to find out who had killed those people. I needed no further proof that John wasn't the killer—it was obvious he was just trying to find out what was going on.

I opened the desk drawers, hoping to find the Cliff's Notes version of his investigation, but no such luck. Instead, he had just about every type of pen imaginable, a bunch of blank legal pads, and a half-empty tin of push pins. In the top right drawer, I found some Post-It Notes and a few sticks of staples. When I went to close the drawer, my hand touched something hard taped to the bottom of the drawer. I knelt down and saw two CD-ROMs in cases stuck to the underside. I greedily pulled them off and wonder what I would find on them.

Then it dawned on me—I had to, somehow, get all of this out of the house and back to Miami without anyone knowing. I hated to disrupt John's organization, but I needed the information—how else was I going to clear John's name? I went back downstairs and found some boxes which had books stacked in them. I emptied the books onto the bookshelves in the basement and took the boxes back upstairs. I took pictures of the walls with my cell phone, making sure to get enough detail so I could recreate the room. Then, starting to the right of the bulletin board, I carefully peeled each piece of paper off the board and stacked it in the box. I resisted the urge to read each document as I put it in the box. One hour later, the room was empty and the boxes full. I filled three more boxes with paperback books from John's general fiction collection.

I went back in the house and re-loaded the closet. If Sheriff Jones returned he would find that I had simply cleaned up after his mess and had gone running back to Miami to spend my money. Loading up the trunk of my rental, I hoped the demon that had attacked me in the night was hiding in its lair. I was well-pleased with myself as I drove back to the Landing. Maybe I could clear John's name, after all.

Chapter Eight
An Investigation

Nothing has such power to broaden the mind as the ability to investigate systematically and truly all that comes under one's observation in life.
Marcus Aurelius, Meditations.

I parked in front of the Landing and went in to find Jessie sitting at the front desk playing solitaire on the computer. When she looked up she must have seen the victory in my eyes because her eyes lit up.

"You found something didn't you?" she asked excitedly.

I decided to play it cool until we were sure of our privacy—Cletus's advice to remember you were always being listened to still fell heavily in my mind. "Not really," I paused, "Is there somewhere we can talk in private?" I asked.

"No one else is here, silly. We can talk here, why?"

"I'd prefer to talk with you where no one can see us—I know I'm being paranoid, but—"

"After being run off the road, I can't say I blame you. How about my office?" she asked, gesturing to a small office behind the counter.

"So long as we're away from these windows and you're sure no one will hear us." When I shut the door behind us she smile and said, "If you're not careful people will think we're fooling around—after all, I'm a young, single woman and you're the handsome man from out of town."

My laugh covered my embarrassment from being called handsome, and the fact that I would not object to fooling around.

"So what's up with the secrecy?"

"I found John's war room."

"War room? What do you mean –" Then the light went on in her eyes and I knew she understood me.

"So? Who's the killer?"

"I don't know is the short answer. The long answer is there was too much to go through in the short time I had there. So I packed everything up in some boxes and threw them into my car. I also piled up some of John's books in boxes too."

"Why?"

"The last thing I want someone to know is I found John's work. Especially if that someone is the guy who tried to kill me once before. So, here's what I was thinking—You're going to tell Dean that I took some of John's books up to the home where your parents live for the enjoyment of everyone there."

"But Dean's not going to go blab that around town."

"I know. But, you're going to tell him when you have dinner with him tonight at Cowan's. There should be a few eavesdroppers in the restaurant. And just to make sure, I've left a message for Cletus with his receptionist that I'm taking the books at your request. I have this feeling that news will make it around pretty fast."

"OK. But I still don't see how—"

"I'm leaving town with a bunch of boxes. I need a rational explanation for those boxes. That's the best I could come up with. And I will be stopping by and donating the books—just I'm keeping the boxes with John's stuff in them until I get to Kansas City. Then, I'm shipping them home—I don't trust the airlines to keep that information safe. It's the only chance I have of clearing John's name."

She sat across from me for a few seconds, not saying a word. Then she stood up, came over to me and kissed me. We melted into each other's arms. Her lips were soft, and the kiss seemed to go one forever. My hands wonders across her back and glided through her hair. We parted, both slightly breathless.

"What just happened?" I asked.

"You're just such a nice guy. Here you are in a small town in the middle of nowhere dealing with the estate of a man you barely know, and yet, you're trying to clear his name. That takes a lot of courage, especially since someone tried to kill you while you were here."

I could not respond. Two complements in just a few minutes caused me to blush. I was not about to tell her that I thought I was run off the road by some monster.

"That, and well, I *like* you. I'm sorry to see you leave. I guess, deep down, I was hoping you'd stick around for a while."

There it was. An invitation to stay, extended by this beautiful woman. It was hard to resist. Aside from the fact I did not want to hurt her, I did want to stay. I knew if I stayed that I would probably end up dead. I had to get some distance to study John's materials. If I could narrow down the suspects, I might have a chance at surviving the next attack.

"I tell you what," I said, choosing my words carefully, "I think I'll stay one more night here. Then I have to go to Miami to work on John's materials. If I stay here—"

"I know what'll happen if you stay here." She said quietly. I could tell she was disappointed that I hadn't agreed to stay much longer.

"But I'm going to need help."

"Help?"

"John's materials are really voluminous. I'll probably need someone to help me determine what is important and what are dead ends of investigation."

"I wonder who could help you with that," she said, batting her eyes at me.

"Well, I hear there's this young lady who could use a vacation in town.

"A vacation, huh?"

"Well, perhaps not a vacation, but I know she could sure use some time away from this town after all that's happened."

"I suppose that's true," she replied, a tint of sadness crossed her face. "What, exactly, are you proposing, Mister Devlin. Nothing improper, I'm sure."

"I wouldn't dream of it." I replied, matching her mocking tone. "You see, I have a second bedroom in my condo and I assure you, my intentions are pure." I smiled, hoping that she would not think that was some kind of line.

"Well, since you put it that way... I'll need to come up with another reason to leave town. I certainly can't be thought of as that type of girl."

"How about this—you make your dinner plans with Dean, then drive up to Jefferson City with me to deliver the books and ship the boxes. On the way, we'll come up with a plan."

"OK, just don't think I'm going to introduce you to my parents—they already think I'm too old to find a guy and get married. In their eyes, I'm already an old maid."

"Well, for an old maid, I'm sure impressed."

We both laughed as we left the office. She headed for the front door and said, "I'm off to start the rumor mill churning, you go get some rest before we have dinner with Dean."

"Rest?"

"You look like hell, Berns, you need to rest. You were almost killed last night. And you spent half the day toting boxes full of books out of John's home. Go, take a short nap."

"Alright. Come and get me, if I don't wake up, OK?"

"I'll make sure the desk knows to give you a wake-up call." She smiled.

As she left, I admired the view. I went upstairs and threw myself on the bed. My mind kept going over the kiss. It had been a long time since I had been involved with someone. I was attracted to Jessie. She was my kind of woman—independent and strong, but also vulnerable at times. Not to mention a knockout.

I fell asleep thinking about the smell of her hair.

I woke to a smoke alarm siren and gasping for air. My muscles screamed as I threw the covers off and dropped to the floor. I crawled over to the doorway and felt to see if the door was hot. Thankfully, it was not. My eyes burned while tears streamed down my face. I pushed on down the stairs to the front door. I couldn't see the source of the fire, but it seemed like it was coming from Jessie's office.

I tried the front door, but it would not open. I started to panic. Each breath was painful. I kept banging on the door, but either no one was there, or they were not going to get me out. Slowly, reason returned and I realized that if I wanted to live, I would have to find another way out of the place."

My mind raced to alternative exits. Jessie's office only had one door to it. I had not seen any backdoors. There was a window in my room. It led out to the roof. I was pretty sure two story drop onto the concrete out front would not be advisable. If I did not get out, I would end up one crispy, and very dead, millionaire. I crawled as fast as I could back up the steps and into my room.

Of course the window was jammed shut. Nothing was going to be easy. I could feel the heat from the fire coming closer and the smoke kept getting thicker. So I improvised. I grabbed the luggage tray and smashed the window. Crawling out onto the roof, I gasped at the fresh air. I looked out into the street and saw there was no one paying any attention to the building. Then I realized there was no reason to—no fire alarms were blaring outside. I wondered whether the arsonist was watching. Moving slowly across the shake roof, I made my way to the edge of the building and looked down. That was a big mistake. The drop looked a lot further from the top down. I figured I better check all options, so I made my way across the roof like a stray cat and looked over the back edge—another drop, this time into a metal dumpster. Now, at least, I could not be seen from the street.

I was panting from the exertion, so I took a short breather and tried to clear my mind. After a few deep breaths, I moved to the edge of the building, and I realized the roof of the building next door was only a few feet below and a few feet across. Then I heard the snap of the fire and looked back to see fire shooting through the window I had just escaped from. I had to move, and fast. Using what was left of my energy, I launched myself across the small alley and onto the roof next door. I hit really hard and got the wind knocked out of myself. At this point, I might survive the fire, but end up killing myself. I lay there, gasping for air.

Off in the distance, I finally heard the fire truck siren blaring. At least someone had noticed the fire. I stood up on my shaking knees and tried to figure out where to go next. There was still a scary drop to the street from this roof. I was so focused on the drop that I tripped over a ladder. I had no idea why someone would store a ladder on top of a building, but I was thankful. I picked up the old wooden ladder and gingerly dropped it off the back into the alley. It landed with a loud crash that was largely muted by the fire truck siren. The rungs were old and soft wood, but they supported me as I slowly made my way down off the roof and into the back alley. I ran out of the alley and into the street, where the town's fire truck was parked. The firefighters were trying to contain the blaze, but it looked like a losing battle. I saw Jessie standing across the street from her hotel, crying. It was then I noticed that my car was missing—which meant John's investigation materials were also missing.

I crossed the street and came up next to Jessie, who was too focused on the fire to notice me.

"It's a shame," I said quietly and put my arm around her.

"Berns!" she hugged me. I could feel her trembling. "I thought you were dead."

"You know us private investigators, we're like cockroaches—very hard to kill."

Through tear-stained eyes she smiled. "I don't know what happened. They're not telling me anything other than they are trying to put the fire out."

"I'm pretty sure it was arson."

"Arson –"

"I was in the place when it was lit up. The front door is jammed shut. I had to crawl out an upstairs window and jump down to the roof next door."

"Jammed shut—but that means someone was trying to kill you."

"The odds are not good, are they? Twice in as many days—I'm beginning to think I'm not welcome in these parts."

"Whoever is responsible is definitely sending you a strong get out of town signal, isn't he?"

"By the way, do you know what happened to my car?" I asked, knowing she would understand what I was really concerned with."

"Oh, yeah. They were going to tow it, so I moved it to a space in front of Cletus's office. I made sure it was locked before I left it.

"Thank you," I said, relieved that the arsonist had not taken the car too. "But I still have the keys—"

"I've hotwired tractors all my life. My dad was notorious for losing keys. Your car wasn't that much different."

"I see." I was impressed with her bad girl side.

The firefighters had managed to take control over the fire and there was a definite feel of victory in the air. Shortly after, the fire was out and all that was left was to sort through the ashes. The fire chief told us that we weren't allowed to go back in until the county arson investigator had a chance to look at the burn mess.

"I didn't see no signs of arson, Jessie. But I'm not expert."

"What about the front door?" I demanded, my rage once again deciding to star back up.

"What about it?" The Chief's voice had an edge of fury in it.

"It was jammed shut—I was in the hotel when the fire started."

"How did you get out?"

I explained my acrobatic act and then repeated my question.

"Well, to tell you the truth, we never checked the front door." He walked over to the door and pulled. It remained shut. "Well, I'll be. It looks like someone jammed the door shut. That's sure suspicious. But it don't mean arson. Could be a practical joke that just happened to coincide with the fire." He was defensive and I could tell I had earned yet another enemy in this strange town.

"You don't really believe that, do you?" I asked incredulously.

"If there's no accelerants, burn patterns, that kind of stuff, I write it up as origin unknown." I could tell he was fighting the same rage that seemed to possess me. "I don't look for nothin' else. This," he said holding the wooden shim in his hand, means nothin'." He leveled his eyes at me. "Got it?"

Jessie took me by the arm. "We understand, Chief." She led me over to Cowan's for a cup of coffee and a break.

Sitting at the small counter, she erupted. "I can't

believe it's gone. You know that hotel was my baby. I bought it with the money I saved from running the farm. The owners had grown old, and, frankly, were letting the place get run-down. So I bought it, fixed it up, and ran it. It makes money. Not a lot, but enough to cover expenses and bring in a very small profit. Definitely not nearly enough to rebuild it. What's going on in this town? Ever since John's death, things have gotten really weird."

"I don't know what the town was like before, but things sure are strange, that's for sure."

We sat in silence as she stared, shell-shocked, out the windows onto the streets of the small town.

"Oh. By the way. We're not having dinner with Dean."

"We're not?"

"You said you wanted to make sure people knew where you were going, right?"

"Yeah."

"We're having dinner at Pastor Mike's house. His wife will make sure everybody knows all about everything you say at dinner."

"I guess that means I should be careful about what I say, huh?

"It wouldn't be a bad idea."

"When is dinner?"

"Around 5:30ish. We've got about half an hour before we should head out there."

"You going to be OK? I mean, after this fire, I'm sure they'd understand if you cancelled."

"Oh, I'm fine. The more this guy tries to kill you, the more I want him caught. He needs to get caught. And if going to dinner with Pastor Mike moves the investigation forward, I'm all for it."

"Only if you're sure," I replied.

"Yeah, I'm sure. Let's go get you cleaned up and changed for dinner. It'll take about an hour to get there."

"An hour?"

"Yeah. They live in a house in the middle of no-where."

I wondered how much more in the middle of nowhere they could be—even in the middle of this town, I felt like I was in the middle of nowhere.

We walked over to the rental car to get my luggage. As I got closer, I saw that some of the boxes in the back seat had been messed with.

"Did you do that?" I asked, pointing to a box that sat open to reveal a bunch of books.

"No."

"Damn it." I popped the trunk and was relieved to see that no one had opened with the boxes where I'd hid the war room contents. I took a deep breath of relief.

"Everything OK?" Jessie asked.

"Yeah. Whoever it was didn't want to spend too much time looking through a bunch of books."

"Good."

I slammed the trunk closed and we got in and drove to Jessie's house. It was another single-story ranch home almost as common as the wheat fields around here. It had another gravel driveway and miles of fields in all directions. Like John's house, you could not see the neighbors.

As we went in, a huge house cat greeted me with a loud yowl. "That's Stormy. He keeps my house free of field mice."

"Field mice? He's big enough to take on a raccoon."

"You'd think so, but the last time he tried, he came out in second."

I was not sure she was joking, but I doubted this cat would have come out second to anything small than a bear.

"The shower's the second door on the left. Take your time."

I headed down the hallway and into the bathroom.

It was definitely a woman's bathroom—small soaps shaped like flowers in a basket next to the sink; hand towels, face towels, bath towels, and all other varieties of towels hung throughout the bathroom. They were in various shades of pastel. It seemed out of character for Jessie, but who was I to judge—the bathroom in my Miami condo had two towels in it—one was for after my shower and the other was for drying my hands.

The hot water felt really good on my sore muscles. I knew tomorrow I was really going to hurt, but right now, I felt pretty good. I washed the dirt and grime off of my body and began humming the Hank William's song I heard the other day on my drive into town. After my shower, I got dressed in a pair of khakis and a polo shirt. As I shaved with my electric razor I realized that my dirty clothes were gone. Jessie must have snuck in while I was humming and must have taken them. Finally acceptable for dinner at the pastor's home, I emerged from the bathroom. I went back into the living room where Jessie sat, listening to the local news on the radio.

She looked up and said, "You clean up pretty, good, if I say so myself." Her smile showed that she had recovered a little from the shock of the fire. "I had to see what they were saying about the fire."

"And?"

"Well, the preliminary report is that the fire was sparked by wires that had been gnawed through by squirrels. But the arson investigator is due tomorrow."

"Squirrels, huh?"

"That's what they are saying."

"I don't buy it. Especially since the front door had been jammed shut."

"You know those squirrels—they're really handy with wood shims." She leaned over and kissed me. Again, I got lost in her intoxicating embrace, her soft lips took all of the cares away from my mind. There was raw electricity between us that sparked something almost primal in me. As the kiss ended, she stayed in my arms, resting her head on my shoulder.

"What was that for?" I asked.

"You almost died, dumb ass." She giggled into my chest.

"Now I'm glad I almost died." We laughed and held hands as we left to go to dinner at Pastor Mike's home.

Chapter Nine
Condemned to Repeat the Past

If a man could say nothing against a character but what he can prove, history could not be written.
Samuel Johnson, Boswell's Life of Doctor Johnson

Jessie was not kidding when she said Pastor Mike lived out in the middle of nowhere. After ten minutes we were in the deep Ozarks. Small hills blocked the horizon and formed dark gullies on either side of the road. At times I wondered how anything could grow in the darkness, but apparently it could. We continued south as the sun set on our right. Another half an hour and I knew could never find my way back—there had been too many bends in the road and the trees were too tall to get my bearings.

"Pretty country, isn't it?" Jessie asked noticing that I seemed transfixed by the wilderness.

"Sure is. But man, it sure is different from town."

"Yeah."

She seemed tense for some reason. "Are you sure you're OK?"

"Oh, I'm fine, I'm just thinking-" she stopped mid-sentence.

Thinking what?"

"Well, you don't think I'm too forward do you? I mean by kissing you that way?'

I laughed. "You can kiss me anytime you want." I smiled at her. "Forward? No. Actually, I was considering kissing you first, but I was kind of afraid."

"Afraid? Of little old' me?" she asked giving me a sidelong glance.

"Well, let's just say, I'm... Well, I'm not sure what I am. I'm not really a ladies' man. Hell, the last real date I had was over a year ago."

"A year?" she asked surprised.

"Yeah. It's not that I'm not interested, just, sometimes its hard work. And after a day of skulking around and prying into people's lives, I usually just go home, watch reruns while I eat at my sink. Then I go to bed."

"I can understand," she said, steering our discussion back to her original question, "I just didn't want you to think—I mean, I don't usually kiss guys out of the blue, it's just, well, I *like* you." Her brows furrowed as she tried to express what she was feeling.

"I don't think any less of you. To tell you the truth, I kind of admire your moxie. I'm not sure I would have ever worked up the gumption to make a move. Especially since the first time we met, I was wearing a hospital gown. I'm sure I looked awful."

"You certainly weren't at your best," she smiled. I could tell she was relieved that we were alright.

"Tell me a little about you," I prodded gently. "I mean, I know you are the only daughter of two parents in Jefferson City. I also know you run your dad's farm, but the folks around town are sure you're gonna screw it up. And I know you own The Landing. What about Dean?" I wondered what their relationship had been.

"Dean?" she asked. "Shute, you don't have to worry about Dean. He and I are second cousins or something like that. We grew up together. He's like a younger brother to me. Not to mention, he's got a thing for blondes." She laughed, and the car filled with her delight.

We drove in a comfortable silence for a few more minutes when I reached out and held her hand. She squeezed it gently. The rest of the trip to Pastor Mike's home we both smiled like teenagers.

When we pulled up the house looked worn down. It

was hard to describe—the paint was fine, but it looked dirty. The yard was mowed, with flowers and shrubs in all the right places. They still looked out of place. The house looked like it might need a new roof. It kind of had the appearance of intentional neglect—like they were intentionally showing they had just enough money to survive, but not enough to get rich.

"What do you think?" Jessie asked.

"Well, it's a nice place, but—"

"It looks like they don't take good care of it, huh?"

"Yeah. It's hard to put a finger on... "

"No kidding. I've been here, gosh, three to four other times and every time I come here, I get the impression that they try, but it's never enough to keep the place up. I wonder if they're impacted by the bitterness that possesses this town, just in a more subdued way"

As we got out of Jessie's pickup, I noticed a curtain move. "They know we're here," I said.

"Well, let's not disappoint—I'd hate to keep them from sinking their teeth into you any longer than I have to." She smiled, and I could tell she was a lot less stressed about everything.

We walked up to the front door as the cicadas hum drowned out all the background noises. Before we had a chance to ring the doorbell it opened to reveal a woman. That was about all I could say about her—her hair was plain and straight, shoulder length. She stood average height and had green eyes. She wore a patterned cotton dress that was a few years out of date. She was not slender, but she was not fat either. I guess she looked a lot like the women you see all over, but you never really see them—they simply blend into the background.

"My name is Sally, I'm Mike's wife," she said in a low voice. "I'm glad you could make it."

"Me too," I said. "I hope it wasn't too much trouble."

"Trouble, of course not. We just love entertaining."

When she spoke she smiled the words at you. As soon as the sentence escaped her lips, her face lost most of the happy expression. It was fairly disconcerting, but, somehow, it fit her. Jessie's thought that the bitterness even infected them came to mind. Bitterness was not my read of the woman. Instead it was a dry and lonely hopelessness. She reminded me of the type of people they do human interest stories on, that combat some deadly disease, and are losing the fight. But still they try.

She invited us into her humble home, where the seemingly intentional appearance of just barely enough continued. The furniture was right out of the 1970's, but it was in excellent condition. The carpet was immaculate, but have off the appearance of been vacuumed way too many times. Even the knickknacks on the mantle gave off a decrepit vibe—they were clean, but worn, like they were regularly handled. not giving into the malaise. As we sat on the old couch, Pastor Mike came into the room, shining like a new dime. It was clear that, despite his household's general disarray, he was the rising sun in the family. His clothes were new, or at least more modern than his wife's clothing.

"Welcome, welcome, welcome," he said, smiling even more widely when he saw Jessie.

"Thanks for having us, Pastor," I replied, realizing that it was probably going to be a very long night. I just hoped his wife was really the conduit for information Jessie said she was.

"Not a problem, please, call me Mike. It is really great to have John's nephew as a guest."

"Thanks," I mumbled, slightly embarrassed at how thick the Pastor was laying it on. He seemed different out here, in his own home. At the church he seemed to be a real person. Here, though, he seemed much more like a caricature of his former self.

"Can I get you something to drink?" he asked?

"Water would be great," Jessie replied.

"Nothing for me, thanks, though." I said.

He turned to Allison, "You heard her, honey. Would you mind?" A subtle undercurrent passed with the request to his wife. I could not quite place what the subtext was, but I made a mental note to keep my eyes open. As Alison left the room, Pastor Mike sat on the loveseat next to us. "I'm sorry, but dinner's running late—Ali was stuck ministering to another in our flock." I sensed Pastor Mike was frustrated with his wife. Home was a hard place for him, I could tell.

Pastor Mike focused on me.

"So, Bernard, tell me about yourself."

"About me? There's really not that much to tell. The most exciting thing that's ever happened to me was getting run off the road into the field yesterday and almost getting roasted alive today. I've lived in Florida my entire life. I work as a business consultant. And now, I guess I'm John's heir."

"Oh, I'm sure you're being modest." He oozed his charm at me, "Life is generally much more complex than we give it credit for. My, life is a good example of that."

I realized that his question about my life was nothing more than a way to transition into his story.

"Mike McLaren, Sr., was born in Pittsburgh. That's my father. He and my mother met in school. He worked in the steel mill until he lost his right arm in an accident. After that, mom went to work as a nurse, while my father raised me. He was a really mean drunk."

Now, I was embarrassed. There are a few things most people agree to not talk about with general acquaintances. Sex practices are one. The other is speaking poorly of one's own family. By breaking down this social constraint, Pastor Mike had forced this conversation into a much more intimate arena than I was comfortable in. I knew that, at some point during the evening, he would expect me to return the favor by offering something similarly intimate about me.

Ali came back in with Jessie's water and sat in a chair off to Pastor Mike's right. She listened with a degree of attention conveyed just how much she was supposed to worship her husband and his stories. I could tell, however, that she was bored.

"But I persevered despite his drunken beatings. When I hit 16, I ran away from home. I don't think the old man looked for me. Sure, I'm not sure he even knew I was gone. As for Mom, well, I know she was heartbroken. But she knew I was better off on my own.

"So I spent a year on the Pittsburgh streets until I got sick. That's when Jesus first came to visit me."

Another social construct was torn down with his mention of religion. At least I had been expecting this violation—he was, after all, in the business of saving souls. As I listened I guessed he was angling for a large donation from John's obscenely rich heir. Despite this, I still kind of liked the guy. His charm was hard to resist.

"They took me in, the First Alliance Church. While I recovered, they kept preaching to me. For the first month, I barely listened to anything they had to say. But the second month I was so bored that I picked up the Bible they'd given to me. I started to read it. I was a very strange collection of words, but it didn't mean much to me. Sure, it sounded like a great way to live in an ideal society, but it didn't jive with the very real world I was trapped in. Every day was a struggle to get enough food. Or to stay warm. Or to keep alive from the marauding gangs of transients, looking for the next easy money to buy drugs.

"Anyways, I got better and they had to discharge me back into the streets with a new used coat and that Bible. It was January and very cold. I froze for a few days before I put that Bible to good use. You see, it started as an accident. I was panhandling outside of a local mall with no success. I took a short break, and with nothing to do, I started reading the Bible. That's when someone came by and dropped a twenty in my hat. It all clicked at that point. For the next two weeks, I spent my time, clinging onto that Bible and getting more money than I had ever gotten before. By the time the mall chased me away, I'd gotten about three hundred dollars.

"You know what I did with that money?"

"If it were me, I'd probably invest in more warm clothing." I said.

"If only a seventeen-year-old runaway had that kind of sense," he laughed. "No, I bought a bus ticket to warmer climates. I ended up in Orlando, Florida. Man when I got off that bus, I was so happy—it was warm. After the cold in Pittsburgh, I felt like I'd never get warm again—the cold seemed to live in my bones." He paused.

"What happened in Orlando?" Jessie asked. Apparently she hadn't heard this story before. Alison, too, was on the edge of her seat, waiting to hear the rest of it. Her movements betrayed the fact she was simply acting; performing the role of dutiful wife of the young Pastor.

"Well, you'd be surprised how easy drugs are to come by down there. It may be the happiest place on earth, but you could get anything you'd ever want to smoke, shoot, or snort. After a while, I got a job as a delivery boy for a Cuban drug dealer. Few cops would look twice at a young kid walking through Orlando towards the entertainment district. You gotta remember that they don't want to cause too much trouble for the big guns in town. I was making a few hundred a week delivering a few pounds of white powder. Once I tried it, though, I never looked back. Getting high was about all I cared about. Then, one day I was set up. I got to the Cheezy Town restaurant and the guy I was supposed to meet wasn't there. I was scared, man was

I scared. You see, if the drugs aren't delivered they think you stole it. And you never steal from your dealer—at least not enough for them to notice. When he wasn't there, I panicked and started to run for the exit. That's when a black van pulled up; they yanked me inside and took me away.

"I was sure I was dead. Until I saw the badges. Then I knew I was pinched, but, thankfully, would survive. They wanted me to talk, but I wouldn't,"

I noticed a tone of pride that surprised me. Here was a man of God, proud that he wouldn't turn on a drug dealer to the Police. I tried not to show my surprise in my face, but, again, noted in my mental notebook to watch the Pastor carefully.

"After two days in jail they charged me with possession with intent to sell. By then I was over 18 and there wasn't much I was losing by getting pinched. Shute, I didn't even have a lease that would be broken. I pled guilty and they send me to the Florida penitentiary for a 24-month sentence.

"It was there that Jesus came back to visit me. While I was there, I decided to kick my habit—I really loved the high, but hated myself for using. I never wanted anything to have that much control over me. So I got clean. I hardly remember the first two months or so, but I emerged from the fog of dependency and much stronger fellow.

"With 22 months left, and not much else to do, I studied and got my G.E.D. I also got trained in machinery. I guess they figured I'd get out and get work as a mechanic. While I was in the shop, I heard rumors of a group of guys that were able to leave their cells during the weekend to go listen to a preacher.

"I looked into it and there was a group that came out and preached at the inmates, hoping it would stick. I say 'preached at' because that was all it was; probably one in thirty of the guys there really listened. Most just used it as an excuse to leave their cells and socialize. I was one of them. At least for the first several months. Then, it started making more and more sense. One day, I realized that I believed. Which was really difficult for me to internalize. Of course, it's kind of easy to believe in prison—you really don't have much else to hope in.

"After a while, they let me out. I was given enough bus fare to make it back to Orlando. And they gave me back that Bible I'd carried with me since Pittsburgh." Again he paused, wanting us to ask more questions.

"Anyways," he continued, apparently taking my silence as interest, "when I got back to Orlando I was back in the so-called real world. And, pretty soon, I was back in the drug scene. With a rap sheet, I couldn't do the delivery thing—they can stop you since you're a felon and search you without any reason. Instead, I spent my time on scheduling and arranging drops. I was a pretty good administrator—I only had two guys get pinched on my watch. I made a pretty decent living and was able to stay clean and sober. But something kept gnawing at me. You know what that something was?"

Before I could answer, he continued, "It was my faith. As strange as it sounds, those sessions in prison kept at me until I could barely sleep at night. I knew what I was doing was wrong, but I didn't have any other skills. I wasn't even that good of a mechanic. So I squirreled enough money aside until I could leave Orlando permanently. One day, I just didn't go into work. I bought a bus ticket to Saint Louis. I chose the bus because I didn't want my employer to find me—you don't have to give your real name to get a bus ticket."

"I ended up in Saint Louis and got a job as a mechanic during the days and got my B.A. through night classes. By then, I was starting to go to church on a regular basis. I learned of a seminary school that might look past my past, and, the next thing I know,

I'm in Texas preaching for a small non-denominational church."

"Where abouts in Texas?" I asked, more out of habit that than real curiosity.

"Near Corpus Christi. You ever been there?"

"Nope. Just wondering."

Unperturbed, Pastor Mike continued. "I was there, oh, three years or so. Along the way Ali and I got married. We ended up being sent here, what, two years ago?" He asked his wife, more for confirmation that real forgetfulness.

"It's been 26 months, hon." She smiled shyly at him. Underneath her comment was the pride of knowing something her husband did not.

"That long, huh?" He replied, conveying that he did not care for her smart comments.

The conversation lulled and I waited him out. I doubted if heever get tired of talking about himself.

"Dinner's ready," Ali said softly and got up to go into the kitchen.

I wondered how she knew—I had not heard any timers. I could smell the roast, but not well enough to know if it was done.

We went into the kitchen and sat at an old, weathered table which was set with miss-matched china. The walls had Norman Rockwell prints in dusty frames spaced sporadically across the room. The roast sat on a platter, the hunk of meat somehow managed to look old and worn too.

"Before we eat, let's pray," said the Pastor, giving me a sidelong glance designed to see if I would pray with them.

"Lord, please bless this food as nourishment to our bodies and accept our thanks for providing this bounty to us. Also bless our friends that sit and fellowship with us tonight. May your blessings pour out on them like rain. Amen."

As our plates were filled with food, I said, "Thanks

again for having us over. Everything looks great. I hope you didn't have to go to too much trouble... "

"Nonsense—Ali loves to cook, don't you hon?"

She smiled dulling in response to his question.

After we had started to eat, I decided to press him for information about John. "Do you think I could ask you some questions about John?"

"I suppose, but Jessie here was a much closer friend to him than I ever was."

"But you and he had long conversations, right?"

"Sure, but they were, well, the big questions that men have when they come to the end of the path of life."

"OK," I said, not sure just how helpful this conversation was going to be.

"For example, the last time I talked with John he asked about redemption."

"Redemption?"

"Yeah," the smile returned to his face when he realized he would get an opportunity to show me exactly how smart he was. "He'd come to me, uh, I guess, it must have been the Sunday before he died. It was after my sermon on Jesus' Sermon on the Mount, remember?" he asked Ali.

"It was a really good sermon," she smiled quietly at him. Her response was practiced and calm. I wondered how many times she had told him that.

"Anyways, I was sitting in my office, going over the next week's tasks when he came in. John had this quiet way about him, where he'd likely sneak up on you without ever trying to. Even in his old age, he walked as quietly as a mouse. When I looked up from my computer, he was standing there, in the doorway, just looking at me.

"I asked how I could help him, and, just by the way he looked at me, I knew we were in for one of his long conversations. He shuffled over to a chair, and sat down. Then he asked me about redemption. I think his exact words were 'Do you think a bad man's good offsets the bad?' I didn't know, exactly, what he meant. But I launched into it with him.

"See, Bernard, we believe that you cannot earn your way into heaven. That only the grace of God is what allows you to go there. That being said, we also believe that the Bible wants you to do good works as well. So, I started getting into it with John, but he stopped me, in fact, he interrupted me." He sounded like he was still hurt by John's audacity at interrupting him.

"He told me, he knew all that, but on a more fundamental level, whether good and bad are offset in a man's character." Pastor Mike paused, making sure we were all listening to him. We were, so he continued.

"So I told him that, at least in my personal opinion, that good and bad were not the same thing at all, so the good a man does cannot 'offset' the bad he does; it simply adds to the complexity of a man's internal psyche when a bad man does a good deed and vice versa.

"John didn't say anything at first, just looked me up and down in that way of his. We must have sat in silence for a few minutes before he asked, what I assumed was his next question, since it was directly related to the first; 'What causes a man to do bad things when he knows better?'

"Even for John, this was a strange question. I'd never knew John to have ever done anything wrong—at least until after Sheriff Jones talked with the papers about John."

"So you think John was the killer?" Jessie asked.

"I think he was, Jessie, and I'm sorry. John was a good man, most of the time. But even good men do bad things. And John's good deeds were of the character of atonement for an awful sin. I mean, how many folks you know would go out of their way to help someone like Rolling?"

"Rolling?" I asked, unsure of the reference.

Jessie jumped in to get me up to speed, "Rolling was not a nice man, usually. He beat his wife, to the point where she had to be transported to Jefferson City for medical treatment. In addition, he was a notorious drunk. John stepped in, after his wife, Lucy, was back from Jefferson City and helped him get help for all of his issues. It took almost two years, but by the time John was finished with him, Rolling was sober and respectful to his wife. But one year later, Rolling had relapsed and Lucy was dead. John paid for Rolling's attorney, who got him a deal and Rolling only served eighteen months for killing Lucy. Now, all he does is sit in his home, staring at the cars as they drive by. As far as I know, he's still sober. John pre-paid all his living expenses and set up an account with the grocery so Rolling gets regular groceries."

Pastor Mike interjected, "Rolling is, by all accounts, a bad man. Not that he's beyond the Lord's love, but he sure is different from those that John normally helped. And to be honest, the only reason I can think of that John would have helped Rolling is if John felt really guilty about something."

We sat in silence while we finished our food. I kept going back over the Pastor's story. There was something that just off about it. John's character would help just about anyone that needed it. I had to wonder why the Pastor thought this was strange. Then again, I did not know anybody in this town very well, and I guessed it was possible that Rolling was an "untouchable."

"I think he was also suffering from some sort of mental illness—you know, the kind that old age brings. After talking about bad people doing good things, he asked me if I believed in monsters."

"Monsters?"

"Yeah. Just like that. I replied if he meant people that acted monstrously, then yes. But actual monsters, you know, ogres, orcs, those kind of things, I said no."

"Why was he asking about that?"

"Like I said, I think he was starting to have mental issues. Because he followed up with questions about whether I thought the devil could make monsters?"

I leaned forward, trying not to show just how intense my interest was. "And?"

"I have to admit, I just kind of laughed, you know the way you do when someone says something ridiculous. I told him I had no idea if the Devil could create anything, since He is the Destroyer of all that is good. He did not seem to like my response, and left fairly quickly after that."

After dinner, we sat around the table and drank coffee, if you could call it that, and Pastor Mike steered the conversation back to me.

"So, tell me, Bernard. Have you decided to stay in our wonderful hamlet or are you planning to return to the big city?"

Here was my opportunity to let the town know I was leaving. "Well, actually, I have to get back to Miami, my business doesn't run itself," I paused, making sure Ali was soaking in my story. "Besides, there's not too much I can do around here—I don't see too much of a need for a private detective." I smiled, hoping the Pastor would believe my story.

"So anyway, I've got to get back to Miami. I figure, I'll hire someone to close the entrance to the caves and, I guess, I'll have to sell the house and the property. But in this market, I'm not sure it'll go very fast."

Pastor Mike looked genuinely sorrowful. "It'd be a shame to see that property sold to some conglomerate. Be weird not to have John own it and tend it. And those caves of his—You got to wonder what he was protecting, don't you?"

"Well, I have to admit, I was curious, but, in the big

picture what does it matter? I figure he just wanted to protect his own property and keep the kids out. And what am I going to do with a bunch of caves? Nothing. That's what I'd do with them. So, I'll close them off, just like John asked, and go back to living my normal life."

"And never come back?" asked the Pastor, leaning forward to better look into my eyes.

"Probably. I mean, I'd like to know about John, but it sounds like he was a nice guy for a while, then became a serial killer."

The Pastor sat back into his chair, smiling again, apparently glad that I had agreed with him. "So, I have to ask, since it is my job, are you a Christian?"

"I've never been involved in any Church. I was raised without religion. And, to tell you the truth, I've gotten along without religion for this long just fine."

"But what about the big questions? Don't you ever wonder why you're here?"

"Can't say that I do. Most of the time, I'm too busy dealing with life to worry much about it."

"That's a shame. Now, I'm not going to force anything on you, but, if, or rather, when, you do start thinking about the big picture, give me a call."

"I'll do that," I replied, with no intention of such thing.

Jessie stepped in to rescue me from the Pastor's conversion attempt. "Did you hear 'bout The Landing?"

"No, what happened?" asked Ali, obviously well informed by her network of small-town spies.

"Well, there was a fire,"

"Oh, gosh," said Ali. "I hope no one was hurt?"

"I was in the place when the fire started," I said, "But I managed to escape relatively unharmed."

"And the hotel is a total loss," said Jessie.

"What started it?" ask the Pastor, again leaning forward with acute interest.

"They're not sure, yet. Gary said it was probably a rodent that had chewed through some wires. But other than that, they don't know."

I was relieved that Jessie decided to keep the fact that the front door had been jammed shut to herself. I needed time to figure that one out.

"Wow," said the Pastor as he sat back in his chair again, and took a deep drink from his cup of coffee. "We'll be praying for you."

"What are you going to do?" asked Ali, wanting to have an exclusive tidbit to share.

"I'll probably rebuild at some point. I've got to submit it to the insurance. Who knows how long that'll take?"

"That's true."

"So where are you staying?" The Pastor asked me.

"Well, I found some books in John's house that Jessie suggested I donate to the facility that her folks are in. So, I'm probably going to take her up to Jefferson City, then just keep driving until I get to Kansas City. I'll catch the next flight to Miami tonight or tomorrow at the latest. It won't be the first time I've spent an uncomfortable night in an airport."

"Well, then, we shouldn't keep you," he replied, starting to stand up. "Not that I don't like the company, but you've got a heck of a drive-in front of you. You get too much of a late start and, well, you'll be driving into the dawn."

Jessie and I also stood up, and made our obligatory comments about how good the food was and how nice it was to spend some time getting to know both the Pastor and Ali. As we walked out, Ali meekly said that it was nice to meet us. By the time we had made it down the three steps, I heard the front door shut and the locks were engaged. I wondered exactly how much crime was out here, in the middle of nowhere. Then, I locked my door too.

Chapter Ten
Homebound

So sweetly she bade me adieu,
I thought that she bade me return.
William Shakespeare, A Pastoral. Part I

Jessie took the wheel again and we headed back to her place. As we travelled down the rapidly darkening roads, we discussed the evening with the Pastor and Ali.

"You were right," I admitted, "Ali sure has her thumb on the pulse of Stillwater."

"Yeah. If you ever needed to know about someone or what they're doing, she's the one to ask."

"He seems kind of hard to figure,"

"Yeah. I think that's what the church liked about him. I remember that he made a similar impression on the selection committee. John talked to me about it a few times when they were trying to decide which of the applicants they were going to hire."

"Oh, yeah?"

"He said that the other Pastor had more book learning, but that Pastor Mike was, different. He was more of a nitty gritty kind of guy. John liked that about him—John was big on having to learn things through life and not just reading about them. Some of the other members objected in light of his past, but John convinced them to forgive and forget."

"So you'd heard his story before?"

"Parts of it. I knew he'd been in prison—John told me that. And in some of his sermons he would talk about wrestling with one's demons with an air of authority that was clear he'd been through it.

"Anyways, after John talked the committee into re-evaluating Pastor Mike, they decided to pay to fly him out for one last interview. I guess he told them everything that night—John never talked much about it since he figured if the Pastor wanted to tell everyone he could. But I still remember John coming to me after the Pastor had been hired, oh, I'd say about a week or two later, and told me that he was surprised that such a young man could have gone through all that and still look like a kid. I never gave much thought about it until tonight. I kept thinking about John's comment and how much like a kid the Pastor looks at times."

"I find it hard to believe that he thinks John was the killer. After all John has done for this community, and all the time he spent with the Pastor. It just seems wrong, you know?"

"I'm with you. I was dumbfounded that he'd even say it, much less believe it." She was angry. "I mean, everyone's entitled to their opinion and all that, but John was no killer. Everybody who knew him knows it." Except for Pastor Mike and Sheriff Jones, I thought.

"Besides, Pastor Mike should know better than to speak out of turn about John. It's just not right, dammit."

It was the first time I had heard her swear. Somehow, it made her more attractive to me.

"You're right. But, if he really thinks that way, I appreciated his honesty. I don't know too many people, when they are in the company of a loved one, will say the truth about someone who died. It was strange, but you could tell he really believed it."

"Yeah," She said dryly. "He went after you, too. Not a good night for the Pastor in my eyes."

I smiled, hoping the anger I kept buried inside myself remained hidden, "Yup. He really wanted to know about my past. But I wasn't sharing. He may have wanted to tell his whole life story, but me, I'm a private person."

"Well, it is his job—to know people, I mean. He was just trying to help you."

"Help me?" I snorted, "He seemed like he was trying to pry into my life. I didn't like it."

"I could tell. And so could he."

We drove in silence for a few miles while she waited for me to broach the subject of my past. I kept my mouth shut. I was not ready to share with her, at least not yet.

After we were closer to town, she started the conversation up again, "So how many people you think know you're leaving town by now?"

"Besides us, you mean?" Smiling, I said, "I'd guess just about the whole town. I imagine the telephone wires are running hot tonight."

"That's for sure—I bet Pastor Mike is already asleep, Ali told me once that he takes long naps at night before going to bed—and she's on the phone, while the dishes wait to be cleaned until tomorrow."

"What's the dynamic there?"

"Huh?"

"Well, I got a weird vibe about those two—like they don't get along or something. Maybe something worse."

"Hm," she had to think about it for a few, "Well, I think there's a lot of hero worship in that house. Ali is obviously enraptured by Pastor Mike. Did you see the way she hung on every word he said? She's always like that. But other than that, I think they're a normal couple."

"Normal? It seemed to me she was more afraid of him than in awe of him." I struggled for an example. "Like when she quietly mentioned how long they'd been here."

"I guess. I mean, I can see it, but I've never seen him do anything but treat her civilly. They seem like the perfect couple, but I don't know."

"No kids?"

"No, but I think that's an issue you might have picked up on. Ali once told me that she wanted kids, but Pastor Mike did not. She said he didn't feel it was fair to bring a child into the world when evil was everywhere."

"That's kind of strange, don't you think?"

"Sort of. After hearing his story tonight, though, I guess it's somewhat understandable."

"I guess."

We pulled into Jessie's driveway. Thankfully, my battle-scarred rental car stood unmolested. We got out to go inside, when she turned to me and asked, "Do you really think you can prove John's innocence?"

"I'm pretty sure of it. Why would a guilty man have a room full of investigation materials—it would be a waste of time."

"I hadn't thought of that," she smiled and planted another kiss on my lips. It still gave me butterflies when she kissed me.

"What was that for?"

She sent a sideways glance at me and said, "The time being."

Suddenly, in the background I heard the wailing noise that had preceded my crash. I whirled, scanning the dark skies for any foreign movement. All I saw was stars.

"Jumpy much?" she asked, joking.

"You heard that, right?"

"Yeah. I was told it's the deer mating calls since I was a kid."

"Is it?" I asked darkly.

She looked at me closely. I hoped she could not see the abject fear that had taken hold of me.

"You mean it?" she asked. "What do you think it is?"

I took a deep breath. "Let's go inside and I'll tell

you. But you have to promise not to think I'm crazy."

She led me inside. "I think you are crazy, but my kind of crazy, is that enough?"

I double checked the doors to make sure they were locked then sat on her couch. "I left out some things from my official report, OK?"

"What kind of things?"

"Well, I went into the caves that afternoon."

She looked alarmed. "You did? But why?"

"I had to know what John was keeping secret there. I figured if he was the killer, there'd be evidence there. When I was there, I heard something It was the scariest thing I think I've ever heard. It was just like that call we heard outside. There was a scraping sound, like bone on bone. It was pitch black and I have no idea what caused it. But it sounded like a monster."

"OK, but what does that have to do -"

"I'm getting there. By the time I made it out of there, I nearly ran to the house. That's when I met Zeke."

"Seriously? Zeke never talks to anyone."

"Well, he talked to me. I wanted to get out of the area, but he seemed to know what it was that I had heard and was sure it would not track me. Anyways, I got in the truck and on my way back to town I got a little lost. As I was backtracking something seemed to come out of the sky and attacked the truck. I'm sure I wasn't asleep when it happened, but I never got a good look at the beast. And by the time I regained con- sciousness I was in the hospital."

"Bernard-"

I held up a hand. "I know, it sounds crazy, but I think John found something," I paused, searching for the right word, "evil in those caves. I think he was trying to kill it when he died."

A dark silence passed before she spoke. "You're right, it sounds crazy. But I can tell you really believe it. As for me, I'll wait and see."

"Jessie, look, I—"

She stopped me with a kiss. "Berns. We'll figure this out, I promise. I'm going to change before we head out, OK?"

"Sure." I figured I could use a few minutes to puzzle over our dinner with Pastor Mike. There was too much there that seemed, well, off. I was unsure what part of the whole ordeal was strange, just that something was not right. Then again, I was not used to religious folk, much less Pastors. I wondered if the whole thing was in my head. John obviously had trusted the Pastor enough to confide in him. John was a pretty good judge of character. I flipped on Jessie's television to see if there was anything going on in the world I needed to know, but all I could find were mindless sitcoms and endless reruns of edutainment. I settled on a police drama. About fifteen minutes into it, I fell fast asleep. My dreams swirled around the mysterious monster who had tried to kill me. In my mind, I was back in the cab of the truck and being rolled over and over through the field which was on fire. With a start, I woke up to find Jessie, gently shaking me.

"You OK?" she asked.

"Yeah, I was having a nightmare about the wreck."

"No kidding, you screamed so loudly, I dropped everything to see if you were OK."

It was then that I noticed she was only wearing her underwear. It was not like it had come from Victoria's secret, but she sure looked good.

I blushed and mumbled, "I'm sorry."

She smiled, "It's OK. I think you are allowed to get a little freaked since some monster's trying to kill you. Anyways, I'm going to finish getting dressed before we go. Unless, of course, you scream again just to catch a peek of me in my skivvies."

I laughed gently, again taking in the sight of her in her "skivvies." "I think I'll be alright. But you never know."

She smiled and walked back out of the room slowly,

so that I could enjoy the view. After about ten more minutes she came back out, this time in a pair of jeans and a blue top. She still looked dazzling.

"You ready for your drive to Jeff City?"

"Pretty much."

"No more bad dreams, I hope?"

"I managed to stay awake this time."

I carried out her suitcase to my beat-up rental. At this point it looked more like it had been through the war than just driven to a small town in the middle of nowhere. I started to laugh—it was comical.

"What's so funny?"

"It's just, well, what did this poor rental car ever do to anybody to deserve this?"

She smiled, "Maybe it was the color—the blue just makes me want to kick it too." She took a good whack at it with her boot. "Try it, it'll make you feel better."

At that we both laughed.

"Before we head out, there's one thing," she said.

I turned to look at her, and the next thing I knew we were kissing again, this time with the renewed passion of young love. At some point we stopped, sensing that, if we continued, we would make a mistake that our relationship wasn't quite ready for.

I cleared my throat, started the car, and backed out of her gravel driveway onto the road. It was about 10:30 pm.

We sat in a comfortable silence for quite a while. I was savoring the memories of those kisses, and the image of her in her skivvies. A sly smile crept across my face as I drove through the small town on the way to the highway. She must have seen me grin. "Now you stop that Mister Devlin—there'll be no fantasizing about me in my underwear, got it?" Her teasing tone made us both laugh.

"I can't promise anything," I replied.

Once we left town and hit the long road to Jeff City, she broke the silence and said, "Tell me more about yourself."

"About me? There's really not that much to tell."

"Sure there is. You've been on this earth for, what, thirty years or so. Something must have happened during that time. I'll make it easy for you, let's start with, where did you grow up?"

"I grew up in Miami."

"OK. What's it like there?"

"Miami can be a very strange town. Its sunny and warm all year round."

"What else—besides the weather. Where do you live now?"

"I have a condo not too far from Calle Ocho. It's a very ethnic part of Miami."

"Ethnic?"

"You know, Latinos, Cubans, that kind of stuff."

"Really?"

"You're in for quite a culture shock when you get to Miami."

"Really?" she replied dubiously. "So now I know you grew up in Miami. Tell me something else about you."

"Nope," I smiled, "now it's your turn. I want to know something about you—and not where you grew up—I know that part."

"OK. Let's see. Gosh, I don't know. There's not much to tell."

"I think I've heard that excuse somewhere—come on."

"What do you want to know?"

"How about you tell me about your relationship with Dean." I said, hoping I was not prying too much since they seemed very close.

"Dean? Well, you know he's my cousin. Let's see. He and I grew up together—he was kind of like a brother to me. After high school, we drifted apart since I went to college and he stayed here to run his dad's farm. But, when I came back we got reacquainted through our friendship with John. We watch over each other, that's for sure. A couple of years ago, he was involved with a gal from Kansas City—she'd driven through and her car broke down. She decided to stay for a while and he fell really hard for her. I didn't like her, though. So I did a little snooping and discovered that she was married and was just living out a fantasy with him. I told him about her, he didn't want to believe me, but, ultimately, she left him. She left him a letter which told him all about her real life and such. It hit him pretty hard. But since then, he's trusted me to 'vet' his girlfriends. I guess that's why he is protective about me—he wants to return the favor."

"You don't seem like a girl who needs protection, that's for sure." I said, "What does he think about me—he has to know that we have a... connection."

"He does, that's for sure. To tell you the truth, he doesn't really like you."

I was stunned. There was nothing in his demeanor or our conversations that even hinted at his dislike. "Really?"

"Yeah. He thinks you may just be here for the money and, once the money's officially yours, you going to run and never look back. He's kind of surprised that you've taken such a strong interest in clearing John's name. He told me he thought that you were just acting concerned. In fact, we had a fight about it. I told him there was no way you were just acting—you actually want to clear John's name."

"I can't believe he didn't like me—I never got that vibe from him."

"He's really good at acting—I told him that he should have moved to Hollywood to star in the movies. He always laughed at that. OK, your turn. Tell me about, hm, how about your job—it must be fascinating to be a private investigator?"

"It has its moments, that's for sure. Once I started doing it, I realized just how much people are, generally, screw ups. Or at least the people I end up investigating."

"Really? I thought you just solved crimes and missing persons for people."

"I wish. That sounds a lot more fun that what I do. Mostly, I do background research on people. For example, I did a surveillance job and caught a guy, who claimed he was disabled after slipping and falling on a dock, sneaking out to have an affair with his neighbor while his wife was away. Needless to say, the case settled pretty quickly after that. I also caught another guy, who said he was hurt so badly that he had to wear a back brace, taking a trip to scuba-dive off the coast of Mexico. At least that job took me to the tropics. Most of my work is computer stuff, with some in the field. Mostly skulking around people's homes and taking video or photos."

"You sure know how to sell it—you don't sound like you like it too much."

"I hate it. Your turn. Tell me about something bad you've done"

"OK. Let's see. I know, I once stole a car."

"Really?" Now that surprised me—she seemed like such a straight-laced girl.

"Yup. I was 18, wanted to go to St. Louis for a rock concert and my parents wouldn't let me go alone. But I had already bought the ticket and I wasn't about to miss the concert. So I snuck over to Dean's house and took his car. He had no idea where it went until he found my note, which I'd left in his history text book. Unfortunately, Dean wasn't much of a student, so he didn't find the note until the following month. But that same night he reported his car stolen and I was stopped by Sheriff Jones coming back to town. We got into a really long discussion about right and wrong, but he let me go. I dropped the car off at Dean's house around two in the morning, snuck back to my house, and got away with it."

"So you're a criminal mastermind, huh?" I said with a smile on my face.

"I guess so." She giggled at that.

We continued to drive in silence for a while until she told me to turn off towards Jeff City.

"I hate visiting my parents," she said bitterly as we passed the city limit sign.

"What?" I was surprised at her outburst—it was out of character for her.

"I guess it's not really my parents that I hate coming to see. It's that *place,*" she almost spit out the word, "It's so depressing. It's worse than a hospital. You can almost feel the quiet death that creeps along the halls, stalking its prey. The place smells like a school cafeteria, looks like an apartment complex, but feels like a graveyard. You know what I mean?"

"Not really. Both my parents died when I was in college—they never got, well, old."

"I'm sorry to hear that. But I think it may be almost better that way. My dad," her voice cracked, "he's just fading away. Sometimes he doesn't even recognize me when I get there. Other times he knows who I am, but he thinks I'm six and we're at the carnival. He used to like to take me to the carnival when it came to town. I wonder how much longer he's going to hold on."

I didn't know what to say, so I kept my mouth shut and she continued, "And it's taking its toll on my mom. She gets older and older every time I visit. The last time, I could see how hard taking care of dad is on her. Not to mention the fact that she's getting confused at times too. Sometimes I wonder if getting old is something I'm ready for. I can't imagine myself sitting in those small rooms, watching a television, or doing crochet, and just waiting to die. That's what it's like. When you walk through the halls, sometimes the doors to other people's rooms are open. You look inside them like you'd look into the entrance to a tomb. Sometimes you see an old man, sitting in shorts

and a t-shirt just sitting there. Staring into nothing-
ness. It breaks my heart to see. I wonder how many of
them ever get visited by their families. I wonder if
they'd know if they had been visited. That's why I come
so often. As much as I hate it, I can't image my mom
and dad sitting there, alone and staring." She began
to cry.

"Turn here, it's at the end of the road."

I turned into a two-lane road which led to a bunch
of small buildings. They were painted different hues of
yellow and green. I could sense the very same thing
that Jessie sensed when she came—it was like death's
foyer. You could almost feel that this was a final
resting ground for the people that lived here. There
was an absence of something—like *life* had somehow
been evacuated from the area.

"You want me to come in with you?" I asked quietly
as Jessie regained some of her composure.

"After the way I described it, you're very brave to
volunteer," she said, trying to lighten the mood.
"That's OK. It's late, they probably will only let me in
anyway. I'll take the books in, you make it to Miami,
and I'll meet up with you in two days. I promise." We
kissed quickly and she ran into the building with the
boxes tucked under her arms.

Chapter Eleven
Service of Process

Our wrangling lawyers... are so litigious and busy here on earth, that I think they will plead their clients' causes hereafter—some of them in hell.
Robert Burton, Anatomy of Melancholy
Democritus to the Reader

I drove towards Kansas City with the thoughts of Jessie permeating my brain. It was a pleasant drive, even if it was in the middle of the night. Under the cover of darkness, the fields were not as menacing as they seemed under the harsh sun when I drove to Stillwater. Since then, my life had really changed. Aside from the money, which, I had to admit was the main reason I had come to Stillwater, I had a new purpose. I had to clear John's name. After all I had learned about John, and what he had done for the community, I could not allow someone to defame him the way they were. As each mile passed, the anger that had somehow taken control of my mind eased. In the back of my thoughts, the evil creature that haunted John's caves swirled.

Much had changed since I had left Miami. I was suddenly very wealthy. I had almost been killed twice. I also, apparently, had a new girlfriend. It was nice. She was a lot different than Bethany. I knew that Bethany would be all over me when I got back to find out what I had inherited. And I was not about to tell her. She would know that I was lying. I wondered if I should have told Jessie about my friendship with

Bethany. I decided that when she came up, I would tell her.

I made it to the car rental place, where I had to explain that the car had been seriously vandalized. I could tell that the woman behind the counter did not believe me. I wondered if she thought I had written 'Go Away" in the paint. Fortunately, she told me that the insurance companies could work it out and let me get on my way. I took the garishly colored shuttle from the rental area to the airport. I decided not to ship the boxes to Miami, but instead to carry them on. If I had to pay extra, I could afford it. Fortunately, they let me take them with me—after all, no first-class passenger is ever denied anything reasonable.

It was just after midnight when I made it to my gate. I plopped down in the chair, hoping I could catch a short nap before the gate became overcrowded. I had just about drifted off, when I felt someone plop into the seat next to me. I opened my eyes and saw a twenty-something guy staring at me.

"You Bernard Devlin?"

"I am," I replied wearily. "Who are you?"

"You've been served," said the guy as he tossed a packet of papers into my lap. He quickly got up and walked away.

I opened the papers and began to read. By the time I had made it three inches down the page, I knew exactly what it was—a complaint for wrongful death against the "Estate of John Lincoln". The families of the alleged victims of the serial killer John Lincoln had gotten together and found an attorney to sue. His name with Richard Welton and his offices were in Saint Louis. The complaint alleged that John "know-ingly, intelligently, intentionally, and unlawfully" killed the victims in his caves. Aside from six pages of legalese and scant facts, all I really knew is that the victims were suing. I wondered exactly how much they wanted—if I had to guess, everything.

154

I could feel a headache developing in the back of my brain. I realized that going back to Miami was not going to happen. I had to get back to Stillwater. This would not end until John was proven innocent. That meant being on the ground, doing what I do, investigating. I had to get up to speed on John's research before I started. I grabbed the boxes which I hoped contained some answers and went back to the car rental counters. I opted for a different company—I figured they wouldn't rent me a car after the sedan I had brought back was so damaged.

I rented a SUV this time—I hoped it would blend in better in Stillwater. As I got in, I dialed Simon, hoping that he would be awake.

"What's up, Mister Moneybags? I hear you inherited more money than I can count."

"Where'd you hear that?"

He laughed, "I have my sources. But if you must know, Bethany called me. Had me look up your inheritance. She's a piece of work, that's for sure. What can I do for you?"

"I need some information—off the record."

"Off the record is my specialty. What's the assignment?"

"I'm looking for a place to buy a gun—nothing too fancy, just a semi-automatic with a clip, not a revolver. And I really don't want to wait the five days."

"Going hunting, huh?"

"I need it for protection—someone's tried to kill me twice since I've been down here. Oh, and I need it tonight. And I'm in Kansas City, Missouri."

"You do realize I don't know anything about KC, right? This could take some time. Give me half an hour?"

"Sure. Make sure you charge me for your time—but charge it as background research on John Lincoln. And do some background research just to make sure it looks good."

"Got it. I'll e-mail you a report on John Lincoln in the morning. And I'll call you back in a bit."

"Thanks."

"You'd do the same for me, Mister Moneybags."

"You bet. Oh, and by the way, it looks like I'm going to be stuck down here for a while—so, give my secretary and call and take all the work you can get from my clients."

"Really?"

"I need someone to run my business while I'm gone—and you're the most honest liar I've ever met."

"Thanks." I could hear the smirk in his voice. "I'll give you call soon. Don't go too far."

"OK."

After hanging up, I drove to a Motel 6 not far from the airport. I got a room and set up a war room. I did not plan on spending more than a few hours in the room, but I had to go through John's stuff before I got back to Stillwater. At least then, I would have a better lay of the land.

I made a pot of hotel coffee, which is only marginally better than muddy water and got to work. The first box contained a bunch of files on several Stillwater residents. There were files on Jessie, Dean, Sheriff Jones, Cletus and Zeke. Then there were files on Levon, Robert, and Frank, none of whom I had met. The files were a veritable rainbow of colors—I wondered if John had color-coded his files. I started with the files on the people I had not met—I figured I needed to start with people I might need to be introduced to once I got back to Stillwater. Levon was John's neighbor to the north. John had done quite a bit of research on Levon. He was born in 1965 and worked as an electronics repairman in town. His shop was three doors away from Cletus's office. Levon went to high school in Springfield, but moved to Stillwater in 1984 to open his shop. After reading a few more pages, I reached the same conclusion that John had—Levon had access to the caves by virtue of geography, but was not likely the killer. No motives existed, and at least on two occasions, he had a verified alibi on a day when one of the killings was supposed to have occurred.

Robert and Frank, both Stillwater citizens, had similar files. Nothing remarkable about them. I could not figure out why John had even bothered investigating them. They were just ordinary folks in Stillwater—there was no connection between them and the killings except for John's investigations into them.

I hesitated before delving into the rest of the files. I knew these people. They had all been, with the exception of Zeke, incredibly nice to me. Even Dean had been nice. John's files were fairly in depth. I was intruding into their privacy. To avoid my discomfort, I started with Zeke, John's best friend. If John could compile this information about his friends, I could wade through it. Anything I could to do would help clear his name.

Zeke was born in 1924 in the wilderness. His parents were immigrants from Russia—his real name was Zavragin, but he chose Zeke early on in life. He had lived off the land, hunting and trapping, since he was 14. He had a small cabin he and his dad had built together in 1938. The cabin was about the only thing Zeke owned—the land it sat on apparently belonged to Levon, who owned about 120 acres of mostly unusable rocky land. Levon knew Zeke lived there and felt that one should live and let live.

Over the years Zeke earned a little money by doing odd jobs for farmers. He mostly lived off the meat of his prey and a tiny garden. He was a nice guy—according to John. Zeke did not have any strange leanings—he did not enjoy killing animals, but did it to survive. John even recorded a prayer he would say before he started cleaning his kill. "Thank you, Lord for creating this animal for my sustenance. It was a noble animal. Amen."

Zeke had gotten married in 1946 to a woman named Justine. She died in childbirth and so did the child. From then on Zeke lived alone—a very somber man. Other than that, the rest of the information detailed certain trips Zeke had taken (all on foot and all hunting trips).

I decided to set the rest of the background files aside and see what was in the second box. The first set of files in the second box addressed the caves themselves. It was almost like John considered the caves were the killer—like some strange supernatural force lived in them.

John discovered the caves shortly after he moved to Stillwater in 1925. As a young man, he actually lived in them until he had scrimped and saved enough to buy the land the caves were on. He made his first fortune by selling the stalactites and stalagmites to cave enthusiasts and scientists—which explained the strange caves that looked like they have been man-made. He knew about the bats and decided that the caves should be left as natural as possible. John decided to keep people out of the caves because of their incredible extent—it would be too easy to get lost. He even detailed his version of Elmer's insanity. It seems like Elmer had gotten himself good and lost in the caves. When the family realized he had gone missing, John went into the caves, found the boy and brought him back to his parents. The kid had not taken a lantern to explore the caves—which meant he had spent three days in the caves in the pitch black. No wonder he went a little crazy. I was only there for a few hours, and look what had happened to me.

My phone rang—it was Simon.

"Hey."

"I've got the information you wanted—got a pen?"

"Yup. Go."

He told me the address of a pawn shop that was friendly to private investigators that wouldn't require the 5-day waiting period if I promised not to kill anyone with the gun during that time frame.

"Thanks!"

"You want me to tell you about John?"

"You've done the background research already?"

"Yup."

"Sure." I didn't think Simon would tell me anything I didn't already know.

"Seems like John was born in Seattle. He ran away from home when he was 13—not sure why. Back then, the records about kids are sparse. Anyway, he was presumed to be dead because the temps were in the lower 20s every night. Next record I get is him buying the property in Missouri thirteen years later. Anyways, he got married shortly after—the wife, Ethel, died seven years later. The report does not give a cause of death, but I it looks like the death was 'suspicious.' After that, John Lincoln became a household name down there in Stillwater. He served on various boards, and ran for mayor. After he retired from politics, he dropped back off the radar."

"How'd you get this information? I did a search when they first called me and got nothing."

"I have my sources—besides, I provide my best work for my obscenely wealthy clients."

"Gee thanks. So you're saying this is gonna really cost me, huh?"

"Yup. But it was worth every penny. You want to hear how John got so wealthy?"

"You found that out, too?" I realized just how much I had underestimated Simon's investigatory prowess.

"Sure did." He paused, wanting to build tension—it worked.

"Well?"

"It seems that he ran booze during prohibition—from Chicago to all points south. It's likely how he came to find Stillwater. The town's along a route that was commonly used in those days. After prohibition, he invested the money- first in the property, then in various stocks, bonds and such. Which gave him a decent return."

"He made all his money in the stock market?"

"Not exactly. My research indicates that he used the investments to cover up less than legal pursuits. Did you stay awake in History class? Do you know who ran most of the booze in prohibition?"

"The mob?"

"Yup. And John was a financier for most of the mobs up until the mid-sixties. Seems he got 250% on every dollar he invested."

"So John was a criminal?"

"Well, that's less clear to me. See, what John was doing was a lot like what Wall Street types do now— they use other people's money to make money. I'm not sure if what he did was illegal—unethical, sure, but illegal—hard to say."

I was stunned. John's past was more sordid than I hoped for, but it wasn't so bad that I was ashamed. "Any chance his mob involvement continued until he died?"

"Nah. He was so far in the background that few people even knew who he was, much less where he lived. See, he lived in the middle of nowhere, which meant that no one ever really saw him. Want to know what his mob name was?"

"He had a mob name?"

"Sure. Everyone back then did. It was 'Racer.' I'm guessing he made quite a mark on the mob during his booze run days."

"Wow. I've got to know—where did you get this information—I've been down here, going through the guy's stuff, and haven't found anything even remotely like that."

"I knew a guy. He was a former mobster—got

twenty years in the federal system and, effectively, retired from the mob. He's a great historian—and loves to talk about the good old days. I called him up when I found a reference to John Lincoln in an article in the Chicago paper. Seems like the two are the same guy."

"Huh."

"You want me to continue my research?"

"Sure—you've gotten a lot more than I'd ever get on my own."

"And, about that place—it's not in the best part of town, so I'd lay low until morning—the cops hang out not too far from the place. It's been rumored that they initiate a stop just because you left the place."

"Thanks, I'll do that."

We hung up. I sat, stunned, at what Simon had discovered. I realized I should call Jessie and tell her I was heading back to Stillwater—her vacation would have to be cancelled. As I hoped, her cell phone was off, so I left a voicemail telling her I was coming back to Stillwater, but leaving out the lawsuit. I figured we could talk about it when I got there. I just hoped she checked it before she drove to Kansas City.

I looked at my watch; it was 3:00 am. I really needed sleep. I took a lukewarm shower, called for a 5:00 am wakeup, and napped on the bed for a few hours. I woke up before the call, but feeling refreshed and dove back into the files I'd saved from John's hidden room.

The next file I picked up was a goldmine—it was copies of the police reports for each of the killings.

The first known victim was Leonard Wokowski. He was a truck driver whose truck had overheated along Rural Route 22. They found the truck abandoned about a month before the remains had been found. The working theory was that he decided to walk back to Stillwater to get some help. He did not have a cell phone. He was 54 years old, had been a truck driver for thirty-three years, and left a widow in Illinois. The background research showed that he, basically, was a hard working guy. No criminal charges except for a few log book violations a few years back.

The remains were found, stacked in a pile along the freeway. They sat, about 30 feet off the roadway in a clearing. They never found his clothes; watch, wallet and wedding ring were also stacked neatly next to Wokowski's bones. No fingerprints were found on anything. No markings were on the bones—they were not hacked apart. The working theory was that the body was boiled to remove the flesh. They did, how-ever, find dust 'consistent' with the caves known to be throughout southern Missouri. There were no clues to go on—no one saw him along the road.

The coroner could not tell how he died—the bones showed no signs of visible trauma. Sheriff Jones had interviewed half the town, including John, but had no real leads.

The next two victims' remains had not been found. In fact, the reports were missing person's reports, not homicide reports. The two students, George Sanderson and Lia Hillsbury had come down from the University of Missouri to study the geography to see if they could find a way to make the Ozarks more productive. They had been staying in Jefferson City and been driving south to various areas to do their research—soil samples and such. Their hotel room looked occupied when the Police entered. The report hinted that Lia and George might have been more than fellow students, but never came right out and said it. They had posted a schedule of places they were going to go—they had a meeting with a farmer south of Stillwater on the day they supposedly went missing. The farmer said they never showed up for the meeting. Sheriff Jones had interviewed just a few people in town who might have had contact with the students.

The next victim, Richard Stokes, was the first of the "in town" victims. Stokes and his common law wife,

Nicole Ferigan had gone missing from their trailer on either a Thursday or Friday. Both had extensive criminal records for everything from petty theft to domestic violence assaults. Stokes had served three years for killing a guy in a bar in Saint Louis. Neither kept a job for longer than three or four months. They, essentially, lived off of the State. Sheriff Jones did not take the report very seriously—he did not even drive by their place for a week after the report. The report never said who reported them missing, but, Sheriff Jones interviewed their parents, so I figured it was likely them. When he finally got around to investigating, it seemed like they had simply up and left, leaving all their stuff behind. Not that what they left behind was any great treasure. Basically, there was the smelly trailer, some ragged clothes, a five-pound brick of marijuana, lovingly wrapped in clean cellophane, and a color TV. Their truck was also in the drive, still on the blocks they had left it on. There was no sign of a struggle. The case remained open.

Damien Stone was the next person to have gone missing in this neck of the woods. He was a travelling salesman; hawking vacuums, brushes, cleaning supplies, and shammies between Ohio and New Mexico. He stayed the night up in Saint Louis and was scheduled to drive through Stillwater on his way to Little Rock. He never checked in at the cheap motel in Arkansas. His car was found, burned to its frame, in a small gully just across the state line. They were able to get some fingerprints off the steering wheel. They did not match Stone and there was no reference in the State databases. They had sent the fingerprints to the FBI, but no results had been returned, even though it had been several months. The body was never found. Sheriff Jones was not really involved in this investigation, so it was more thorough. Stone had no real family—he lived alone in a small apartment just outside Cincinnati. His employer reported him missing—

apparently they suspected he had taken the car, which belonged to the company, and was planning on selling it in Mexico. Apparently other employees had tried the same tactic. The report concluded that the case was still open, but it was likely that wild animals had carried off the body from the car crash.

The most recent victim was Steven Holcomb. He was a tourist from Nebraska. He had come to Kansas City for a convention of antique farm tractor collectors. The working theory was that he had driven south to see if he could find an antique tractor to buy. He was driving a rental car, which suffered a similar fate as mine—the car was beat up, like it had rolled several times, and left abandoned in the same field as the remains were found. Holcomb was survived by two adult children—his wife having died of cancer a few years ago. They reported him missing when he did not return from the convention. The Kansas City Police had interviewed the hotel and got virtually no inform-ation about Holcomb. He was just another body filling a room. There was not anything remarkable about him. Not even the bellhop remembered him. I found that incredibly depressing.

It took a week for the rental car to get reported, towed back to the rental agency, and for the Police to connect the car to Holcomb. By then, they car had been crushed by the rental company and any evidence in the car had been compromised Four weeks, almost to the day, after that, Ed Nile discovered a pile of bones, stacked neatly as before, along the edge of his field. There was no clothing stacked next to it. It was at this point that Sheriff Jones' obsession that John was the killer began. Holcomb had approached John to ask if he knew anyone with an old tractor. It was the last known contact Holcomb had before he died. Sheriff Jones' report was a layer upon layer of sus-picion, innuendo, guesswork, and speculation. He was able to connect John to every one of the missing people. John had been in town, made a strange remark, or otherwise was around when each of the victims had gone missing.

Aside from the background on John, the police reports had various photos, sketches, and various notes. Nothing too remarkable. Then I found a report signed by Sheriff Jones. The writing was cramped, tight, like he was excited when he took the notes. Apparently, on an April night, when John was at a church function, he came out and did some snooping in the cave. He recorded the bat cave—they pooped on him when he was crawling into the caves.

He made it into several different caves, but, ultimately, found nothing but a bunch of empty rooms. He even got a little lost coming back out—apparently he tried to keep a map, but his powers of observation were not as astute as he thought. Regardless, he still thought John was killing the men in the caves. Interestingly, however, it was Sheriff Jones who had the sample of the dirt from the caves to compare to the dust supposedly found on the bones.

As the sun started to outline the drawn shades, I realized I still had a gun to buy. I never travelled without a stash of hundreds stored inside the sole of my shoes. I pulled out the carefully folded bills and put them into my wallet. I took the paper on which I wrote the address, locked the door behind me and got into the rental car.

As I drove to the place, the city was slowly waking. The bums still slept in some of the store fronts, others were being chased away by the shop's owners. The cars were all filled with men and women dressed sharply for their day jobs. The traffic was still light, but there were enough cars for me to blend into them. I could tell when I left the business corridor and entered the darker side of town. The bars and clubs were all closed, leaving nothing but a vague taste of noise and alcohol in the air. A few more blocks and I was in the old part of town, which exuded hope and desperation in every weed-choked lawn or dilapidated front porch. Police tape hung like party streamers from the occasional tree.

The traffic had changed too. Instead of newer model sedans, I was awash in Buicks the size of small countries, vans with painted murals on their sides, and the occasional low rider Honda. I hoped the SUV I was driving would not draw too much attention. The pawn shop sat by itself along the side of the road. If the street was ever widened, the shop would lose the remaining three parking spaces. I pulled in next to a 1970s Dodge and got out.

The air hinted at the incredible heat that would soon permeate the City. Three steps and I was inside the dark shop. The shop did not have any air conditioning and you could feel yesterdays heat still emanating from the various objects for sale. The clerk sat at an old bar stool listening to a bottle-blond whine about how little he was offering for her wedding ring.

"He said it was real. That's a real diamond, dammit!"

Not in my book. Lady, look, the guy rooked you. Best I can do is a hundred fifty bucks."

"That son of a bitch," she paused, looked over her shoulder at me, "But I really need to money. I can't buy the stuff at a hundred fifty—I need two hundred to get enough."

"Enough? Lady, you couldn't buy enough coke to make you happy. 'Sides, wouldn't your old man notice you don't got your ring?"

"Him? Nah. He's prob'ly already drunk on the cheep booze he likes. I need it man, c'mon, two hundred."

"Can't do it. Go over to Henry's shop—He might think it's real. Give you more. Me, just not worth it." He made eye contact with me to communicate just how silly the whole transaction was.

While she continued to plead her case, I wondered
over to the case holding the guns. Simon had been
right—the guy had quite a collection. Everything from
a small 0.22 to a .44 magnum. There were even old-
style cowboy revolvers. The only thing he did not have
was ammunition. Behind the counter, in a large,
locked cabinet were a dozen shotguns and rifles. If you
wanted to start a militia, this was to place to go.

The blonde slammed the door behind her as she
went, thumbing through the hundred and fifty dollars
he had paid her for the ring. The wrote the transaction
down in a spiral notebook, put the ring along with the
other jewelry in a glass case and made his way,
shuffling, to me.

"You lookin' for anything in particular, or just
browsing?"

"I need a clean gun. Something that hasn't already
been used. Completely off the books."

"Well, you know, there's a waiting period?"

"That's funny. I was sure that private eyes got an
exception to that."

"You a private? I ain't ever seen you around." His
eyes roved over me to see if I stood like a private
detective.

"Yup. All the way from Miami." I showed him my
credentials. "Seems I've run into a bit of trouble down
south. I need something to keep from getting killed."

He stooped over the credentials, moving his lips as
he read the tiny print. "Well, I might be able to help
you. Who sent you here?"

"My associate, Simon Briggs, said you could help
me out."

"Simon?" An ugly smile broke across his face. "How
the hell is Simon these days? I knew him way back
when."

"Simon's good, that's for sure. He's out in Miami,
too."

"Miami, huh," he savored the taste of the word as

he said it. "I knew that boy wouldn't stay in Ohio long."

"Ohio?"

He eyed me suspiciously, and then confided, "that's where we met. We both failed the police academy. C'mon." He pulled at my arm and led me to the door in the back. "You don't want to look at any of those—they're all pretty, uh, well known. I got the good stuff back here."

We passed through the doorway, where he opened an old army chest, labeled, clothing, to reveal an impressive array of handguns, semi-automatics and snub-nosed revolvers.

"Now these, they, I guarantee, are clean. Most of them have never been fired, even."

"Great. I'm looking for a 0.44 caliber. Something that holds a good-sized magazine."

"I thought you said it was just for protection?" he looked sideways at me.

"I do. You ever been down in South Missouri?"

"Drove through once."

"If you had, you'd see the need. The guys down there, well, let's just say they'd laugh at one of those short barreled numbers."

"I get it. The bigger the gun, the better."

"Yup."

He dug through the guns. "This'll do ya. It carries thirteen bullets in a magazine." He sniffed the barrel, "probably never been shot."

"Good. And it looks intimidating. That's the effect I'm going for."

"OK. That'll be $600 bucks." He looked greedily at me, hoping he hadn't set the price too high. Which meant there was room to bargain. I had to bargain anyway. If I just paid the cash he'd be sure to remember me. If I bargained, there was a chance he'd get fuzzy on the details.

"$600? That seems king of high for something like that. I'd go $600 for a decent rifle. How about $300 and you throw in a hip holster."

"$300? You kidding? $600's a steal for a piece like this. Course there's the, what they call, instant gratification. I'm taking quite a risk here. How about $500, and I'll throw in the holster you want."

"I'll go to $425. Most I can afford for this job."

"$450 and we're there.

I signed, emphasizing how much I hated having to concede the last twenty-five bucks. "OK. And I still get the holster."

He smiled an ugly, tobacco stained smile at me, we shook hands, and we went out to the register. "OK. Here's the deal. All I sold you was this fancy holster—you don't know where you got the gun, okay? I don't want no trouble, see?"

"Got it. And you won't remember anything except I paid cash for the holster, deal."

"I like the way you think, son."

I handed over the money and he gave me the gun, wrapped in a fine leather holster—probably the most expensive holster I would ever buy. He did not offer a receipt.

"Thanks again," I said, heading for the door.

"Not a problem." He paused, "Just in case you need to do more than just scare with that piece, there's an ammo shop three-four miles south of here."

"I'll keep it in mind," I replied vaguely.

Back in the SUV I drove straight to the shop, which was in an even more colorful area of town than the pawn shop. The streets were littered with cars that looked like they had not run in several years. I bought five boxes of bullets for my new gun. As luck would have it, the ammo shop was affiliated with a gun range in the basement and offered a free half hour at the range if you bought enough bullets. I qualified and went straight there—I needed to see exactly what type of gun I had bought.

After fifteen minutes, I knew the gun was a solid

piece—the guy had really sold me quite a weapon. I just hoped I would not need to use it.

Chapter Twelve
Change of Luck

Ill-luck, you know, seldom comes alone.
Cervantes, Don Quixote. Part I, Book, III, Ch. 6

I made it back to the motel; it was time to pack up and head back to Stillwater. No matter how much I wanted to leave with the money, take Jessie away, and never come back, I had to, the day's heat was just beginning to increase, slowly revealing its burn. I checked out, paying cash, and began to drive back down the highway. I still had not heard from Jessie, but figured she probably got my message.

Once I left the main highway and was back on the rural roads, the feeling of impending doom crept into the car with me. The fields remained slightly ominous and I sped past them, like there was some sort of beast hiding in the crops, just waiting for me to leave the relative safety of the SUV. With each mile left behind me, the more anger seemed to build, until I was primed to explode. I noticed my knuckles were white as I gripped the steering wheel. Trying to combat the strange rage, I took a few deep breaths and tried to calm myself.

To distract me from the dark anger trying to consume me, I turned the radio on. It was an unwise move.

The news report pierced the quiet cabin of the SUV.

"The news out of the tiny community of Stillwater is that their local Sheriff, Robert Jones, has gone missing. Sheriff Jones has been a very vocal investigator looking for the suspected killer of seven. Bernard

Devlin is considered a person of interest in the disappearance. Devlin is the nephew of John Lincoln, the
man suspected of being the serial killer. The County
Police are actively looking for Bernard Devlin. If
anyone knows of the whereabouts, they are encour-
aged to contact Sheriff Forrester of the County
Sheriff's Office.

"Devlin is supposed to have been going back to
Miami, where he lives. He checked into the gate, but
never made the flight."

I smashed the buttons, letting the radio take the
abuse I wished I could unleash on fate. I tried Jessie
on her cell phone, but it went to her voicemail
immediately. I left a rambling message begging for her
to call me back. As I shut the phone, it alerted me to
a new voicemail I had. Dialing in, I had no idea how
my day would get worse.

"Berns, it's me." Bethany. Great. I wondered what
she would want. "I'm here in this po-dunk town and
no one knows where you are. I heard you inherited a
fortune, but might need some help getting everything
sorted out. I figured you wouldn't mind if I came, you
know, to give you a hand. Seems like the only hotel in
town burned down, so I'm staying at a woman named
Jessica's house. She said she used to run the hotel.
Call me when you get this, I'm worried about you."

No wonder Jessie was ignoring my calls. I wondered what sort of lies Bethany had told her about us.
Especially our relationship or lack thereof. My guess
was that I was elevated back to 'serious boyfriend'
when she learned how much I had inherited. I knew
now why Jessica had not returned my voicemail.

I decided to call Jessie one last time and try to
explain. After leaving a second rambling voice mail
where I tried to convince her that Bethany was a gold
digger who dropped me years ago. I told her that I
really cared for her and wanted to talk with her. When
I hung up, I knew I would have to explain it all in

person. That is if I was not arrested on sight by Sheriff Forrester.

In my rage, I had pressed the accelerator to the floor. Looking down I saw my speed in excess of 110 miles per hour. I eased up, slowing as quickly as I could, without slamming on the brakes Not three minutes later I passed a State Patrolman.

Seeing the police made the think of Sheriff Forrester. I hoped Sheriff Forrester was not like Sheriff Jones. If he was, I would be serving my time in a Missouri state penitentiary before the evening meal. I realized I needed to get ahead of this before I got to town. So, I decided to call the only Missouri lawyer I knew. Cletus answered with his customary booming drawl. It told him about the lawsuit—he already knew since they had sent him a courtesy copy.

"Can you defend against it?" I asked.

"Sure, sure, sure, son. That's not a problem at all— I'll put in a notice of appearance this afternoon."

"What do you know about the Plaintiffs' attorney?"

"It's a firm out of Saint Louis. They probably had to go that far to find someone who'd take the case. I never worked with the specific attorney, but I've heard the firm will file against anyone for anything. Strictly a Plaintiff's firm. They are just after the money, son, not likely to settle, especially when you consider John's estate."

"How'd they know how much money John had?"

"It wasn't much of a secret that John was rich; but 'round here, rich is a relative word. I doubt they realize exactly what a gold mine they found. 'Least not yet."

"Great."

"You need to talk with Sheriff Forrester as soon as you get here, son."

"Yeah. It'll be my second stop—I've got to see Jessie first."

"I heard there was a young lady in town lookin' for you."

"An ex-girlfriend. She's after the money too. What a day."

Cletus let the thread of conversation drop, and resumed his advice about Sheriff Forrester.

"What's he like?" I asked.

"Forrester's a good guy. Came out of a good family—a local. We all thought he'd be the next Sheriff, but Jones came up, you know the big city cop, wowed the counsel, and got the position. Anyway, Forrester's reasonable—pro'ly gonna ask you some hard questions 'bout where you been all night, stuff like that. I know I needn't ask, but, you didn't have nothin' to do with Sheriff Jones going missing did ya?"

"No," I laughed, "I was at the airport when I got served with the lawsuit documents. I decided to come back today and deal with this damn thing here." I decided not to share with him that I had John's investigation files. He may be my lawyer, but that didn't mean that I could trust him just yet. I was not about to share the fact I had bought a gun illegally.

"Well, you've got an OK alibi—the proof of service will put you up there. Course they'll say you killed Jones and ran away."

"Yeah." I couldn't believe that I needed an alibi. Things had sure changed since yesterday.

"Tell you what, I'll give Forrester a call, tell him you're on your way back from Kansas City and will check in once you get settled—by the way, where you gonna stay?"

"I'll be at John's. Give Forrester a call and as soon as I see Jessie, I'll stop by the station."

"Sounds good, son. You drive safe, now, you hear?"

"I will." We hung up and I was left in the cabin of my SUV, with a gun tucked into the center console, alone with my thoughts. The last thing I needed was Bethany messing everything up with Jessie. In a small town like Stillwater, I knew my name was mud. I had gone from the nice young man, related to John, to the philandering cad from Miami who had led Jessie on. Never mind that it was all untrue. I figured I should get a cut of Southwestern Bell's profits for the past seek. I bet I could double John's fortune.

My mind made a sharp turn to the left and began analyzing John's history. A prohibition alcohol runner turned into mob financier. Hard to believe a guy so, well, good, could have been involved in the mob. I wondered if, just maybe, John's history had come back to haunt him in his old age. That would explain his generosity to the various residents of the town. What it didn't explain is why someone had ripped his throat out that dark night. The boxes of John's materials had been helpful, but hadn't really helped in solving the mystery. Unless the solution lay in the files I opted not to go through, since I knew the people. My instinct told me that I was right, that none of those folks were the killer. It had to be someone, or something else.

I decided to burn some more mobile minutes and called Simon.

"How's my favorite fugitive?" Simon asked.

The rage erupted. "What is your problem, asshole? I yelled. I'm here trying to keep my life in line, and you give me shit?"

Simon was quiet on the other end.

After the eruption, I felt much less angry. It did mean I had to eat crow. "Look, Simon, I'm sorry -"

"Hey, not a problem. I was just kidding, but I get it. Besides, being near Bethany would do that to me."

"You knew she was here?"

"She asked me to hook her up with you a few days ago, so I figured she'd head down there. Probably causing you trouble, I'd guess."

"You have no idea." I turned the conversation to the work at hand. "I've got another strange research request, OK?"

"I'm here to serve at my reasonable hourly rate, my

friend. Whatta you got? Need info on the Plaintiff's suing the estate?"

"Not yet. Actually, I'm looking for information on the animal kingdom."

"OK... you know I'm not a zoologist, right?"

I laughed. "Yeah. What I'm looking for is info on what lives in the caves in Missouri."

"Bats." he replied instantly. "Flying vermin that shit their brains out. That's what lives in the caves."

"Seriously," I replied. "Something big, maybe with horns?"

"Horns?"

I related my experience in the caves, leaving out my own panic. The line turned very quiet.

"Simon, you still there?"

"Uh, yeah." He replied. "Give me an hour, OK?"

I glanced at the clock on the dash. You've got 43 minutes before I hit town, how about half and hour."

"On it." He hung up. That was one of the things I liked about Simon—when he was working, he got to it quickly.

I tried Jessie one more time, but this time exercised restraint and did not leave a rambling message. I wondered what sort of animal might live in the cave. I wondered if it was big enough to kill a man. In the back of my mind, I kept running over the Pastor's story about John's interests in monsters. Even in my line fo work there were no real monsters. People were evil enough. A monster, well, that was so unlikely.

As I pulled onto the Rural Route, I wondered just how equipped I was to hunt down a monster. Simon's call broke me out of my reverie.

"Well, you're not going to like this, OK?"

"OK," I replied cautiously.

"Nothing with horns lives in caves."

"OK." I could tell there was more.

"At least nothing that's been proven."

"Proven?"

"Well, when I got nothin' on my first search, I expanded it. Found something odd in the historical record, I'd guess you'd call it."

"Simon, if you tell me its bigfoot, I'm going to throttle you."

"Not bigfoot, no. A piasa bird."

"Excuse me? A bird?"

"In Illinois, the Illini had a legend of a creature that lived in the caves and attacked the village. The village was prosperous. Then one day, an earthquake shook the village and an animalistic scream emerged from the west. Out of the sky came a dragon that attacked the tribe. The dragon had the body of a horse, with long fangs jutting up from its lower jaw. Supposedly, flames shot from its nostrils and it drooled incessantly. They named it the piasa bird. Each morning, just before the sun rose, and after the sun set, the Piasa bird would, it would attack the village, taking the indian warriors one by one back to its lair where it would consume them, leaving pile of bones, with no flesh across the countryside.

"Ultimately, the chief wounded the beast with poison arrows, and it fell into the Mississippi, never to be seen again by the Illini."

The Indian lore had sent cold chills down my spine. The crude description seemed to match what I had experienced. That made no sense. It was legend, not reality. In real life, monsters are not real.

"Hello? Berns, you there?" Simon asked.

"Yeah, thanks. I—"

"Dude, your taking this seriously, aren't you?"

I saw no reason to lie. "Yeah. I'm just, well-"

"You don't have to justify anything to me. Life is full of weird stuff. Piasa bird or not, you be very careful. You need a second gun?"

"No," I paused, back up would be nice. "I've got it for now."

"Good luck, man. And be careful."

I hung up, trying desperately to reconcile the real world I lived in, with the monster I now believed existed in John's caves. I wondered if John had encountered the beast before he was killed. The mental picture I built of the creature was not calming my nerves.

I pulled into Jessie's gravel drive, anxious to tell her about Simon's discovery. I also hoped she would understand. I hopped out of the SUV and bounded up the stairs to her front door. It opened before I could even knock.

"How could you?" she asked, her eyes red from crying. She sniffled, "I trusted you."

"You can still trust me. Jessie, you got to believe me, Bethany's old news."

"She's not here," she replied, sensing my unstated question. "Said she needed to get some pretty underwear for later. I don't like her. And right now, I don't like you."

"Seriously, Jessie, Come on. She,"

"Dammit, she said she'd just stayed over at your place before you flew here."

"That's a lie! What the hell—"

"She knew all about your place—even described the bathroom that she helped decorate."

"She did help me decorate my place," I admitted, "But that was, what, two years ago now. Let me in, let's talk about this."

"I'm not letting you in here," she replied, blinking back angry tears. "I still don't trust you. You never even mentioned her. You hid her from me. I told you about my old boyfriends, and you didn't say anything."

"I know, I should have, but—" The door slammed in my face. I pounded on the door, "Jessie! Dammit, I want to talk to you about this! Come on! Please?" I was reduced to begging. The door remained closed. "At least come with me to see Sheriff Forrester, let's put aside this *thing* and clear John's name. He's being sued! And I think I know what's in the caves."

The door opened a crack. "What?"

"I got served with a lawsuit last night. Wrongful death. Seems the victims' families found an attorney to sue John."

"Let me see," she demanded, holding her hand out. I grabbed it with mine and kissed the palm.

"You've got to believe me. She means absolutely nothing to me."

"Just give me the lawsuit," she said quietly.

I handed her the papers and the door shut again. Like an idiot I stood outside the door, hoping she would come with me. I needed her to be with me. After a few minutes, the door opened and she stormed past me saying, "Come on. I owe this to John. But I'm not talking to you about her. I want to hear about what's in the caves."

We got into the SUV and I filled in the details that Simon had told me. I hoped whatever Bethany had told her was not going to destroy what I had built with her. We made it to the station without her saying a word about the Piasa bird theory. We went inside.

"I'm here to see Sheriff Forrester."

An older woman, who bore an uncanny resemblance to Cletus's secretary, replied, "Who may I say is here?"

" Bernard Devlin."

Her eyes widened just a bit before she resumed her disinterested gaze. "I'll let him know. Have a seat."

We sat down and Jessie began leafing through the Missouri Conservationist magazine. I chose to follow her lead and sit in silence, waiting to clear John's name.

After a few minutes, Sheriff Forrester emerged from behind a closed door. He stood six foot six and was built like a line-backer. He was the kind of guy you wouldn't dare challenge.

"Bernard?"

"Yes, sir, nice to meet you." I stood and we shock hands.

"Jessie," he smiled, "Good to see you! It's been ages. What brings you here?"

"I'm here to clear John's name."

"OK. You know you can't come back with him, right?"

"Yeah. He's a good guy, though." She gave me a look I could not quite read.

"I'll treat him just fine. Unlike Sheriff Jones, *I* happen to believe that the killer is still out there. I figure it's my job to figure out whom. And with Sheriff Jones missin', well, I guess I'm in charge."

"Follow me."

We went into an office that looked like it was, at one time, been designed to be an interrogation room. After years of not really having to interrogate anybody, it had been filled with office supplies, reams of paper, and file folders.

"Have a seat, Mister Devlin."

"You can call me Berns," I replied, trying to break the ice.

"Thanks for coming in," he sat as he against the wall directly across from me. "Do you know why you're here?"

"The radio said I was a 'person of interest' in Sheriff Jones's disappearance."

"Yup. Where were you last night?"

"Well, I drove Jessie to her folks in Jefferson City, then I drove to Kansas City, and I checked into my flight back to Miami. That's when I was served with the lawsuit, and I decided to come back and see this thing through to the end."

"About what time would you say you checked into your flight?"

"I guess it would have been around 12:15 am."

"And it was for, what, a 5:45 am flight, right?"

He knew more than he was letting on. I realized

that Sheriff Forrester was the real thing—a real detective who knew how to dance the dance in this tiny room. "Yeah. I didn't want to waste any money on a hotel room."

"I see."

I decided that I would play his game. After many years as a PI, I knew my share of tricks. We sat in silence for a while, his eyes boring into mine. I never broke eye contact with him. He finally conceded the point to me and asked "Then what?"

"Well, after I got served, I decided to come back to Stillwater to handle this thing. So, I checked in to a motel to get a little sleep," I figured there was no reason to tell him about John's investigation just yet. I still needed time to look through it all. "I knew that I shouldn't drive as tired as I was. Especially since I got run off the road the day before."

"Which hotel?" he interrupted.

"It was a Motel 6 off of the highway, not too far from the airport. I have a receipt, I think." I shuffled through my wallet and handed the receipt to him.

He looked it over carefully, then said, "It's got a timestamp of 1:15 am, or so. You got a receipt before you checked out?"

"Yeah, I paid cash for the room, and knew I was going to be leaving at between 4:00 and 5:00 am to come back here."

"But, you didn't get back here until, what, 2:30 pm, or so, right? You stay longer than you expected?"

"Yeah. I didn't wake up to the first alarm I had set." I hated lying to him, but I wasn't so sure I wanted to tell him about the gun.

"I see." He never broke eye contact with me, trying to push me to tell the truth. "Let's switch gears, OK," he sat down. "Who do you think is killing everyone 'round here."

"I have a theory," I admitted. "But I'm afraid you may not like it."

"Try me," he smiled warmly. He was trying to change the dynamic between us—he wanted me to believe we were no longer on opposite sides, but were friends.

"OK. I think there's an animal doing it."

He looked at me coldly. "An animal? That's what you're going with?"

"I'm pretty sure it was the animal that attacked my truck and caused my truck to roll off the road."

Levelly, he said, "Big animal. What, like an elephant?"

"No, A Piasa bird."

"Now it's a bird, not an elephant? Damn big bird, huh? Did it have yellow feathers and a friend named Suffuluphogaus?"

"I'm serious. Apparently it's a monster from Native American lore."

"So it's an big, old bird monster." Skepticism dripped as each word left his lips.

"Look," I said, "I know it doesn't make any sense. But, I've been out there, in the caves, with it. There's something in the caves. If it's not the Piasa bird, then it's something else. And its killing people."

"OK. But how do you explain Sheriff Jones going missing on the one night you leave town?"

"I'm guessing he knew I left town -"

"How?"

"We told Pastor Mike and his wife-"

"I see. Go on."

"And Sheriff Jones went out to search the caves."

"So where's his car?"

"I have no idea."

Forrester looked at me sharply. "I believe you. At least that you don't know what happened to him." He opened the file and pulled out a photograph. "We found his truck at John's house. He's probably lost in those damn caves. I'm planning on forming a search party to go rescue him."

"I can't allow that." I replied meekly.

"Why?"

"John's will says I'm supposed to keep everybody out of the caves."

"What happens if I get a warrant?"

"Beats me—you'd have to ask Cletus, I guess." I looked him in the eyes. "But that doesn't mean that I can't go in the caves to rescue him."

"You?" He laughed, a dry raspy noise. "You want me to let the man suspect in Jones's murder go find him in the caves that he may have been killed in? You have to admit, that's insane."

"Look, I don't have to go alone, I could take Jessie. You trust her, right?"

"You'd risk her life against this monster? And if you killed Jones and her and barely escaped with your life, I'd look even more insane. Not going to happen, OK."

"Fine." I replied. "I've established I couldn't have killed Jones, right?"

He nodded. "For now."

"And you're not arresting me for anything, right?"

"Nope."

"Then I'm out of here." I stood up quickly, causing the chair to rattle behind me

He reached out a hand and placed it on my shoulder. "Look. I think you really believe its a monster. Unless I see it for myself, I'm gonna be a skeptic. Don't do anything foolish, OK?" He removed his hand. "And don't leave town, got it?"

"Yeah, sure." I replied. I was already wondering how much of a head start I would have before his rescue party would make it to the caves.

"If you go in the caves, though, I'm pretty sure you won't find Jones." He frowned, rubbing his hand across his face, like he was trying to wipe his nose off his face.

"What? How can you be sure?" I asked suspiciously.

"See, Sheriff Jones isn't really missing."

"What? Is this some sort of twisted mind game to screw with me? What kind of—"

He held his hand up, allowing me to swallow the unkind words I had been planning on blistering him with. "You see, we found Sheriff Jones about an hour ago."

"Where was he?"

"Dead." He let that word sail across the room and sink into my thick skull.

"Dead?"

"Yup. Now, my gut tells me several things. First is that you're not a killer. Second that John didn't kill those folks. And third, I think I can trust you. You've been as honest as I would be in your circumstances. Of course, you didn't tell me about the gun you bought up in KC, but..."

I was stunned—he had found out about the gun.

He continued, "Let's see, you were almost killed twice while you were staying here. I'd probably buy a gun too. You have stellar references, though. It seems the cops you worked with back in Miami, well, they all thought you were one of the best and said as much when I talked with them. And I always trust the instinct of cops. But anyways, see, I'm going to tell you something about the details of this investigation. I like you. I think you'll keep it under your hat. But, I'm going to need something from you. I need you to prove to me that it is this Piasa bird, got it?"

"Absolutely," I affirmed, regretting my lack of honesty with him. "What happened to Sheriff Jones?"

"Well, his bones were found about an hour ago. It was not too far from John's place, actually. Bones isn't exactly what I'd call it. Kind of like a puddle of a body. Most of the muscle and fat were gone, but the sinew and gristle was still attached. The bones were covered in a slime that the crime lab is still trying to identify. Reminded me a owl pellets—you know what those are?" He continued, not waiting for my answer. "An owl eats a mouse whole. While it's in the owl's guts, the meat is digested, while the fur and bones are vomited out later.

"And now you tell me of some legendary bird-beast. It starts to make sense. The piles of bones were probably out there long enough for the scavengers to take what they could, leaving on the the bones. I'm not convinced by your theory, but it makes more sense than anything else I can think of. But you can't tell anyone about Sheriff Jones' fate. We're keeping it quiet until we can get a handle on whatever it is that's living in those caves."

"Can I tell Jessie?"

"Sure." We stood, two equals trying to figure out where we go from here.

Chapter Thirteen
Weeds

We have a choice: to plow new ground or let the weeds grow.
Jonathan Westover, Plowed Ground

Forrester and I tried to formulate a plan, but combating a mythical monster was neither of our wheelhouses. So, he let me go, telling me he would be naming me as a 'person of interest' to the media. We both hoped that would keep people satisfied and away from our investigation. I also told him I was going to go through the caves with a fine-toothed comb, and hopefully, take Jessie with me to help me kill the demon that haunted the town. My headache returned as I thought more about the quest before me.

I walked out with Jessie, who was still mad at me, but I could read curiosity in her eyes. I decided to use that curiosity to my advantage and stayed quiet. I figured if she broke the ice, it might help my cause, and we could go back to being a couple. Of course, I still had to deal with Bethany.

As we got back in the SUV, she finally asked, "So? What happened?"

"Sheriff Jones isn't really missing—"

"He's not?"

"He'd dead. He was killed last night."

"Dead? How?"

"Like the others—a pile of remains. Sounds like it has struck again."

"It? He bought your crazy Piasa bird theory?"

"Sort of. Forrester, I guess, thinks its an animal of some sort. Whether or not its this bird-monster I just don't know.

"Hm." She paused as we passed the fields on the way back to her place "We're in danger then?" she asked quietly.

"Could be. But I have, at least, some protection. I bought a gun up in Kansas City."

"A gun?"

"Don't worry," I smiled, and took her hand. "I've been trained; chute, I used to carry one of these for my job."

"Oh." She left her hand in mine, so I knew we were slowing emerging from her anger, and cooler heads might prevail. I hoped I could repair the damage Bethany had caused.

"I was thinking, are you up for a little adventure?"

"Adventure? Maybe." She looked sideways at me, a slight grin on her face. "What do you have in mind?"

"Jim and I agreed that someone needed to go through the caves to see if we can flush this thing out. If we can kill it, wound it, or something, and then the murder issue is off the table. He hopes there's some evidence we can show that it's something wild. I'd go alone, but I may need someone to help kill the damn thing."

"And you think I'm a killer?" she smiled at me.

"I'd bet you've been hunter a far piece more than me." I smiled back.

"A far piece?" She giggled. "You are so not from around here. I'd stick to east coast jargon from now on you sound like a dork."

"Fair enough," I conceded.

"Why not take Bethany, your *girl*friend?" she asked. The edge of her anger remained, but at least she was willing to listen to me.

"She's not my girlfriend... you are." She squeezed my hand, so I continued, "Bethany is, well, a friend, sort of."

"Sort of? Some friend."

"See, we did date, what, three years ago, I think it was. She broke up with me when my earning potential went down. It was hard on me, but we stayed in contact, and occasionally still see each other, but only as friends."

"Friends with benefits, though, I bet. She told me you tried to seduce her last week."

"I..." I had not expected Bethany to be so brutal. "Well, it has been a long time since I've had a girlfriend. A really long time." I exhaled heavily. "And I did try to, uh, rekindle, but I knew it was a mistake. And since then, well, I met you, and I really like you. More than I've liked anyone in a long time."

She squeezed my hand again, but looked out the window. Since she kept silent, I decided to continue, "And I like you, a hell of a lot more than I ever liked her."

She giggled, which kind of startled me. "You are such a—"

"Such a what, you minx? If I recall, you tried to seduce me yesterday, after all, didn't you?" I laughed. "Running around in your undies, really."

"Now hold on a minute," she said, her smile lighting up the car, "You were the one who screamed bloody murder, making me come to save you in my under-wear."

By the time we pulled back into her driveway, we were well on the way back to normal. When I stopped, she turned to me and said, "OK. The true test. You get rid of *her*."

"Not a problem. I'll tell her the get the hell out of Dodge."

She giggled again. "You do that."

We got out of the car and went back into her house. Bethany was still not there—apparently she was still out shopping. "When do you want to go into the caves," I asked.

"How about first thing after sunset? This thing

maybe nocturnal—it'll be better if we can catch it in the open, where it might be more vulnerable. I'll pack my gear. We'll need my camcorder to record anything we find. We should also bring some extra food and water, in case we're there for quite a while. And any weapons you can tote."

"Don't forget some waterproof stuff—there are underground streams in the caves, too." she said.

I stepped over a kissed her. She kissed me back, letting me know, in not so many words, that we were OK.

"So, what did you tell her?" I asked, curious how she had reacted to Bethany.

"Absolutely nothing. All she knows is that I'm just someone who used to own a hotel."

"That's too good. What else did she tell you about me?"

"That you are real freak in the bedroom," she smiled, obviously joking.

"And I'm sure she mentioned my incredibly large porn collection." I replied, laughing.

"Oh, yeah, she said you had truckloads, but most of it was animated."

We kissed again.

"Is there a historical society or library around here that I can go to?" I asked, deciding to do my own legwork instead of relying on Simon.

"Uh, sure. Two doors up from Cletus is the historical society. Why?"

"I want to see what I can dig up on the Piasa bird. Maybe there's a how-to guide on how to kill the damn thing."

"You really think that's what this is?"

"I've got no choice but to think so. Something attacked me on that road that night. And it all makes sense—the noises I heard in the cave, the bones being deposited away from the caves."

She shuddered in my arms. "I—"

"It'll be OK. The Indians were able to beat it, so can we."

"I'd skip the historical society. Go find Zeke."

"Zeke?"

"Zeke is descended from the local Indian tribes. He might know something."

I recalled my moonlit meeting with the man and realized she was right. "Where can I find him?"

She glanced at her watch. "This time of day, he's probably home watching TV."

"TV?"

"He loves talk shows. He lives about five miles that way." She pointed to the west.

"Got it. I'll deal with Bethany, get some supplies and meet you back here. OK?"

"I'll make dinner, then we'll go." She kissed me again. "Dinner for two, got it?"

"Yes, ma'am," I said, putting my best effort at a southern drawl. She giggled and kissed me one last time.

I headed out to get some answers out of Zeke. As I drove off, relieved that Jessie and I had worked things out. I was not looking forward to Bethany, but at least I was going to be rid of her. As if the mere thought of her conjured her presence, my cell phone blared Bethany's ringtone. I pressed the ignore button and drove on to Zeke's house. By the time I had gotten there, Bethany had tried to call six more times. I had five voice mails from her, too. I swear the woman was a nut job.

Zeke's house was less of a house and more of a shack. I doubted it had more than two rooms. Out to the left I saw an outhouse. Zeke's place was as rustic as it came. I stepped up to the door and it opened before I could knock. The old man stood, his eyes sharp and piercing. He said nothing.

"Zeke," I stammered, taken aback but this strange man. "I need to know about the Piasa."

He spat in disgust, barely missing my shoes. "No such thing." He started to close the door.

I pushed the door back open and stepped into his face. "Bullshit. I'm going to find and kill the monster that killed John, your best friend. So if you know anything at all that'd help, now's the time. You owe it to John."

His eyes widened ever so little, but my words had hit home. He stepped outside and gestured to me. "Piasa doesn't exist."

"OK. So what is it?"

I walked behind him, along a well-worn path as he spoke over his shoulder to me. "Do you know where the Piasa story came from?"

"I don't." I admitted. He was quick for an old man; yet our pace quickened.

"White man." He spat again. "White man came, corrupted the legend. Made it comical. Something to laugh at."

"If the Piasa doesn't exist, what is it?"

"Wapipinzha."

"Huh?"

"Wapipinzha—real lynx."

"A lynx? So it's a real animal."

He stopped, arriving at a shady spot where he, apparently sat on a regular basis. He gestured at a stump, so I sat. He leaned against the tree. "Wapipinzha lives at the bottoms of lakes. Drowns those not careful. Frightful creature. Very dangerous. Sharp teeth. Tail made of copper."

"How do I kill it?"

"Hard to say. Legends are not very clear."

"I heard poison arrows were used to chase it away."

"Maybe," he shrugged. "Could be its nothing more than an animal." He spat again. "Could be something worse."

Zeke was not being overly helpful, so I tried another track. "You seem to know more about this thing than anyone else. Why did not you come forward?"

"No one is going to believe me." It sounded so simple in his plain voice.

"Why not? John did." I guessed, hoping to coax more information out of him.

"I'm old. Foolish as some would say. John, well, he was old too."

"Was the lynx why John closed off the caves?"

"Not exactly."

I waited, hoping he would give me more. Instead he stretched, causing his back to pop. He took a deep breath, and started walking back. I jumped up and followed as quickly as I could.

"Why did he, then?"

"He didn't want people in them."

"And?" My headache was pounding, causing my temper to flare. "Damn it, Zeke. I'm trying to help, here. You've got to give me more information. Damn it." I had grabbed him by the shoulder.

He whirled, much quicker than he should have, his eyes a blaze. "I don't got to help. John tried to help. It killed him. It'll kill you. I just want to be left alone. I'll die on my own terms." He threw my arm away and tromped off.

I called after him. "I'm going to kill it."

"Good luck. Better men than you have tried."

On that note, he quickly outpaced me. By the time I got to his shack the door was closed and I could hear the TV blaring an obnoxious daytime talk show about who the father was. I figured there was nothing more to be gained so I jumped back in the SUV and headed to Walmart. I already had two more messages from Bethany when I turned into the parking lot. I remembered what it was like to be with her. She had always been like this, always calling, checking on me, trying to make sure I was where I said I would be. I had to be nuts to want to get back together with her. I turned my phone to vibrate and went on a small spending spree.

I had two carts full of stuff to lug back to the SUV. I had rope and flashlights, waders, propane containers and a camp stove, sleeping bags and even camping silverware. I did not know how long we would be gone, but I planned on three days, if necessary. I also picked up a digital camera and camcorder with extra batteries—if we did find something, I knew we needed to be able to document it.

As I drove back to Jessie's house to deal with Bethany, I realized just how crazy this actually was. Here I was, in the middle of nowhere, intending to go exploring a network of caves, hoping to prove John's innocence. With my luck, we would spend a few days wondering around in the dark and find nothing. Then we would be back where we started from, with no leads on who the real killer was. I pulled into the drive and I saw Bethany standing at the door, waiting for me. She had a big smile plastered on her face and one of her red, 'you-know-you-want-me,' tops on. It did not work for me. As I got out of the SUV, she started down the steps, almost at a trot.

Before she could come any closer to me, I held up my hand and said, "Stop."

Her entire body stiffened as she came to a halt about five feet away. Her eyes grew wide with shock. She knew this was something new to her—I was rejecting her. She decided to give it a try, "Bernie! I'm so glad to see you! Give me a hug." She stepped forward at the same time I stepped back.

"Bethany, what are you doing here?" My tone was flat, almost dead.

"Well," she said, slightly confused, "I... I... Simon told me you had run into some trouble with the inheritance and, well, I, thought I would come down and help."

"Help, huh?" I said dubiously as I walked to the back of the SUV and started taking stuff out. "And you thought you would help by telling everyone we're boyfriend and girlfriend, huh?"

"Well... yeah." She was defensive now, obviously upset that I had not gratefully accepted her help. "I figured no one would help me if I told them I was just a friend."

"I see. So you told a bunch of lies to a bunch of people so that you could help me, that sum it up?"

"Don't you talk lawyer to me, you asshole," she said angrily. "I took a week off of work to come down here and help you out. And the thanks I get is a bunch of B.S. and absolutely no gratitude."

Her cheeks flushed red. I was getting to her, I could tell. I knew she hated it when I started cross-examining her. So I pressed on, determined to force her to want to go back to Miami. "Gratitude? You know what I think? I think you heard about the inheritance and you thought, hey, Bernard is finally going to be the rich guy I always wanted to marry. So, let's see, I know, I'll go down, insinuate myself into the situation, old Bernard, he's such a push over. And, what the heck, he still has a thing for me, I'll see if I can't become Misses Devlin—better yet, the rich Misses Devlin."

She stood silent, staring at me with eyes that burned with rage. I decided not to wait for a response, instead I would put an end to this. "But that isn't gonna happen. See, I'm wise to you. And I'm tired of it. You keep me around, just in case. You think I'm some sort of patsy. Not anymore. I'm just not interested. Got it? Now, get into your car, drive back to Kansas City, catch the next flight home. And I don't want to see you again." I moved toward the front door.

Suddenly, I was attacked from behind. Apparently, I had pushed too many of Bethany's buttons, and she was pissed off. Her nails dug deep into my arm and she tried to spin me around. I come from the old school, where you never hit a lady, but I doubted very much if Bethany could be called a lady at this moment. Her face was twisted in rage, her makeup smeared from her tears, and her lips were pulled back from her teeth like she wanted to take a sizable bite out of me. I shook her off me and continued up the walk, but she was determined.

She hit me several times in the back, hard enough to trip me, causing me to drop to the sidewalk. I hit my knees and could feel the aches from my recent car crash reignite. I turn around to see her coming, once again, directly at me, her long red fingernails flashing in the evening air. I hoped my eyes did not get plucked out.

Before she got to me, she suddenly fell to the ground, gasping for air. Jessie had come out to give me a hand and had delivered a single punch in the bread basket. She towered over Bethany, her golden hair hanging free and said, "You heard the man. Get!"

Bethany regained some of her composure and some of her breath and stood up, glaring at both of us. "What? You mean this—"

"Careful what you say," I said quietly, my stare hard and cold.

Bethany instantly became suspicious and leapt to the conclusion. "You... and her," she sneered. "You could have this," she gestured at herself, "and you chose her? She's nothing more than—"

"Careful." I said again.

"To hell with you. Who needs you, anyway? I'm going back to Miami. And trust me, you won't ever see me again." She whirled dramatically and stormed off to her car, slamming the door shut. She peeled out of the drive and drove off.

Jessie started laughing. I looked at her puzzled, "What's so funny?"

"She's headed the wrong way—that is a loop. Give her, say, five minutes at that speed, and she'll pass this way again."

As she helped me back up.

"You alright?"

"Yeah. Nothing that a back rub won't cure."

"Oh? You think you deserve a back rub? You got beaten up by a girl. And I'm the one who saved you. I think I deserve the back rub."

"I didn't get beat up by her—" I protested, smiling.

"Which one of you was on the ground, huh, tough guy?"

"Good point. I guess you do deserve a back rub. Especially since we're going caving later."

She kissed me. "Look, I heard most of what you said to her. You did good."

"Thanks," I said, embarrassed. "I guess it was a long time coming."

She looked over her shoulder as she got more of the packages out of the back of the SUV, "But don't you ever turn lawyer on me. I'll deck you the same way I decked her."

I chuckled, taking the rest of the stuff and closing the hatch. "Deal."

"And don't get a big head since you had two girls fighting over you. I'd have hit her even if it wasn't over you. I found her disgusting."

"Good to know."

We unpacked the various items from their boxes, Styrofoam, and bubble wrap, then re-packed most of them into the camping backpacks Jessie had pulled out. By the time we were finished we had two really large packs, with enough supplies to last for three days. She agreed that we should plan for a long trip, but hope that we could be done in one.

I told her about my last trip through the caves and emphasized exactly how easy it was to get lost. She suggested that we take some duct tape with a marker, that way we would draw arrows on the rock leading us out of the caves. I wished I had thought of that when I had gone the first time.

We had a light dinner and talked about nothing in particular, just talked. It felt good to be with her again. I was glad that hurricane Bethany had not done so much damage that we could not be fixed. After dinner, she wanted to know what I had learned from Zeke. She, like me, felt we had to kill it. Or at least try.

Chapter Fourteen
Voyage to the Center of the Earth

O'er many a frozen, many a fiery Alp,
Rocks, caves, lakes, fens, bogs, dens, and shades of death.
John Milton, Paradise Lost

We sat at her dinner table, warm cups of coffee steaming in our hands. The sun was setting, cooling off the fields outside. It was hard to leave the comfort of the house, and we both had reservations about what we would find. The more I thought about it, the more I was certain that we would find it. I was not so sure I would be prepared for what we saw. The beast of Indian legend was said to carry off men in its talons. Its horns were sharp weapons that delivered certain death. Despite the hot coffee, I shuddered.

Across the table, I saw Jessie's eyes widen slightly. She, too, was afraid.

"You know, you don't have to go," I said quietly.

She looked sharply at me. "You're afraid, aren't you?" It was not an accusation, but more of an observation.

"I—" I hated to admit it, but I was terrified of the creature I imaged lurked in John's caves. "I guess. I mean, I don't know. Look, its a monster, for God's sake. A monster that has been killing for a very long time."

"I know." She placed a gentle hand on my forearm. "Its OK to be afraid."

We took sips of our coffee.

"In fact, my daddy told me once about his time in the War."

"OK."

"He said if you weren't afraid, you would be the one who got killed. Being afraid isn't a weakness, its an awareness."

"Makes sense I guess. I just—"

"Berns," She took my hand. "We'll be OK. I'm scared, too." She kissed me. "But we can kill this thing. In fact, I'm sure we'll kill it."

"How can you be so sure?"

She smiled. "Because, just like John, you know it has to be done. And no matter how unpleasant, scary, or just plain stupid it is, it has to be done."

With that, she stood up, took my coffee and rinsed the cups in the sink. "Let's get packed an on our way, OK?"

I stood up and held her. Her warmth gave me more confidence in our mission. After picking up our packs and ensuring that we had everything we might need, we left her house. She locked the doors and glanced back at the home. In the dwindling light, the shadows give even her cheery farm house a sinister pall. We drove in silence to John's house. The gun felt heavy and cold in my hands. We pulled into John's drive and parked. Our long shadows preceded us down the dirt path that led to the cave. I looked over towards Jessie and saw she was carrying a crossbow.

"Where'd you get that?" I asked.

"Second at State my junior and senior years. I've had it since I was a teenager. My dad taught me."

I chuckled. "Not something I expected."

In the low light I could see her smile. We were both tense, our smiles were too tight, and each movement conveyed nervous energy. I tried to break the tension, "So, how about a nice, romantic walk in some, dark, dank caves, huh? Maybe get eaten by a monster, sound like fun? And people say I don't know how to have a good time, huh?"

She laughed, nervously, "Yeah. You're a laugh a

minute. I can hardly wait to see what you decide to do for our second date."

I could feel the earth cooling.

I decided to break our reverie and start the journey. "So. You sure you want to do this? You don't have to come with me, you know."

"Damn it," she replied. I'm coming, OK?" She paused, "I wouldn't miss this. I owe it to John." Her serious tone turned into a smirk, "Besides, a night alone with you in the dark sounds kind of fun."

I did not know what to say to that, so I just grinned. She took my hand and we pushed our way through the entrance. As soon as we both could stand in the small cavern, we put on the disposable ponchos I had bought. I figured that there was no better way to avoid getting bat poop all over us. I turned on the lantern to reveal a small cave with guano several inches thick on the floors and walls. We worked our way through the bat toilet and into the next chamber.

Once there we shed our shit-covered ponchos and piled them neatly under a small rock. The lantern showed what I already knew—the room had been systematically destroyed. Where there should have been stalactites or stalagmites, round scars emerged where the geologic formations had been forcibly knocked over, the remains shattered across the room.

"Do you think John did this?" she asked.

"I don't know," I replied. "It seems out of character for him to remove all these features. Maybe they had already been removed when he purchased the place."

"Maybe."

I pulled out the painter's tape I had brought and taped a small blue arrow, pointing to the way out. We both agreed that we needed some, non-permanent, way to ensure we did not get lost. I hoped we would still be alive to return the way we came. We pressed onward. The next cavern we entered was not scarred; the geologic formations littered to room in an impressive manner. Columns extended from the floor to the ceiling fifteen feet above. We had to duck under stalactites, avoiding the pools of water under them, then dodge stalagmites, just to get to the other side of the cave.

"Look!" she said, pointing at the far edge of the cave. A well-worn path had been made along the edge of the room, big enough for the monster to pass through. On the walls, deep scratches marred the natural surface.

We rarely talked, both of us too amazed by the caves. When we did it was to consult on which way to go next. Neither one of us had a system of exploration that we thought we should use. Instead, we bumbled along, amateur explorers in this strange subterranean world. After a few hours, and countless numbers of chambers and an entire roll of blue painter's tape later, we decided to stop and have some coffee and rest. It was not like it was a simple hike. It seemed to me that we were steadily heading downwards, but we had to climb over, under and through a number of obstacles. I was tired. Most of the chambers were damaged like a small child had gone in and tried to smash the features.

We were in a small chamber, no more than ten foot by fifteen feet. It looked a lot like all the other caves we had already been through. In one corner was a small, flat outcropping, kind of like a desk. We used that as our table top. We both set our packs down and I worked on getting out the thermos of coffee while Jessie sat on the floor. I could tell she was thinking about something.

"Something on your mind?" I handed her a steaming cup of coffee.

She took a sip, then replied, "Sort of. We've been going through these caves, for what, an hour or so. And, even at the slow pace we've been forced to go, we probably have walked over three miles. And there's no end to these caverns, yet. I wonder just how big of a search area we have. I mean, if this system is as large as it could be, we could be down here for days and still not find anything. Not to mention the fact that we might have already taken a wrong turn, and already missed the damn thing. It's been bothering me."

"Hm." I had not thought that far ahead. I was too focused on the trek we were on to look to much farther ahead than the next cave. Her analysis was correct. We might have bitten off more than we could chew. "So what do we do?"

"You'll know," I said quietly, my mind recalling the few murder scenes I had seen during my stint as an investigator for the prosecutor's office. "There's got to be something we'll see. So much has been destroyed, we've got to be on the right path. The creature has to have been struggling to get out through some of these tight spaced. That'd explain the condition the caves are in. So, I'm looking for blood stains, blood spatter, something. It's not easy to kill someone without make a mess. Never mind taking all their flesh off and vomiting up their bones." I shined the flashlight along the walls. "And these deep scratches are in all of the caves—I think itis the horns. That's what I heard when I was down here before."

Jessie was quiet, but I could see her eyes widen as I told her what I was looking for. I hoped she was ready for it when we found it. I hoped I was ready for it too.

"So, I say we keep wondering around until we find it." I continued, "Once we find it, well-"

"We'll kill it."

As we finished out coffee and started to get our gear strapped back on our backs, she grabbed my arm, "Listen!"

Off in the distance it sounded like thunder. It was too short lived to be a storm. Then it dawned on me. Cave in. The scratching was faint, but I could hear it, and it send chills through my entire body."

"What was that?" she asked, even though I could tell she knew the answer.

"Cave in. I think. It's moving around somewhere."

"What if it blocked our exit?"

"We'll find another way out. Or we'll dig our way out."

"What are the odds..." She began.

"This has nothing to do about odds, Jessie. We're not alone down here. It's here. And it might know we're here, too."

"Do we go back, check it out?"

"No. That could be exactly what it wants. We continue on. If we find the chamber, we might get an advantage. We kill it, and then we work our way out of here. We've got food to last, what, three days?"

"Yeah, if we ration it right."

"OK. Good. Let's head out." I took the gun out of my pack and strapped it on my belt. There was no reason to go into this unarmed. It seemed like the air had gotten colder.

We ventured on for another couple of hours before we came to a huge cavern with an underground lake standing serenely along the side of it. We decided to have another rest by the shores of the lake while we planned out next move. Especially since there did not appear to be any other exits out of the cave other than the one we came in at. Since the cave in we had not heard anything. We sat and ate crackers, beef stick, and water. Neither one of us felt like talking too much. I went over and touched the water—it was really cold. It was so cold that you would not just swim in it. A wetsuit might make it bearable. Disgusted that we were at a dead end, I decided to pace, which sometimes helped me think. I left the lantern with Jessie and took a flashlight to shine onto the cavern walls.

As I walked back and forth, I could hear the water moving slightly. I stopped and drew my gun.

"What? What is it?" Jessie asked, grabbing her

crossbow.

"Shh. Listen."

The water splashed slightly, and we could see small ripples disturb the surface. Then it stopped. We waited, our breaths held, until we were sure it was gone.

"Maybe a fish. It'll be OK," I lied. "We'll get out of here. That much I'm sure of." Whether we got out of here on our own accord, or simply as a pile of bone, was another matter entirely. Jessie packed back up, while I walked the perimeter of the cave, I let my wind wonder to all the other chambers we had gone through. There was no evidence anywhere that John had ever ventured into these caves. No litter, no debris. Not even markings that would allow him to figure out how to get back where he came from. There had to be something. I respected John's reputation, but there was no way he could have regularly gone into and out of these caves without a map of some kind. Lost in my own thoughts, I almost missed it. The glint of metal reflected my flashlight, almost blinding me.

Excitedly, I shone my light over the wall until I found it again. There it was. In a small alcove was a satchel with, what looked like an oxygen tank, next to it. "Jessie!" I said excitedly.

"What?" she whirled, again, pointing the crossbow at the water.

"Not there. "I found something. Hang on, I'll bring it over to you."

The satchel was remarkably heavy, even without the air tank. I drug both to our impromptu site. We both tore into the bag like greedy children at Christmas time. To both of our surprises, it was an old rubber raft, with a small rubber oar folded within. The oxygen tank was not just a tank. It was a compressed air tank to inflate the raft.

"Do you think this was John's?" Jessie asked.

"Had to have been John's raft."

"How do you know?"

"See the markings on the raft?" I asked, pointing to white block lettering painted on the side.

"Yeah."

"It's from World War II. Which means it was purchased a long time ago. Which means John probably had it down here for years." I connected the compressed air to the raft intake and it inflated rapidly.

"I guess we get to go for a boat ride." I said. "There must be an opening over there," I said, pointing to the back wall where the lake met the chamber wall.

"This is too weird," Jessie replied. "I mean, whoever heard of an underground lake leading to other chambers. And it's called a water lynx, right? I'm not too sure I want to cross that lake if it's lurking below the surface."

As it the monster had been listening, the surface of the water rippled ominously. We both jumped and gaped at the water, lapped at the edge of the underground lake. We looked at each other, the lantern casting menacing shadows across our faces.

"We've come this far, I'm not about to let some monster scare me." I said, with much more confidence in my voice than I actually had.

She looked back at me, her eyes hard and determined. "I'm in."

Then, in the darkness, with danger seemingly lurking just outside the dim light of our lanterns, she kissed me.

"So, danger is an aphrodisiac for you." I mumbled between kisses.

The kisses came to a natural stop and she sighed. "I suppose we should get on with it."

"At least I'll die happy,"

She slapped at my shoulder. "C'mon."

We drug the raft over to the shore of the lake. I dipped my hand into the water. "Damn. It's cold."

She pulled out her gun. "I suggest that we be fully

prepared." She paused. "You know how to shoot?"

I took out the pistol that I had purchased in Kansas City. "Well enough. It has been a while, but it comes back quick."

"So long as you don't hit me, I'm good."

"Very funny."

We put our packs in the raft and started to get in.

"Wait." I said, dropping back.

"What?" she spun, pointing her gun at the darkness.

I picked up a rock from the floor of the cave. "Let's see if its home, OK?" I launched the stone in the path of the beam of her flashlight. It splashed loudly, echoing across the cave. We waited in the darkness, as the ripples subsided. Nothing broke the surface of the lake.

"Either it's gone..." She said, leaving the alternative to hand in the air.

"Yeah, I know." I replied.

We got into the raft and launched across the icy waters. Neither one of us spoke, instead, we strained our attention to any hint that the beast was here. We made it to the other side uneventfully, which somehow made the trip even more scary. We pulled the raft to the edge of the cave, leaving the silent water behind us.

We made eye contact several times before we left the cave, but chose not to speak. The next chamber was smaller than the one on the other side of the lake, but had two different openings. Once we were away from the water, we saw there were two different paths. We chose the opening to the left, and stumbled around for about an hour. From that point on, each cavern had only one entrance and one exit. So we just kept going until we came to a dead end.

I was breathing pretty hard. The air was cold and damp, like getting slowly smothered with a wet blanket. Jessie was also breathing pretty had. I suggested we take a short break and Jessie agreed. As we sat in the lantern's light, we looked at each other, not wanting to talk about the monster.

We hiked back to the lake and decided to have dinner and decide if we should continue on tonight, or camp there for the evening. After a spare camp dinner of cold cuts, chips, and a cola, we sat around the lantern looking at each other. We were definitely a sight. We were both covered with sweat and cave dust. Somehow, she still looked good to me.

"What are you smiling at?" she asked.

"Nothing," I lied, trying to buy time. "I'm just glad that I've got company in this crazy adventure."

I think she could tell I was lying, but she let it go. "So, oh great leader, what do we do now?"

"Well, I'm not particularly fond of camping along this lake." I shivered, as if to emphasize my point. "How about we press on and look for a smaller cavern that we can stay in?"

"Sounds good to me." She paused and arched her eyebrow. "Besides, we may need to share our body heat to stay warm."

"Now that you mention it..." I replied, a grin slashed across my face.

"You just make sure you keep your hands to yourself, mister," she smiled back, "I may be the type of girl that lets a strange man lead her through a bunch of dark, creepy caves, but I'm not crazy."

We both laughed, which echoed across the cavern and emphasized just how alone and scared we really were.

We grabbed our packs and left, this time choosing the right cavern. It led into several other smaller chambers. I kept an eye out for a place where we could bed for the night. Someplace that would be hidden from the view while we slept. After another hour or so, we found a small cave where a small niche had been carved into the side of the cave. It looked like it was just large enough for us to sleep in and was out of the view of anything that might pass through. No guarantees, however.

We discussed whether or not to stop there for the night, and decided it would be the best place for us to stop for the night. After unrolling out sleeping bags and stowing the packs in the back portion of the niche, we lay next to each other and let the darkness swallow us. I wrapped my arm around Jessie and she snuggled into me. We laid there, silent for a few moments, listening to the natural sounds of the cave. I could hear groundwater dripping down into the caves, creating the geologic formations we had picked out way through. Occasionally a wind whistled, like these caves were breathing.

"You still awake?" Jessie whispered.

"Yeah."

"What are we doing down here?"

"What do you mean?"

"Do you really think we'll find it? I mean, let's see, this thing has eluded people for centuries. What if we reach the end of this cave and find nothing? What if its hiding from us?"

At first, I did not know what to say. Jessie was right. If this was all in vain, we would have wasted a few days and the monster would still be out there. Not to mention that the civil lawsuit would proceed against the estate. They would probably win; John was just weird enough to warrant suspicion that he was a serial killer. I put on a brave front for Jessie's sake.

"I've got a good feeling about this," I lied. "We'll find it. And kill it." Not even I believed what I was saying.

"I guess," she said doubtfully.

"What's the matter?"

"It just seems so hopeless. We wondered around in the dark for almost a day, and besides being likely trapped by a cave-in, we have nothing."

"I understand. It's the dark—it gets to you after

while. I don't know about you, but I'm dying for some sunlight. Not to mention it's just plain cold in here."

"Yeah, that's for sure," she said, turning towards me. "How about we warm things up?"

Chapter Fifteen
The Lair

We learn wisdom from failure much more than from success. We often discovery what will do by finding out what will not do; and probably he who never made a mistake never made a discovery.
Samuel Smiles, Self-Help

The next morning I woke, still enveloped by the dark, wet, and frigid air of the cave. Our bodies were still entangled and the warmth of her body seared my skin. I did not want to move. I wondered if we could do this forever. The mere thought left me dumbfounded. Never in my life had I felt quite like this. She stirred in my arms, and I instinctively held her tighter. She hugged me back, making a low purring sound.

"Mornin'" I mumbled, hoping my rank breath would not be too much of a turn off.

She kissed me. "Morning. You feel up to beast killing today?"

"Always," I replied, trying to sound much braver than I felt.

We got up, put ourselves back together in the cold. I felt old, as the aches from laying on the stone shelf wracked my body. Jessie, too, stretched, trying to get the kinks out of every joint. The darkness was oppressive. Even the slightest movement echoed off the walls, seemingly coursing through our minds. The longer we stood idle, the more fear seemed to grow in my mind. Each drip from the ceiling plucked at my nerves.

Too sharply, Jessie said, "You ready?" Her voice conveyed the fear we felt.

"Yeah," I replied. "Let's go kill the beast, shall we?"

The lantern cast weird shadows as we walked cavern after cavern. Hours drug by as we walked through a seemingly endless twisting path over the cold and rock terrain. We had just stopped for a short rest when a low and dark moan shattered the cave's silence. The call was part animal, part something worse. The moan cascaded off of the cave walls and continued on for what seemed like minutes. Instinctively, we both raised our weapons and stood back to back, peering into the unknown.

The moan subsided, leaving us to our thoughts. My heart pounded in my chest and I could almost feel the adrenaline course through my veins. Jessie, too, was shaking. I reached out in the darkness and took her hand. She squeezed it hard.

"That sounded close," I whispered.

"Uh huh." She paused, placing her crossbow back into her holster. "What's our play?"

"I'm hoping we can sneak up on it, maybe get a chance to observe it." I holstered my gun. "And then we kill it."

"How?"

"The legend says poison arrows killed it, right?"

"No..." She swallowed hard. "It says it drove it away into the Mississippi. Not killed it."

"I'm betting our superior firepower will do more damage than those arrows."

"Do was have a backup plan?"

"Run like hell," I quipped, trying to be funny.

"Seriously," she replied, more serious than I ever heard her.

"OK. If the guns and crossbow don't work, brute force might work." I shined by flashlight up to the stalactites. "I'm betting we can cause a few of those to rain down on it."

"Bury it? What about us?"

"If I have to kill it, and it kills me, well..." I left the

sentence uncompleted.

"But—"

"No arguments, OK?"

She did not respond. I could tell she did not like my back up plan.

"Besides, we don't need out back up plan," I tried to lighten the mood. "We've brought our kick ass, right?"

Another silence permeated the darkness.

"Come on." I urged. "Let's get this over with."

We moved on, pushing our way through the caves. With each step, the gravel crunched underfoot. It seemed like we had stopped descending, and instead, were slowly climbing. I held my breath, trying to move a quietly as I could. Jessie followed behind, her breathing just as quiet as I was. Then the scraping began. The sound of bone being pulverized by rock echoed throughout the caves. The noise sent shivers down my spine. The scritch and scratch got louder and louder as we passed through each cave.

"We're almost there." Jessie said, her voice as tight as a wire.

"Yeah."

As we entered the next cave, ahead, faint light scattered the darkness, causing us both to squint. The scratching stopped and a large wail echoed through-out the caverns. We both dropped to our knees, placing our hands over our ears. Finally, the wail stopped, the silence descending on us as welcome relief. In the lantern's glow, we stared at each other, not daring to say another word. Before I could say anything to Jessie, we heard what sounded like a large bird flapping its wings, accompanied by another deafening wail. The light ahead flickered and some-thing passed. This time the silence was significantly darker and deeper. I was breathing heavy, my heart thumped in my chest, and my hands were shaking. Neither of us wanted to move.

The cold cave air sent chills down my spine as the sweat tricked down to the small of my back. The monster had left its lair, giving us an opportunity to scout ahead and, just maybe, lay a trap for the beast. Jessie looked closely at me, assessing if I was ready. Our eyes met and we locked gazes. The fire in her eyes burned with an intense mixture of anger, determination, and fear. I imagined my eyes reflected the same fervent desire mixed with fear.

"It's time," I said. "It's gone, you know that? Let's see where this thing roosts, nests, or whatever the hell it does."

She nodded, her knuckles white from gripping the crossbow. "And that's daylight," she whispered. "How?"

"I'm guessing a sink hole, or cave in, something like that. We are too deep for it to be an exit."

With more boldness than we actually felt, we stepped, ever so slowly, towards the next cave. The smell of must and dankness gave way to an odor that burned at my nostrils.

Jessie sniffed at it. "Smells like the slaughterhouse, but," she gagged, "much, much worse. Mixed with really bad body odor." She spat.

"Huh." I replied I swallowed hard, trying not to puke. "Damn."

We entered about ten feet above the floor of the cave. Below a small shoreline was bathed in the midday sun. The lake it illuminated was wide and calm. Littered alone the edge were piles of decaying carcasses. I recognized cows, sheep, a horse, and even a few foxes. Some had been partially eaten, others were killed, left to rot in the sunshine. Looking up, I squinted at the opening, about 50 feet up. I could see the roots of trees pushing through the opening. At some point in the past, the cavern roof had collapsed, leaving the hole, covered only by the woods above it.

I pointed up. "You think it was trapped here until

that?"

"Could be. What do we do now?"

The think ledge we stood on was no place to face the beast. Below us, the water lapped at the cave wall. "I guess we swim." I glanced over at her. "You can swim, right?"

She smacked me on the arm. "Of course I can swim. But it'll get our guns wet. And without those..." She let the end of the sentence fall into the chasm.

Before she could react, I wound up and tossed my pack, gun and all, across the water, where it landed with a thud next to what looked like a rib cage of a horse. "Not a problem," I jumped into the water below.

The water was cold, and I nearly cramped up. More by force of will than anything, I paddled over to the shore.

"It's cold," and said, trying not to shiver too much.

"Of course its cold, moron," she replied, "its rain water. Probably contaminated with hoof and mouth, or some other dread disease."

"So what, your gonna leave me down here?" It sounded less manly than I had intended.

"Course not," she said. "Catch." She tossed her bag to me. I watched as she shimmied along the edge of the wall. As she crept along, each step caused shards of rock to fall. A few times, I was sure she was going to end up in the drink. Finally she perched almost directly above me. With a quick glance over her shoulder, she jumped into my arms.

"Good catch, but, ew, your wet." she said. "Now lets get set up to kill this thing."

Stumbling along the carcasses, I found a shadowed alcove which gave us a clear view of what looked like its nest, while also keeping us out of the direct sunlight.

"You stay here," I ordered. I'm going to swim over to the nest, and see if I can hide there."

"That is the stupidest thing, I think I've ever heard,"

she said, grabbing my arm. "You'll be in my line of fire. And I'm sure the damn thing will know your there, in the same way that you'll know if a predator was in your bed." She paused and smiled. "Unless her name is Bethany, of course."

"Very funny," I snarled playfully. "What do you suggest?"

Looking around the cave, there were few hiding places suitable. Then I saw a strange smile cross her face. "How do you feel about playing dead?" she asked.

"Playing dead?"

She pointed out a carcass where the flesh still hung loosely on the bones. "You'd fit behind, it, I'd bet. We can both hit the same target from different angles, and I don't have to worry about hitting you."

Having never killed a mythical beast, I figured it was as good of a plan as any. Clouds obscured the sun, and the cave dimmed. We both flinched slightly. The grip on my gun tightened. With a sigh of relief, we both relaxed.

"How long you think it'll be gone?" she asked quietly.

"Hard to say." The digital number on my watch showed it was early evening. "I guess it'd depend on when if finds its prey."

"What's the deal with that," she wondered, pointing to the half-eaten livestock strewn across the shoreline, and piled around what looked like a nest on the far shore.

"Don't know. What I can see, there's not too many broken bones. Maybe it can only swallow so much before it has to stop." I kicked at the limp hind leg of what might have once been a cow.

I walked over to the edge of the water, trying to peer into the deep. A thin greasy film floated across the surface. I would need a chemical shower after this to feel clean. "Looks pretty shallow," I said, shining my flashlight at the tips of stalagmites about 5 feet under the glass-like surface. Suddenly, something moved under the water, and I found myself aiming.

"What?" hissed Jessie coming to my side.

As our eyes focused, we both realized what it was I had seen. The bloated head of a bobcat floated back by, its cloudy eyes reflecting my flashlight beam.

"Damn," she mumbled.

I rubbed my eyes, trying to unsee what I had just seen. It did not help. "We should get into position." I said, more to distract us fro the awful place we were in, than for any other reason. I walked her over to the shadowy alcove, and got her set up. She sat on my back pack and rested her crossbow on a notch in the rock. "This looks like I've got a pretty good aim at it." She placed her reload arrows next to her.

"How fast can you get off—"

"Fast enough."

We kissed. I could not tell if it was the danger, but the kiss lingered, like we were afraid of parting. As the kiss broke, I could see tears in her eyes.

"Are you—"

"I'm fine, damnit." She wiped at her eyes. "Now go hide, so we can get this over with."

I picked my way along the half-eaten detritus strewn across the floor. The smell was powerful, but even so, I could still smell the stale water that i had jumped into on my skin. Nestling next to the rib cage of the beast I marveled at how few bugs were there. The cave must keep all but the most hardy of them out. I could see Jessie, holding her crossbow protectively in the shadows. We made eye contact, and seemed to communicate without saying anything. She looked scared. I probably did too. Neither one of us was looking forward to our encountering the beast. Yet, I felt thankful for this adventure. As scary and impossible it all seemed, I had a cause. A purpose. Something that would help define me for the rest of my life. And it had brought Jessie into my life.

As I lay next to the rotting side of beef, I marveled and how much I had changed over the short few days. I had come to this town, intent on leaving as a multi-millionaire. Now I was a monster hunter. I did not care whether I saw one penny of John's fortune. Instead, I cared that John's name would be cleared. I cared that this town would survive and that they would accept me. I cared whether Jessie would go out with me next week. For the first time in a long while, I had a purpose.

As I lay there, thinking bout Joh, I saw them. Bullet wounds peppered the carcass. I followed the body until I saw what looked like a skull. This was one of the beasts. I remembered the bullets I found in John's kitchen. He had killed it. Of that I was sure. Which mean the creature had not killed John for food, but for revenge. That explained why he had been mauled unlike the other victims. The creature was more complex than I had expected. It was capable of feeling anger and seeking revenge on John.

I glanced again over to Jessie's hiding spot. I marveled at how brave she looked. I'm pretty sure I looked more like a scared school boy instead of the next Van Helsing.

The cave quieted. All I could hear was the slow, regular drip of water filtering through the ceiling and dropping into the lake. Something inside me settled, too. A strange calm came over me as I tried to prepare for the fight ahead. We heard it before we could see it. A low growl, mixed with a sickly wheeze echoed through the cavern. I gripped the gun tighter as it approached, my heart thudding in my ears. Small pebbles fell from the opening above, dropping into the lake like tears. Suddenly, something fell from the hole to hand on the rocky shore of the underground lake with a corpse-like smack.

Above, and still unseen, the beast screamed like a tribal warrior returning victorious from the hunt.

Jessie, too, screamed. The look of horror on her face conveyed the depths of despair I had not seen. I could barely make out what she was screaming, until I followed her gaze to the nearly lifeless body between it. It was Dean,

It seemed as if Jessie and the monster moved at the same time. She was running to help Dean, it stalked her to claim its trophy and enjoy a meal. Its leathery wings beat against the still air of the cave. It landed with the grace of a swan on the rocks. It was unlike any animal I had ever seen. In a broad sense it was shaped like an elk, but it stood eight feet tall, with another two feet of twisted antlers atop the mangled face. Its wings curled around its scaled body and it snorted derisively toward Jessie and Dean. A thin, snake-like tail trailed behind it, coiling sinisterly.

It carefully approached Jessie, who was trying to assess just how badly Dean had been injured. Its hooves were covered with what looked like sharp claws, but at irregular and unnatural angles. Its legs were muscular, but also seemingly bent at irregular places. Its neck was scarred and bloodstained. Perhaps the most striking feature of its twisted face were numerous fangs jutting out of its lower jaw. Like the rest of the creature, they were spaced randomly and each slightly askew. Each of the fangs dripped with filmy slime. A pungent odor wafted off the beast in powerful and musty waves, making the rotting flesh in the cave seem less objectionable.

It pawed angrily at the ground, and then, for the briefest of moments, our eyes locked. In that second I realized we were not fighting some mutated beast. Its eyes were cold and filled with a hatred that was all too human. Then, after another short, soggy wheeze, it lifted its head and let out another tremendous cry that reverberated in the cavern. In a movement that was much too graceful for such a repulsive creature, it spread its wings and grabbed Jessie around the waist and plunged into the water.

Without thinking, I dropped my gun and dove after them. The cold water tried to seize my tired muscles, but I forced them to keep working. The lake was fairly shallow, but the murkiness made it difficult to find Jessie or the creature. I could not help but notice the bottom was littered with the bones of easier prey. The murky water made my grasps random and careless, but, almost out of air, I found the slick and hard antler of the beast, and grabbed on tightly. It tried in vain to shake me off.

I could barely make out Jessie, fighting against the thing's clawed hands, trying to get out of its deadly grasp. I yanked hard on the antler, trying to get the damned things attention—I had to make it let Jessie go. I yanked again, this time snapping the tine of the antler off in my hand. It worked. Jessie was free and kicking hard towards the surface. The leathery wings snapped around my biceps, its claws digging in deep and drawing blood. It launched upwards out of the lake and landed in its nest, made of the fur and remains of a myriad of other forest creatures. It held me directly in front of its hideous face, assessing me with the cool intelligence of something more than mere animal.

It crossed my mind that this was how John had died. Face to face with this awful thing. It slammed me down into its nest, the sharp bones of prior kills, bloodying my back. It did not let go. Instead it drew me closer, its evil intent clear. I barely felt the claws sinking deeper into my arms. My forearms were slick with my own blood. The slime oozed more quickly out of its mouth. As I struggled, I saw a hint of amusement in its eyes; it knew it was an apex predator. Clearly it enjoyed both the hunt and the kill. It wheezed as it sniffed at me. A dark green tongue slipped out of its mouth as it opened its gaping jaw, presumably to take a chunk out of my soft and delicious flesh.

Blindly, I twisted, using what little leverage I had and hit at the beast's eyes. My wild attack hit soft eyeball as I heard a disgusting, but satisfying, pop, I had forgotten I still had the antler fragment in my hand. Somehow I had managed to stab it in the eye. It dropped me immediately and wailed loudly. I scrambled out of the nest and back into the cold water. The water stung at the cuts. I felt weak. By the time I made it across the short span, I barely could see where I was going. All I knew was that I needed to get away from that thing. Jessie pulled me out of the water, her eyes brimming with tears.

"I'm OK," I said weakly. I sat, looking at the ugly creature that was half blind which somehow made it even more ugly. It finally dislodged the antler shard and stood, reassessing us both. Jessie turned back to Dean, who was still breathing, but just barely. I stood on shaking legs and stared defiantly back at the thing. Slowly I crept back to where I had lain in wait, hoping to ambush it. There, still dark and deadly, was my gun. Without breaking my gaze with it, I stooped and picked it up. The beast roared again, sending long streams of slime into the water to mix with the water. I decided to scream back.

"Come on, you ugly son of a bitch!" I hollered, clearly getting its attention. I stepped sideways, trying to draw the attack, when it happened, away from Jessie and Dean. Its stare followed me. Clearly I was the threat now. "That's right, you pile of excrement, look at me. I stabbed you! I took your eye!"

It snarled, and bucked on its hind legs, spreading its massive wings, and roared back at me, as if trying to shout me down. I was still shaking from the attack, and it was just far enough that I could miss, so I kept the gun at my side, hoping I could bring it up in time to kill it before it got me.

Chapter Sixteen
Settling

Virtue and riches seldom settle on one man.
Machiavelli

Just as it looked ready to pounce, gun fire rattled across the nest and the creature whirled and escaped down a tunnel halfway up the wall behind it. Looking up I saw Forrester repelling down a rope, his gun drawn. I sat down, on the rock and stared at the hole, sure the beast would come back.

Forrester radioed up to his support. "We got three down here, one's gonna need the stretcher. Looks pretty bad."

He turned to me. "What the hell was that?"

"That," I said, "Was a piasa."

He whistled. "Ugly thing."

"How'd you find us?" Jessie asked.

"We didn't. I was out at Dean's talking to him about him," he said, nodding my direction. "As I was leaving the thing came out of nowhere and grabbed him. I radioed for back up and tried to follow. In the end, we pinged his cell and have been searching the area where the pings stopped. Then I heard some maniac shouting," he smiled at me, "I saw that thing again and took some shots." He spat into the lake. "But I missed."

"Yeah," I said more sharply than I intended. "And chased it off."

"Good thing too, you both could have been killed."

I whirled at him. "It has to end now. No more death, no more killing." I was standing so close to him I could see the blood vessels in his eyes. "I will kill it. It has to die."

He backed up and put a hand up. "Now, Bernard, look, I want it—"

"No," I interrupted quietly. "I am going to kill it today."

"And how are you going to do that?" Forrester asked, his voice filled with both concern and condescension. "It just scurried through a hole halfway up that wall and you have been ripped to shreds? Your arms are coated in your own blood."

The truth in his words stung more than my wounds. I turned away and dove back into the water.

"Bernard!" Jessie yelled. I ignored her. After looking this beast in the eyes I knew it had to stop. After wounding it, it now had a reason to hate. I had no doubt if we left the caves now, it would wreak havoc on Stillwater. Too many people had already lost their lives to this evil creature. Once I got to the other wall, I found a handhold and began to scale the wall.

Behind me I head Forrester cuss. Then he dove in and soon we both were scaling the wall towards the hole the beast had ferreted away through. Once I crawled into the hole I saw it was less of a hole and more of a tunnel. Unlike the caves Jessie and I had trekked through, the walls were strangely smooth and regular. Forrester soon was standing next to me. He shined his tactical flashlight down the length of the tunnel, showing it led around a corner about sixty feet away. It hit us both at the same time; this was not a natural tunnel. This was carved into the rough rock by the beast. We truly were entering the lair of the beast.

He looked at me, deep concern in his eyes. "You sure about this?"

Instead of responding, I started down the path. He grabbed my shoulder. "You're gonna need this," he said, handing me my gun, which, in my rage, I had left behind.

"Thanks," I replied and turned back. He kept the light shined on the passages turn as we got closer.

"You think its right there?" he asked quietly, shining the light.

"No." I said, "You would hear its wheezing."

We continued around the tight corner. At that point we did, in fact, start to hear the wheezing of the creature. As the beam of light hit the end of the tunnel, illuminating another cavern, the beast roared again. Forrester fumbled his flashlight at the sound.

"It's OK," I lied. The beast was injured and danger-ous. Before our attack it was a man-killer. Now, however, it was wounded, which made it ever more deadly. I was not going to stop. John had tried and failed in killing this thing. Sheriff Jones had been killed by the damn thing. Jessie had nearly died. Dean might still die. The only thing between death and Stillwater were Forrester and I.

Forrester inched forward, summoning up the cour-age to face the monster one more time. He said, "Let me go first, I'll see if I can't take it out. You cover me." He did not wait for my answer and poked his head out of the hole, shining the light trying to find it in the dark. Almost immediately his flashlight fell to the cavern floor as powerful wings from above grabbed him and threw him across the cavern. I heard him hit the wall, and I heard his gun clatter across the rocky floor. Then it was quiet, which was not a good sign.

The flashlight, though, illuminated the cave better. Thanks to Forrester's ill-fated attempt to be the hero, I knew it sat perched above the passage, waiting patiently for its next victim. I had few options, and the beast knew it. There was no way I could leave the passage where it could not grab me. I was not going to leave Forrester in there to be devoured. I sure as hell was not going to leave without killing it.

Bile rose in my throat. This beast needed to die. In

my life there have been few times when true hate coursed through my blood. Now I relished in the anger. It fueled my continued resolve. Long shadows were cast by the flashlight, giving me a point of reference. The creature was diabolical. Aside from having a perch above the passageway, a large rock sat in the way, so you would have to turn in order to avoid getting grabbed. In the dark you would never know it was coming. I slung along the edge of the cave, trying to see if I could somehow get a shot off. The wheezing had quieted—the creature was trying not to give away its position. The wings slapped down, grabbing at me. I fell back, the wings barely missing my face. It did tell me something valuable—it could not reach the bottom of the passage—the perch was about two feet too high.

That meant I had about two feet of purchase to crawl and maybe, just maybe, have a chance to kill it. I took a deep breath and lay down on the ground. I pushed myself out, face up, into the kill zone. Almost immediately, another scream followed by the terrifying wings striking at me. I could feel the wind as they swiped at me. I had over-estimated how much space I would have, though. Instead of a good foot between the claws and my face, it was more like six inches. The beast screamed in frustration and took off to land about six feet away. I sat up as quickly as I could and tried to aim at the beast. I pulled the trigger twice. The first shot ricocheted of the back wall. The second shot, however, hit. Blood began to flow out of the beasts left side. It wailed in pain and reared up on its hind legs. I fired again, the shot seeming too loud in the shadow cave. Another wound opened, causing more blood to flow out of the beast. It flailed its wings again and screamed. In the dim light I could almost see fear in the beast's one good eye.

When it stumbled, I knew I was close to success in vanquishing the creature. I took a step forward, took a more careful aim, and fired. The bullet tore through the creatures face, and ruining the other eye. In a literal blind rage, it dropped to its front knees, hitting its jaw on the hard floor. Two of the misshapen fangs broke off and rolled across the floor. I walked closer to it, aiming the gun at its head. It never once whimpered, instead, it's wheeze was slower, and it growled angrily. With a lack of pity that surprised even me, I fired one last time. I felt that John had been vindicated. It spasmed once, and slipped into a crevice that I had not seen. It hung there, held up only by its antlers. I picked up the flashlight and shined it down the crevice. Below, there appeared to be an underground river. The crevice was only two feet wide. I hurried over to Forrester, who was slowly regaining consciousness.

"You OK?" I asked.

"I've been better," he said. "I think that I've got a few broken ribs." He sighed loudly. "But I'll live. Did you kill it?"

I helped him up and we walked over to its carcass. I shined the light on the body, its position had twisted its neck into a grotesque angle.

"Damn. Thing's ugly, huh?"

"You know it."

A sharp crack broke our stares as the antlers broke and the body fell down to the river, disappearing quickly under the water. By the time we made it back to the nest, Jessie was wrapped in a rescue blanket and Dean was being treated by the National Guard. I dog paddled over to the shore, pulling Forrester behind me. As soon as we got close, other guardsmen help us out of the water.

"Is it over?" Jessie asked.

I nodded. "It's gone. It won't be back."

I remember them airlifting us out of the cave. Somewhere along the way I lost consciousness. I woke up to the sun shining on my face through the hospital windows. I ached everywhere. I looked around and saw the terrible mess I truly was. Each arm was covered in bandages and were somewhat immobilized. An IV stung my left arm and was pumping some other liquid into my body. My stomach wrenched and cramped. I wanted to go back to sleep, but I also wanted to know if Jessie and Dean were alright. I tried to call out, but my throat was so dry I could barely croak. I wondered if this had all been some sort of weird drug induced dream after rolling my pickup. Maybe my arms were hurt from that accident and none of this had happened. I couldn't reach the call button on the remote since it had slipped over the to side. The more I struggled, the more hurt.

Then the door opened and Jessie came in, looking more beautiful than I had remembered.

"You awake finally?" she asked.

I croaked as I tried to respond. She gave me a sip of water. "The doc said to take it slow."

"What happened?"

"You don't remember?" she looked alarmed.

"Was it... real?" I mumbled. "How long have I—"

She kissed my forehead. "Yes. You really did it. It's been a week, but it's dead. And I'm really mad at you."

"Mad? Why?"

"You left me on that shore and went to kill it. You could have been killed yourself." She said, running her hand along my face. "It's been a week. You lost a lot of blood. And that water was infected with awful things. We've all been on antibiotics."

I tried to sit up.

"No. You stay put. Doctor's orders."

"Dean?"

"He'll live, but not like before. He's going to need a cane for the rest of his life. His pelvis was shattered. But he's going to make it." She smiled. "And I think he likes you now. You saved all of us."

"Forrester?"

As if on cue, he stepped into the room. "How's our

226

hero feeling?"

"Like I went ten rounds with Mohammed Ali, Mike Tyson, and a mack truck. You?"

"Well, let's just say I don't think I'll go caving for quite a while."

Jessie sat next to me and held my hand. "So, what brings you around, Sheriff?" she asked.

"Well, I always check in on Bernard, here about this time. And today, the official report has been submitted. OK?"

"Official report?" I asked. "You mean to tell me you filed a report about that damn thing?"

He smiled. "Look, I know you know no one would ever believe us about that thing. And without a body, well, it's hard to not be skeptical. So," he ran his hand through his hair. "The official version is that the killings were the result of a herd of rabid deer that have been killed and their bodies burned to destroy the virus. John's name is in the clear. The lab results came back to deer-like DNA. Any differences were written off as contamination, so no worries there."

"OK," I said. I was slightly disappointed that no one would hear about our heroics. No one would know that John died trying to protect the town from this awful creature. Jessie squeezed my hand. In the long run, I could live with it. "Thank you, Sheriff. Clearing John's name means a lot to me."

He stood painfully up. "You ever need anything you know who to call. You saved my life."

"You too, Forrester," I replied.

As he left, I turned back to Jessie. "Are you OK?"

"Never better, now that you are OK. You worried me, you know that? Don't do that again, got it?"

I smiled. "I promise never to go hunting after a monster in the dark caves again."

"I'd smack you, but I'm pretty sure it might kill you, in light of the condition you're in." She kissed me again.

We sat together, enjoying the sun, which for the first time felt warm and welcoming, not harsh and evil. I took a deep breath. A great weight had been lifted off of my shoulders. My life was finally falling back into place. Jessie was with me and that's all I cared about.

Apparently I drifted off. When I awoke, Jessie was still there, her long hair tucked behind her ear, looking at a stack of papers.

"What's that?" I asked.

She turned, her brow furrowed. "Cletus dropped them off."

I could tell from her tone that it was not good news. "Here, let me see."

She handed me the documents. As I paged through them, the first several were simply estate settlement forms, closing John's estate and transferring his immense wealth to me. Then I saw the document she was fretting over. It was a settlement agreement. On top of it was a short-typed letter, with Cletus's signature underneath. I read each word slowly, letting his advice sink in. He wanted me to pay out $40,000,000 to settle the wrongful death claims against John's estate. His recommendation was based on the fact that John's will required me to close the caves to the public. During the lawsuit they would want access to the caves, which would mean I would lose the money. He also pointed out that if John knew the monster was there, he had a legal obligation to warn people who came onto his property.

"I'm so sorry, Berns." Jessie said softly.

I looked at her and smiled. "If I could move my arms, I'd sign it right now."

"What? Why? John did nothing wrong..."

"It's not about that. Think about it, John would have given every last cent he had to help people. And if this will help the families move on, then why not? There's still a good amount left over—enough to live on. Maybe start a farm. I hear cotton is a good crop out here." I dropped the documents on the floor. "Besides, I found real treasure in Stillwater. Now come here and kiss me again."

The Caverns of Stillwater

CPSIA information can be obtained
at www.ICGtesting.com
Printed in the USA
BVHW040812300320
576345BV00006B/22/J

9 781951 384234